Praise for India's Sum

"*India's Summer* is a furious, fast-paced, fun romp through the excesses of life in the Hollywood fast lane, with some thought-provoking wisdom interspersed throughout."
– Jane Green, *New York Times* bestselling author

"A book has an energy field all of its own and *India's Summer* has a really great one."
– Ekhart Tolle, spiritual leader and *New York Times* bestselling author

"*India's Summer* offers a timeless tale of women supporting one another – delivered in a way that makes it feel fresh, alive, and utterly of the moment."
– Arianna Huffington

"India's fascinating character is what makes *India's Summer* a compelling read. She is trying to make a big shift in her life, in her career, in the choices she's making. She's funny, clever and vulnerable and you are rooting for her every step of the way."
– Goldie Hawn

"*India's Summer* avoids the familiar clichés of LA and yet captures the character of the city so well."
– Orlando Bloom

"I love how India learns to trust her inner voice and begins to let her light shine."
– Miranda Kerr, Victoria's Secret "Angel" and author of *Treasure Yourself*

"I loved this book. India made me smile."
– Kim Eng, Presence of Movement Workshop Leader

Letter
from
Paris

Letter from Paris

Thérèse

THE
STORY PLANT

The Story Plant
Studio Digital CT, LLC
P.O. Box 4331
Stamford, CT 06907

Print ISBN-13: 978-1-61188-141-7
E-book ISBN-13: 978-1-61188-142-4

Visit our website at www.TheStoryPlant.com

First Story Plant printing: June 2014
Printed in the United States of America

For Ken, James, and Kate.
I love you more than words can say.

*"It is important to have rain the first day in Paris
and never an umbrella."*
— Audrey Hepburn as *Sabrina*

Hotel de l'Abbaye
Saint Germain
Paris

December 15, 2013

Dear lovely reader,

Letter from Paris is the continuing story of India Butler who has not long turned forty, and is technically still single.

India has always longed to be French, to have that illusive *je ne sais quoi*, a signature style of dressing, a certain confidence. She dreams of an apartment in Paris with its air of "benign neglect" and casement windows she can fling open to breathe in lavender-scented air. She longs to speak better French, to cycle down Rue de Rivoli with her baguette tossed casually in her basket, her hair swept up in a casual chignon, her lover waiting for her in Brasserie Lipp on Boulevard Saint Germain... If you ask me she's watched far too many Audrey Hepburn movies, but a girl can dream can't she?

If you have yet to read *India's Summer*, then no spoilers; all you really need to know is that India is back from LA, living in London, and in a long-distance relationship with Adam Brooks. She'll tell you the rest herself.

Writing this sequel has been a labor of love for me. I've thoroughly enjoyed living vicariously through India again and I hope you will too. Do let me know. I'd love to hear from you. You can contact me at www.thereseblogs.com.

A bientot mes amies
Bisous

Thérèse x

1
—

"Are you okay? You shot out from nowhere. I could have killed you," the biker shouted, wrestling to unfasten his helmet.

"I'm fine...I'm fine," the girl stammered, scrambling to her feet and collecting the strewn contents of her purse. "It's my fault. I wasn't looking. I was distracted by the fountains."

"Are you sure you're all right?" he asked anxiously, wiping his brow with the back of his hand. "Let me see you. Have you hurt yourself?"

"No. I'm fine. Absolutely. I promise," she said, brushing the dust off her pants and lifting her bag over her shoulder. "I'm okay, just a bit shaken up..."

"Here. Catch your breath a minute," he said, taking her by the elbow and helping her back onto the pavement. "I'm Adam. What's your name?"

"Natalie," she said, running her hands through her hair and attempting a smile. "I wasn't looking where I was going. I really am okay."

"Are you sure?"

"Yes. Thank you," she said, looking around in something of a daze. "I think I should go back to my hotel. I'm clearly not safe to be out on the street."

"Let me get you back there. You'll be perfectly safe," he assured her. "I do know how to drive."

"You certainly know how to stop." She laughed. "I'm

really sorry. I feel so stupid. Yes. Thanks. It's just up the street – The Paris," she said, pointing across the Las Vegas strip.

"Okay. Here. Put this on," he said, handing her his helmet. "Let me fasten it for you."

He snapped the strap under her chin, climbed back on the Harley, and fired up the engine.

"Okay? Take your time," he shouted.

Natalie swung her leg over the wide leather seat.

"Are you on?"

"Yes," she yelled back.

"There are foot pegs. Got them? Great. Hold on to me and lean into the curve."

Natalie put her arms around his waist as the engine gave a throaty growl. In the few short minutes it took to get back to her hotel, she became acutely aware of the strength of his muscles under his cotton shirt.

"Thanks for the ride," she said, climbing off and shaking out her long hair. She handed him back the helmet.

"Can't stop here," he said, nodding toward a truck reversing in his path. "I really want to know you're okay. Can I catch up with you later? Are you doing anything tonight?"

Natalie shook her head. "Not especially," she said.

"How 'bout I take you to dinner? Would seven o'clock work?"

"Yes," she said, nodding.

"Great. I'll pick you up over there by the lobby. See you later," he said, revving the engine and negotiating his way around the truck.

Natalie didn't waste a second grabbing her phone from her purse.

"Hey Monica," she said, breathless with excitement. "Omigod. Never, as in never, are you going to believe what just happened to me."

"Let me guess. You just won a million dollars on a slot machine?"

"Ha! Not exactly...Okay...so I tripped in the street and this guy on a motorcycle almost killed me...and he's just given me a lift back to the hotel...and..."

"Are you insane?" Monica screamed. "The guy nearly kills you and you get on his bike?"

"I didn't finish yet. It wasn't his fault and the GUY was Adam Brooks."

"Adam Brooks? As in...Adam BROOKS? Omigod, that changes *everything*. Are you sure it was him and not some lookalike? Maybe you have a concussion."

"Too funny, Monica. Yes. I'm positive. It was him all right, right down to his six pack. Okay. Are you sitting down? I haven't even told you the best part yet." She paused for effect. "Ready? Wait for it...he's taking me to dinner tonight. Adam Brooks as in *People Magazine's Sexiest Man Alive*...is taking me to dinner."

"Cool, as in really cool. But sorry to break the news Nat, he's in a serious relationship. He's got a thing with Annabelle Butler's sister. What's her name? India. I think they might even be engaged."

"Monica, he could be married with kids for all I care. All guys cheat," Natalie said, examining the long scrape up her elbow. "Anyway, gotta go. I'm mad late for my meeting."

Natalie left herself plenty of time to get ready for the evening. After a long shower, she took time doing her makeup and shimmied into a tight cocktail dress. She checked her reflection approvingly before jostling her way through the packed casino to the hotel entrance where Adam shouted to her from the open window of a black Mercedes.

"Over here. Climb in. I guessed you'd feel safer on four wheels." He grinned.

"Good call. I'd have had to have ridden sidesaddle in this dress anyway." She laughed, sliding in next to him in the back seat and arranging one long tan leg over the other.

Adam turned to her. "Hungry?"

"Yes. Where are we going?"

"Le Cirque. I think you'll like it. I did think of taking you to MIX. I was at a party there last night."

"With Prince Harry?"

"Not that kind of party. I'm working this week." He laughed. "Anyway, I thought you'd like to see the fountains properly."

A short while later, the car turned into the entrance for The Bellagio. The driver slowed down to let them see the cascading water as Pavarotti's aria built to a penetrating crescendo.

"Awesome," Natalie said, as the car continued snaking up the driveway. "Thank you for thinking of that."

"Least I could do," Adam said.

They made their way down endless corridors, past the heaving bars and roulette tables to a vivid canopied restaurant where the maître d' led them to a quiet corner table. He shook Adam's hand and pulled out a velvet chair for Natalie.

"Bonsoir Monsieur Brooks. C'est un grand plaisir. On est honore que vous avez revenir. Bonsoir Madame."

"He seems to know you well," Natalie observed.

"I've eaten here most nights this week. My character's French, so getting the French vibe helps me stay in role."

"Are you in a show in town?" she asked.

"No. Filming. We're doing outtakes for a movie. It's based on Omar Sharif's life, his horses, gambling...women."

"Is he still alive?"

"Last time I spoke to him." Adam laughed. "What are you drinking, red or white?"

"Red, thanks."

Natalie glanced at the menu, her eyes widening at the price of the starters.

"Flat Evian for me. Early start tomorrow," Adam told the sommelier who had appeared at his side. "Please bring a glass of your best Merlot for my guest."

Their drinks order taken, he turned back to Natalie.

"How are you feeling? I've fallen off a bike more times

than I care to admit, but running someone over would be a first."

"I really am fine," she assured him.

"Okay. Good. So, what brings you to Sin City? Are you here with friends?"

"Work. I'm a publicist. My client is speaking at the convention center in the morning."

"Where're you from?"

"Arizona. I went to school at UCLA. Went back home afterward. Big mistake."

"Oh really? I love Arizona."

"Too hot for me." She shrugged. "I'm planning on moving back to LA just as soon as I can. I'm talking to Ogilvy Mather, Saatchi's, and a few other ad agencies, putting it out there. It's time for a change."

A waiter was hovering behind her, waiting to take the order.

"So have you decided what you want yet?" Adam asked her.

"Yes. To get out of corporate representation and into advertising."

"I meant to eat," he said, smiling.

"Oh, sorry. Yes. Okay. Let me look," she said, casting her eyes down the menu. "I'll have the sole, please."

"Starter?"

"Caesar salad."

"Le Filet Mignon. S'il vous plait et le potage du jour. Merci," Adam said, handing him back his menu.

"Merci Madame," the waiter nodded, lifting Natalie's menu. "Merci Monsieur."

"So where were we?" Adam picked up. "Ah! Yes. So tell me more about your job."

"I'm sure yours is a lot more interesting," she said, cocking her head to one side and tossing her hair over her shoulder. "Why don't you tell me about the film? It sounds super cool."

"It's a challenge, that's for sure," he said. "Very different from the other characters I've played and of course there's the accent. I'm working on that one."

As they chatted, Natalie began to forget that Adam was one of the biggest stars in movie franchise history. He seemed so down to earth, so normal, until a couple of hours later when they were leaving the hotel and he grabbed her hand.

"Quick," he said, pulling her toward the waiting car. "Get in fast."

Turning around as she scrambled into the back seat, Natalie was momentarily blinded by the whirring flashbulbs of paparazzi cameras.

2
―

So. Here we go again, India thought, hurling a copy of *The Mail on Sunday* at the wall. She flung a copy of *Hello* magazine in the same direction, picked up her phone and speed-dialed Adam Brooks.

"Hey you...how's it goin'?" he said sleepily. "Is everything okay?"

"Not sure," she said. "You tell me. I just saw your photograph in the paper. You were in front of a hotel holding hands with a half-dressed woman. A former Miss Arizona it says. I need to know. Is *she* the reason you're not coming to Paris with me? Is that the real reason?"

"Of course not, Indie. It's not how it looks." He yawned. "I almost killed her on my bike the other afternoon. She came flying out in front of me. I felt bad about it. I bought her dinner. It's not what you think. Now can I go back to sleep?"

"So why was she wearing your jacket?"

"Because she was cold, India. It's freezing here at night. It's the desert. Stop it already."

India said nothing.

"You've got to trust me at a certain point." He sighed.

"You're right. I'm sorry. I'm just feeling a bit raw that you aren't coming to Paris. It's been two months and I miss you...and..." Her voice trailed off.

"I don't pick the locations, Indie. You think I like shooting my scenes around a fake Eiffel Tower when I could be going to the real Paris with you?"

"No. Okay," she said hesitantly. "Well anyway, I've decided to go for a few days by myself. Just letting you know."

"Okay. Fine. Look, I'll call you later. It's the middle of the night here." He clicked off.

~ ~ ~

India lifted the booking confirmation from Hotel de l'Abbaye off her printer. How very generous of Annie, she thought, remembering the previous evening's conversation and how sympathetic her sister had been about her ruined plans, how she'd suggested the boutique hotel in Saint Germain and insisted on treating her.

"Take a breath, darling," Annie had told her. "It's tough for Adam too, remember? It's lonely and exhausting being on location. I understand that only too well. You know how the paparazzi twist everything. Remember the craziness of that last summer you were in LA? Don't be too fast to jump to conclusions."

Annie was right. Maybe she shouldn't have been so quick to believe the worst of Adam. He certainly sounded convincing. She was tired. She needed this getaway. Folding the receipt carefully into a wallet, India took her cup of tea over to the couch, pressed the television remote and snuggled up under a throw to continue watching her movie. An image of Owen Wilson froze on the screen as she scrambled around for the phone vibrating under a stack of French fashion magazines. She located it and sank back into the couch.

"Bonjour Sarah," she said.

"Hey Indie. How's it going?"

"Tres Bon. I'm watching *Midnight in Paris* to get in the mood for my trip next week."

"Are you on a kind of *Eat, Pray, Love* mission?" Sarah responded.

"Sarah, ma petite amie. Alas, no 'love' as you know. I am making this trip purely for the intellectual rigor, for the galleries, the museums and to practice my French. I am committed to the life of an aesthete."

Sarah laughed. "Well whatever that is, it doesn't sound like you. Anyway, do you fancy joining Roger and me down the pub? I'm waiting for him now."

"Okay," India said, jumping up and stretching. "Give me half an hour. Order me chicken curry pie and chips please. I'm starting my juice cleanse tomorrow."

She twisted her long dark hair into a clip and went to take a shower. An hour later, the three of them were crowded into the benches of The Cat and Lion pub. Roger raised his martini glass in India's direction.

"To a whole new adventure. We're going to miss you Miss Butler. Hackney Community College will not be the same without you."

"I'll miss working with you too, Roger. It's been great. Be sure to let me know if you get wind of any more maternity leave I can cover," she said, taking a sip of her Chardonnay.

"Back in a sec," Sarah said, pushing away her plate of fries. "Need to go to the loo."

India stood up to let her squeeze past.

"Roger, did Sarah tell you Adam's not going to Paris with me now?" she said, bouncing back down on the leather banquette.

"She did. Dahling, I feel your pain. Long distance relationships are the worst. You've hardly been out at all these last few months. Frankly, it's a waste of one hot mama. Believe me if I were straight, I'd snap you up like a shot."

"Why thank you, Roger!" India said with a smile.

"Seriously. You're absolutely beautiful. When you walked in just now, every man in the place looked up. You've legs up to your armpits, porcelain skin, cheekbones to die for... that Adam should be so lucky. You're fabulous, darling. Fabulous."

India blushed. "Now you're embarrassing me, Roger," she said. "I'm sure you must be sick to death of me talking about him all the time."

"Not at all. That's what we're here for, isn't it, Sarah?" Roger said, leaning across and giving India's hand a squeeze as Sarah joined them again.

"So what did I miss?" Sarah asked, sitting back down and pouring herself a glass of Pellegrino.

"Are you okay?" India said. "You look a bit pasty."

"I'm tired. It's been a long day." Sarah smiled. "Now tell me all about your plans for Paris."

3
—

I should have taken the Eurostar, India thought, nervous as ever about taking off and squirming in her tiny seat as the Air France plane taxied down the runway. I can handle this, I can, she told herself. It's only a short hop.

Briefly making eye contact with the man squashed next to her, India pretended to be absorbed in her copy of *Le Monde*. She flicked over the pages, determined to look as French as possible as the flight attendant approached her.

"Bonjour Madame. Aimeriez-vous quelque chose à bois? Peut-etre voulez un verre de vin ou de certains canapés?"

"Non Merci." India smiled sweetly, thrilled she had been addressed in French but not at all sure what she had just declined. She sighed as she opened *Parisian Chic*, the book by Inès de la Fressange that had become her bible in the last couple of weeks. India had copied all of the basic style tips and was surprised at how many of the key elements she already owned: the biker jacket, the white jeans, the navy sweater, the little black dress. It seemed somewhat formulaic, but who was she to argue with the muse to Chanel, the supermodel who had graced so many catwalks?

This is such a beautiful book – the red leather cover, the bookmark ribbon – everything she does is so special, she thought wistfully.

After a mercifully smooth flight and landing, India stood up with a wave of excitement, lifted down her carry-on case

and made her way along the glass-walled terminal to join the
passport control line. At baggage claim, she scoured the line
of waiting drivers and finally located a sign with her name
on it. The short man holding it announced himself gruffly
as 'Emanuel.'

"Bonjour Monsieur." India beamed at him. "Merci," she
said, pointing to her cases on the carousel and smiling gratefully as he dragged them onto a cart. Thank goodness for
Annie. I'd hate to be getting a shuttle right now, she thought.

Taken by surprise at the fierce wind and driving rain as
they crossed the concourse to the car, India reminded herself
she was not in Paris for the weather. Even if the sky were
a cloudless blue, there would be no romantic walks in Les
Jardins de Versailles or picnics at Pont des Arts with Adam.
Pushing that depressing thought to the back of her mind,
she climbed into the back of the Peugot.

The traffic was surprisingly light and as they left the auto
route from Charles de Gaulle Airport way behind, India,
with mounting excitement, began recognizing landmarks –
the Louvre, the Place de la Concorde, the Egyptian obelisk,
the Champs-Élysées. She could hardly contain herself when
the car swung over the arched bridge of the Seine to the left
bank and she was finally in the Sixth Arondissement.

They pulled up to the cobblestoned courtyard of the
hotel, where the driver deposited India's suitcase on the side-
walk and, without ceremony, took her euros and drove off
into the night. India was negotiating the stone steps while
struggling with the wheels of her carry-on suitcase when the
door opened and a porter helped her inside.

This was not at all the entrance I was planning on making, she thought, running her hand through her bedraggled
hair and taking in the elegance of the foyer and sitting room
where a few couples were relaxing on luxurious couches in
front of a roaring log fire.

"Bonsoir," India said with a smile to the concierge.

"Good evening, Miss Butler. I hope you will enjoy your stay with us," he responded in clipped English while reaching for a set of keys from a wooden cubbyhole.

India registered quickly, then followed the bellman down a short hallway. As the door closed behind him India looked with delight around her room, at the floral wallpaper, the exquisite drapes, the gilt mirrors, the marble bathroom. It's like a doll's house, she mused. Like stepping back in time.

After pulling off her boots, she threw down her raincoat and opened the window, drinking in the damp air of the leafy courtyard. She was in Paris, in Paris for four whole nights. Dismissing the nagging feeling that dinner would be a whole lot more fun if she were not alone, she began to plan out her evening. She would shower, then order a vin blanc before dinner.

4
—

Luella's eyes filled with tears as she watched the closing scene of the movie. A girl wrapped in a shawl was cradling her newborn baby.

"They'll take her from me; I know they will," the girl cried.

"Well now, we can't allow that to happen, can we?" the older woman replied.

God, that was intense, Luella thought as the credits rolled to the haunting strains of an Irish lament. She switched on the side-light and glanced around the walls of her study. The shelves were lined with the novels she had written, the foreign language editions displayed next to the Brassai print, the paperbacks, hardbacks, audio tapes and CDs arranged in chronological order.

There isn't a single sentence in one of those books that comes anywhere near the power of that final line, she thought, repeating it softly to herself. "Well now, we can't allow that to happen, can we?"

Dragging herself up from the armchair, she checked her phone. No messages. Peter won't have landed yet I suppose, she thought, gathering up a pile of Sunday papers and a coffee mug. Going into the kitchen, she emptied the trash-can, cleared a few dishes from the countertop and glanced up at the clock. God, weekends are interminable when he's not at home. The house feels so empty.

Going into the hallway, she pulled her coat out from the closet, wrapped a scarf around her neck, grabbed her purse and left the house. She walked a couple of blocks to the newsstand and bought a pack of cigarettes and a magazine. Maybe Peter's right. We probably should get another dog, she thought.

Luella smiled remembering how she had argued the merits of slobbering Labradors over flatulent bulldogs. How they had agreed to disagree, both of them understanding it was too soon to fill the gaping hole left by Chester, the Pointer who had been their 'baby' for so many years. She unwrapped the packet, took out a cigarette and cupped the lighter against the wind.

"Hey careful," she snapped as a girl flew past on roller skates almost knocking her into the wall.

"Kids," she muttered, taking a drag and watching the teenager race past the bus stop and disappear around the corner. Seconds later, hearing the screech of tires, Luella's stomach lurched. Running the few yards down the street, she took in the scene instantly. The driver was dashing toward the girl.

"Call 999," he yelled. "Someone. NOW!"

Rummaging in her purse, Luella found her phone and called the emergency number. Then she crouched down next to the girl and held her hand. "You're going to be okay," she whispered. "Help is on its way. Don't be frightened. Keep your eyes open. Keep looking at me."

The paramedics were on the scene quickly. Luella watched as they laid the girl onto a gurney and with a deafening wail of sirens raced off in the direction of Ealing General Hospital. She answered a few questions from the police. Yes, she had made the call. It all happened so quickly. No, she didn't know her. Sorry she couldn't be more helpful.

When there was nothing more to be done, Luella turned back in the direction of home. Picking up the pace, her walk turned into a run as she reached her front door. She threw down her coat in the hallway, dashed to her desk and began writing – *Fate, serendipity, fragility, frozen moment in time, hopes dashed, plans changed.*

She was startled out of her thoughts an hour or so later when her phone vibrated and slid across the desk.

"Hey Lu..."

Her husband's voice was as clear as if he were in the same room. Luella sank back in her chair.

"Hi sweetheart," she said. "How's Hong Kong? How's the hotel?"

"They've put me up in the Residences here at the Shangri La. The room's pretty amazing. I've a great view of the harbor. How are you getting on with planning the new book? Have you been working all day?"

"No. It was frustrating. I gave up in the end and watched *Albert Nobbs.* You remember the movie I wanted us to see a while ago, the one where Glenn Close plays a woman pretending to be a man? She really should have won an Oscar for it."

"Good for you. You work too hard. You sound exhausted."

"I'm a bit rattled. There was an accident down the street this evening."

"What happened? Are you okay?"

"Yes. I'm fine, but it was awful. This kid went careening into the street on her skates. She was almost knocked unconscious by a car. I called the ambulance."

"Will she be all right?"

"I'll never know. I don't know who she was. I really hope so. She was so scared, so helpless, and her leg was at a peculiar angle. I haven't been able to get the image out of my head," Luella said quietly. "Makes you think how life as you know it can change in a millisecond."

"I'm sorry, Lu. You couldn't have done anything more."

"I suppose not, though I do wish I could find out how she's doing." She took a sharp intake of breath. "Okay. So... take my mind off it. Tell me how your meetings are going."

"I've just had an eight-course dinner with the Shanghai

client. I thought it would never end," he said. "They're keeping me pretty busy in the daytime too. The line's not good. I was just checking in to say good night. I miss you."

"Me too. Sleep well," she said. "Love you. I'll text when I get to Paris."

~~ ~~ ~~

Luella was in a deep sleep when her alarm went off the next morning. Remembering her hair appointment, she showered quickly, dressed and dashed down the street.

I wonder how that girl's doing, she thought, passing the newsstand and turning into the salon. Please let her be okay.

"Luella?" The hairstylist jolted her out of her thoughts and spoke to her reflection. "Shall we smooth it with the flat iron?"

"Sorry. Yes please. I was miles away," she said, forcing herself back into the moment. "It'll last longer. It always amazes me how just an hour or so on a plane from London can wreak havoc with my hair."

"Lucky you, off to Paris. I'm so jealous," he said, clicking off the dryer. "It's so romantic."

"I wish." Luella grinned. "I'm not going for romance, sadly. I'm going there for meetings and to work on my next book."

Luella crossed her legs underneath her and turned back to her magazine as Joseph pulled her chestnut bob into sleek strands.

"Where are you staying? Somewhere exotic with all those little cafés and bars and cobbled streets?"

"Saint Germain."

The woman sitting next to her with a head covered in silver foils leaned across. "Excuse me, but I couldn't help overhearing. You're a writer?"

Luella turned her head and winced as she caught a stream of hot air. Joseph swiveled Luella's chair around so she was facing his other client.

"I've written a few books." Luella smiled. "What about you?"

"Travel journalist," she said, scribbling on the back of her card. "I'm just back from Saint Germain. If you do need a hairdresser, look up Studio Thirty-Four and ask for Marcel."

"That's so kind of you," Luella said.

"My pleasure. I'm Helen. Helen Davis. Tell them I sent you."

"Will do, and I'm Luella Marchmont."

"Goodness," the woman gushed. "Are you really? I'm so thrilled to meet you. I've read all your books."

"Thank you." Luella smiled. "I've a new one coming out in September. I have your e-mail address now, so I'll arrange for a copy to be sent to you if you'd like."

"That'd be wonderful. Thank you. And if it isn't too cheeky of me, could you sign the copy?"

"I'd be delighted," Luella said. "My pleasure."

Leaving the salon, Luella decided to walk home through the park. It was early March – too soon for the daffodils – but there was a signal from the budding sycamore trees that spring was on its way. She walked quickly past the children's playground area toward the lake, narrowly avoiding some cyclists.

How could it possibly be more than twenty years since we moved here? she thought, remembering the weekends watching her husband play football or sitting with his sister Maisie and having lunch in the garden of the Kings Arms Pub. Where had the years gone? Luella could hardly remember a time when Peter had not been around – growing up a mile away from each other, walking to the village school most mornings, riding their bikes down the lanes. Nobody was surprised when they announced their engagement. It was a given.

They were still so great together even now. Sure, with his international travel for the bank and the pressure of her career, they didn't exactly live in each other's pockets, but that was probably why they'd lasted. Space was important to them both. He was her best friend and as he reminded her so often, she was his soul mate.

Of course if we'd had kids, the whole dynamic would be different by now, she mused, distracted by the excited shrieks of a little boy as his dad unraveled a kite. Sitting down on a wooden bench, she pulled her coat around her tightly, watching them run back and forth across the grass together, struggling to catch the breeze to get it airborne.

Luella felt a rush of adrenalin as the multicolored dragonfly swirled into the air. She watched it swoop and curve effortlessly, its tail trailing against the clouds. Tomorrow I will be flying too, she thought, and then feeling the chill in the air, she stood up and walked briskly back home. She closed the heavy double doors behind her, threw her coat on the hallstand and ran up the stairs.

Joseph's right, she thought. I AM very lucky to be going to Paris. I should never take my wonderful life for granted.

Going into her bedroom, she made a mental list. Okay. What do I need for carry on? Nightie, underwear, tights, layers...space for my coat...she thought. Then balancing on a wicker chair, she reached up to a high cupboard and pulled out her suitcase. Remembering the broken fastener, she slung it to one side and dug around for another. Spotting Peter's Hermès Holdall crammed at the back of the shelf, she stretched up and made a grab for the strap. The chair swayed as she tried to reach it and catching her balance just in time, she managed to fling it across the room.

If Peter were here he'd be furious with me for being so stupid, she thought, climbing down and catching her breath before picking up the bag. Then noticing the bundle that had landed at her feet, she leaned down and picked up a sheaf of envelopes. Untying the ribbon around them, she fanned them in her hands. Each one was addressed in the same cursive handwriting. There was no stamp and no address, simply a first name, *Peter.*

Luella recognized the feeling in the pit of her stomach, the sense of premonition she had felt years ago, seconds before the doctor told her she had lost her baby. A wave of panic swept over her as she leaned against the edge of the bed and caught her breath.

Dropping the letters onto the quilt, she went into the bathroom and began dispensing cleansers and toners into travel-sized containers. Realizing she was pouring nail varnish remover on top of moisturizer, she stopped and splashed her face with cold water.

"Open the letters. You know you want to. You know you must," her reflection seemed to be saying. Another louder voice was clamoring in her head. "They're addressed to Peter; they're none of your business. Put them back where you found them."

She dried her face and stared in the mirror hardly recognizing her reflection, feeling strangely detached. Surely this is happening to someone else, she thought, leaning against the sink for support, her heart pounding. Returning to the bedroom, she lifted a single envelope and turned it over in her hands. She sat down, pulled out the letter and ran her finger over the embossed logo of the hotel letterhead, *Le Meurice. Paris.*

I'm sorry for doubting you, Peter, but I have to know, she thought. Please, please don't let this be what I think it is.

Moments later, unable to control the violent tremor in her hands, Luella let the pages drop to her side and stood up. Walking unsteadily downstairs, she leaned for a few seconds on the newel post before crossing the hallway. Switching on the dining room light, she headed for the drinks cabinet where she downed a double shot of brandy. It burned the back of her throat. It was good to feel something – the rest of her was numb.

5

—

Maybe the secret of *savoir faire* lies in body language, India thought sitting in the bistro on the corner of Rue Cassette sipping her coffee. She was having a sartorial crisis: her navy blazer was far too predictable, her Breton T-shirt a little clichéd, the square silk scarf too considered. She observed that the young woman across the table had broken all of Inès de la Fressange's rules with her tousled hair and sheepskin jacket, although with her air of insouciance, she still looked decidedly French.

Standing up carefully, straightening her back and walking briskly in the direction of what she hoped was Rue de Rennes, India eventually found Monoprix without having to ask directions and was soon the proud owner of a long beige linen scarf.

A woman approached her as she was handing over her euros. "Excusez-moi Madam. Ou sont les produits de beauté?" she asked.

"A bas," India answered, gesturing to the back of the store.

How wonderful, India thought. She must have assumed I was French. Her phone rang as she was leaving the store.

"Bonjour," she said. "C'est moi, India."

"Bonjour ma petite." Adam laughed. "Je suis desole. Je ne pouvais pas etre a Paris."

"Desole?" She laughed. "You feel desolate? Sorry always

sounds much more extreme in French don't you think? Do they have a word for when they are feeling REALLY bad?"

"Not sure, but I AM pretty cut up about it," he said. "Where are you right now?"

India looked around at the crowded street, unsure of her bearings.

"Not far from the hotel. You?"

"Don't ask. I'm by a miniature Arc de Triomphe in ninety-degree heat and it's still early. I can only stay on for a minute. I just wanted to check in, make sure we're okay."

"We are. I'm sorry I lost it the other day. I was so disappointed."

"I'll make it up to you, Indie. We'll do Cannes together. You'll love it."

"Great. Okay. Great," she said. And this really was great, wasn't it? She could relax and enjoy the trip now that they had cleared the air properly. She must learn not to overreact if she saw tabloid pictures of him. It was as Annie said, just par for the course when someone was famous.

"A bientot," he said.

"A bientot," she chirped.

I will practice my French – impress him with my fluency in Cannes. What a beautiful day, she thought, walking in the direction of what she guessed was Rue Bonaparte.

India spent the next several hours striding the streets at rapid Parisian speed, stopping occasionally to browse in bookshops or to step inside the doorways of the many delicatessens to savor the sugary aroma of bonbons and artisan chocolate. By the time she arrived back at the Hotel de l'Abbaye she was on a high, greeting the doorman with a cheery "Bonsoir Monsieur" and adding "D'accord" for good measure. Then sweeping through the foyer, she allowed herself the thought that if she were any more 'almost' French, she would be French.

~~ ~~ ~~

"Susie, I'm completely thrown. How can I have lived with a man for all these years and not have had the slightest inkling he was gay?" Luella said with a deep sigh, pushing away the over-spilling ashtray and her coffee cup. "Tell me. How can this have happened? How?"

"Luella," her friend said, "I'm not sure what to say. I've known you both since forever and I'm totally shocked too."

"Thing is... it's challenged everything I thought I knew about myself. I hate to admit it, but I'm wrestling with all these emotions. At first I thought the letter was from another woman, the handwriting was so delicate." She paused. "I mean, why should it make any difference? A love letter's a love letter, right? An affair's an affair, but the thought of him with a man makes me feel nauseous. I'm hoping I haven't discovered some deep-seated prejudice in myself. I thought I was more broad-minded than this."

"I'm sure it's just shock, Luella. I mean you weren't even expecting him to be having an affair at all, let alone having one with a man."

Luella rolled the edge of the sepia paper placemat in front of her.

"Well, if I'm honest with myself I chose not to ask too many questions. I always allowed for the possibility; he's away from home so much. But this is different. It means that I never really knew him. It's torturing me."

"Lu, are you sure you don't want to tell him you found the letters?"

"Certain. I'm not ready to talk to him yet. I can't. I just can't deal with that right now."

A group of tourists scraped out chairs and sat down next to her.

"Susie, this is impossible to discuss in public. I'm at Café de Flore and it's getting busy. I'll call you back from the hotel tonight."

"I'll be here for you whenever you want to talk, day or night. I can only imagine what you must be going through."

"Thanks, it means a lot. Oh. And by the way, did I tell you Air France lost my bags too? Least of my problems right now I suppose. Bye Susie. Thanks for being there."

Luella waved for the check and put her phone into her purse. She sat for a while absently watching a pigeon scavenge bread from a nearby table. Then quickly finishing her glass of Evian, she settled the check and set off across the cobbled streets to Monoprix for a few of the toiletries she needed while she waited for her suitcases to arrive. She pulled her scarf around her to ward off the chilly evening air.

Leaving the store, she resisted the overwhelming urge to go back to the hotel and curl up under the duvet. Instead, she wandered across the footbridge among the throngs of tourists toward the Louvre.

Luella's love affair with Paris had begun years back when she'd found grainy photographs of her grandparents in wartime Paris. She had often imagined the two lovers running toward each other or locked in each other's arms under the foggy light of a lamppost, oblivious to the people around them. Her grandmother's story had been the inspiration for *One Night in Cap d'Antibes*, the romance novel that had been her first bestseller.

Today she was thinking very different thoughts as she pulled her scarf tighter around her neck and dug her hands deeper into her coat pockets, racked with questions, questions that may well have been answered if she had read the other letters. The thought of that made her throat constrict. One letter had been all she could take. Any more would have been pure masochism.

As she crossed the Place des Pyramids in front of the Regina Hotel she wondered how often Peter had strolled here with his lover. Who is he? she asked herself. Is he French? Why was he staying at Le Meurice?

She walked across the square, drawn toward the gilt monument of Fremiet's Jeanne d'Arc charging on her horse, sword in hand, French flag waving above her head. Gazing up at the monument, Luella remembered the quote from Joan of Arc she had used to open one of her books: *You say that you are my judge, but take good heed not to judge me ill.*

"I will do my best Peter," she whispered. "I will try not to judge you."

As the sky began to blacken, Luella turned back in the direction of her hotel and managed to flag down a cab before it began to rain. Throwing her shopping bag onto the backseat, she climbed in wearily next to it.

~ ~ ~

India would be dining alone again tonight, a woman of mystery, an international traveler with *un histoire*. She rehearsed out loud the phrases she had learned from her online Language 101 course many times before calling the concierge to make her reservation. Lifting the phone, she took a deep breath.

"Bonsoir Monsieur," she said.

"Good evening, Madame Butler. How can I help you?" Jean-Paul responded.

"Je voudrais faire une reservation pour sept ce soir," she said in her best accent and at speed.

"Of course, Madame, a table for seven people tonight. What time would you prefer?"

"Non, la table pour un a sept heure," she said, enunciating slowly.

"Of course, a table for one at seven o'clock. Merci Madam." He clicked off.

India put down the phone. Damn. Okay let's try again, she thought, picking up once more and dialing room service.

"Good evening Madame Butler, Jean-Paul here. How can I help you?"

There's no escaping him. All the calls seem to go via the concierge, she thought.

"Je voudrais un verre de Sancerre, s'il vous plait," she said, confident his reply would be a simple, "Oui, bien sûr Madame."

"I am sorry, Madame Butler," he answered. "By the glass, we only have a house white. I assure you it is an excellent wine from the Loire valley. I would be pleased to have it delivered to your room."

Frustrated at her inability to reply in French, India settled for "Merci Monsieur" and put the phone back down on the receiver defeated. Give up. Jean-Paul is clearly not going to let you win this game, she thought. Opening the closet, she picked out her knee-length silk black dress and laid it out on the bed. She rested her patent leather high-heeled pumps alongside it.

Even though I shall be dining alone, it is important to make a good impression, she thought. Inès is adamant that much of French élan is the emphasis of style over comfort on all occasions.

After dressing and paying particular attention to her makeup application, outlining her eyes with a kohl pen and applying two layers of mascara, she sipped her wine slowly. Inès had also been clear that while French women enjoyed their wine on a daily basis, they would be horrified at the idea of appearing tipsy in public and drank only with food. India was tipsy within minutes but decided that as she would not be speaking to anyone this evening, it would not be apparent and her fall-back position was that at the end of the day she was, well…English.

The dining room was quiet. India took in the room with a sweeping glance: the young couple with immaculately turned out children; the ancient woman with the younger companion leaning in to help steady the water glass that she was gripping with trembling hands; the distinguished-looking gentleman swirling his wine glass.

The barman greeted her politely. "Bonsoir Madame But-ler," he said, coming out from behind the bar and leading her to a table near the window. India took her seat and smiled up at him as he handed her the menu. Fiercely deter-mined to order in French, she scanned it for words that she could say with confidence and was delighted when he made no attempt to speak to her in English. A little while later the *Saumon en croûte, the pomme de terre* and her *verre de vin* were presented exactly as ordered.

Feeling a little awkward, she pulled out her iPhone and began checking nonexistent e-mails. She looked around as she ate. Tomorrow she would pick out a leather-bound book at Melodies Graphiques to bring with her to dinner. She would emulate the stylish woman at the next table who was also alone.

It was still early when India finished dinner. She decided she would take her *digestif,* a port perhaps, by the fire in the sitting room. She sank into the downy cushions of an old armchair with a contented sigh. The perfect place to journal, she thought, pulling out her blue mini Smythson notepad inscribed with the words "Travels and Experiences."

India glanced up as a woman about her own age sat down on the opposite couch. She watched her polish off one drink and order another. She could not be certain, but from the distinctive bob, the red-rimmed glasses and the air of distraction, she was pretty sure it was the same person who had asked for directions earlier in the day at Monoprix.

6

Luella undressed quickly, climbed into bed and stared at the ceiling, listening to the rain pounding the windowpanes. She was drifting into an uneasy sleep when the hotel phone rang.

"Hey Lu. How are you?"

She propped herself up on the pillows and fumbled around for the switch on the bedside light. "I think I was asleep," she mumbled.

"Sorry. I thought I had the time right. Are you getting my texts? Is everything okay?"

"No, Peter," she said quietly. "Far from it."

The silence reverberated in the room.

"I found letters," she said eventually, realizing her voice was slurred.

"Oh...Lu...I don't know what to say..."

"Neither do I, Peter. It's why I've not been answering your texts."

There was an achingly long pause.

"Lu. I can explain. I'm sorry."

Luella sighed. "Peter, we can't do this on the phone. We'll both be back in London in a week or so. Can we leave it 'til then?"

"I'm sorry, Lu. I really didn't mean for you to find out this way. This is very bad timing."

"Is there ever a good time to tell your wife you're sleeping with another man? One thing though, now that I think of it. I need you to move out of our house as soon as you get back."

"Lu. I need to talk, Lu. I still love you. I..."

Luella hung up, cutting him off midsentence. Awake now, she climbed out of the bed and pulled a sweater, her jeans and a pair of boots from her suitcase. Rifling through her purse for a packet of Marlboros, she dressed and left the room. Reaching the courtyard, she put up her umbrella, struck a match, lit a cigarette and inhaled deeply. She walked through the gateway onto the empty street and carried on walking toward the river to the water's edge as the sky lightened and a weak sunrise gave way to daylight.

~ ~ ~

India had planned on visiting the Rodin museum the next day, had imagined sitting outside in glorious sunshine surrounded by sculptures, perhaps sipping a *limonade* before wandering around the gallery. As soon as she pulled back the drapes, she realized she would need a change of plan, as the rain was clearly settled in for the morning. Negotiating your way around a miserable Paris crowded with hundreds of visitors over the Easter holiday would require more careful planning than she had thought.

She dressed quickly in Inès de la Fressange's suggested 'go to' uniform of a navy V-neck cashmere sweater, blue jeans and ballet flats, then piled her hair into a topknot, secured it with a clip and threw her trench coat over her arm. She would have breakfast in the hotel and then make a new plan for the day.

A middle-aged man was shaking off his raincoat in the foyer as she approached the busy dining room where the waiter gestured her toward a window table. Once seated, she observed the English family at the adjoining table who were planning out their afternoon trip. The father was tapping away on his iPad booking tickets for Disneyland Paris while their mother was encouraging the girls to eat. To her left, a couple about her own age was cooing over a baby in a bassinet.

An unexpected wave of loneliness came over her. She shifted awkwardly and picked up the menu. She gave her order for coffee, boiled eggs and a chocolate croissant in passable French, then sat back and stared out into the courtyard where a woman was sitting alone on a bench, barely sheltered from the rain by a canopy. India recognized her once again, the same woman who had been drinking brandy the previous night. She glanced up at India as if sensing she was being watched, then stood up and walked away.

India finished her breakfast, signed the check and went back to her room. The day stretching ahead seemed less full of promise than it had the evening before. Traveling alone was not as easy as it appeared. Your head filled with thoughts you needed to share with someone else. You kept thinking of all the things you wanted to do and the sites you wanted to see with another person, particularly if that person were, well, Adam Brooks.

She flicked through her guidebooks. There were so many wonderful restaurants, but eating alone was not romantic or much fun. There were majestic churches, but after years of attending mass at school she was in no rush to check them out. Museums. That would be a start. India's mood lifted when her phone buzzed and she saw the text from Adam and the image of the Eiffel Tower, incongruous against the potted palm trees.

This sucks, it read.

We'll be together in Cannes soon. A bientot mon amour, she typed.

Setting off on foot in the direction of Musée National d'Histoire Naturelle, India fought the wind with an umbrella. Pulling it down defeated, she stopped by Compton des Cottonier to buy a hat. It was so much fun speaking Franglais with the shop assistants that the prospect of a museum teeming with school parties seemed a lot less inviting than a morning spent shopping. She decided to leave the cultural pursuits for the afternoon.

When the stores closed for lunch, she walked back to the hotel. The wind had died down, the sun was coming out and she was now the proud owner of a whole new closet. A French closet. Yes, shopping was the one thing that was better done alone.

Reaching the hotel, India realized she had not eaten for hours. Lunch, a little glass of wine and a quick snooze were the order of this spectacularly beautiful day. She walked in the direction of her room to drop off her shopping when someone opened the restroom door onto the cramped corridor and she careened straight into them, spilling her bags and making the whole thing worse by tripping over them.

"I'm so sorry," she said. "I really am overloaded here. I didn't see you. I'm terribly sorry."

"It's okay."

India looked up. "Oh! Hello. I'm India. India Butler. We keep bumping into one another. Well, I know I actually just bumped into you. Oh! Sorry. Etes Vous Francaise?" she added, realizing she possibly wasn't being understood.

"Luella," the woman answered. "I'm fine. Sorry, I wasn't looking either."

India scrambled to her feet.

"We're neighbors," she said, nodding her head to the adjoining door. "How long are you here for? I'm on vacation for a week."

"Me too," Luella said, "though it's not vacation – work."

"Oh! What do you do?" India asked, relishing the opportunity to speak in full English sentences while attempting to balance her bags on top of one another.

"I'm a writer. Novels. Can you manage all those bags?"

"Yes. Thanks," India said cheerfully. "Great. Well, see you."

How romantic, India thought wistfully, turning the tasseled key in the lock. To be in Paris writing a novel. That would make traveling on your own so much easier. You could sit around in cafés with all the other writers, just like Hemingway or Sartre had done years ago. You would blend in seamlessly.

After a lunch of yet another Saumon Fume, smoked salmon being the only meal she could order with absolute confidence at speed and with a decent accent, India decided not to waste time napping. She set off for the Musée d'Orsay. Walking along Rue de la Paix, her eye was caught by the dance display in the window of Repetto. Time to buy a new pair of ballet flats, she thought.

Coming out a while later carrying her delicately wrapped new shoes, she took a stroll around the market stalls. Perhaps it's too late to go to a museum. May as well stop in APC for a little gentle browsing, she thought.

An hour or so later, India emerged carrying several shopping bags with a spring in her step. Another perfect day, she thought. Tomorrow I will most definitely get to the Pompidou.

At the hotel, the doorman allowed her to struggle with the handle for only a few seconds before pushing open the door for her. I wonder if I'm supposed to keep tipping him everytime I go out, she thought. That could get very expensive.

"Merci beaucoup," she said with a smile.

After arranging her purchases on the bed and carefully removing the many plastic tags with a tiny pair of nail scissors, India showered and put on her new APC sweater with the silk trim, then turned her attention to the unexpectedly complicated issue of dining alone again.

Maybe, she thought, glancing at her watch, maybe there will be more people eating at the hotel this evening, perhaps some other travelers. Luella might be there. I wonder what kind of novels she writes. Then remembering to pick up a book for appearances sake, she closed the door behind her and went across the hall to the dining room.

~~ ~~ ~~

Luella ate in her room. After the trays had been cleared, she leaned her head out the window of the conservatory and smoked a cigarette. The rain had turned to sleet. Springtime in Paris. Huh! she thought, wrapping a sweater around her shoulders before turning on the table lamp and opening her laptop. She thumped at the keyboard for a while, then shoving back her chair pressed 'delete.' She took her cognac over to the bedside chair and sank into the cushions.

I can't even write, she thought. On top of everything else, I can't write. She glanced at her watch. "Shit! I forgot to get back to Susie." She took another sip of brandy before calling her friend.

"Sorry to call so late," she said.

"It's fine, Lu. It's perfect timing actually. The kids are finally in bed. I'm having a nightcap and watching a rerun of *Downton Abbey*. I'm all yours. How're you managing?"

"I spoke to Peter," Luella said.

"You did? Did you find out anything?"

"No. I was half-asleep when he called. It didn't go so well."

"But you told him you knew?"

"Yes."

"And?" She paused. "Lu, you don't need to tell me if you're not up to talking about it right now."

"I want to talk. I've been spending too much time alone. Another of life's cruel jokes don't you think...me having to come to Paris the same time I find out about all this. Everywhere I go, I wonder if Peter was there with his lover. I mean, that man could be right here, right now in this hotel. I might have passed him in the street. Can I ask you something?"

"Anything. Anything at all..."

"What do you think is important? I mean, tell me what I should I be focusing on."

"I'm not sure I understand," Susie said quietly.

"I don't know quite what I'm trying to say."

Luella stood up and paced the tiny room, sitting down on the side of the bed, then getting up again and wandering into the conservatory. She opened the window, shut it again and went back to the bedroom.

"He's been unfaithful. He's having an affair. He's been living a lie. Over and over. I keep asking myself does it make any difference if it's with a man or a woman? I'm really wrestling with it. I've been trying to imagine how I'd feel if it was another woman, and I think I'd be angry, I think I'd be hurt but I don't think I'd be feeling so helpless."

"I'm sure it makes things different, but honestly Lu, the best I can keep suggesting is that you talk to him, listen to what he has to say."

Luella flopped onto the bed. She flung the cushions onto the floor and leaned back on the pillow. "Well I'll have to at some point I suppose, but I need time. It's not like I can save our marriage. There's something so final about knowing I can't compete, knowing he needs something that I'll never be able to give him. It's all so complicated."

"It is and at the risk of sounding like a broken record, it will take time, and the only way you're going to attempt to understand it is to talk to him."

"I keep asking myself how come I didn't know."

"Lu. I'm no expert on this, but I think you're right. It is complicated and maybe in ways you're not seeing right now. I mean a lot of people are bisexual."

"That's true. I know that, but I've never really thought about what that means. I'm not even sure I want to. I've always believed that what two consenting adults do behind closed doors is none of my business. Now it turns out it kind of *is* my business."

"Lu, I'm thinking you should get some professional advice, someone you can talk to about your sex life."

"What sex life?" Luella quipped. "Sorry, lame joke, over

share, you're right. I'm sorry. Look, I'll let you go, it's getting late. Thanks for being a sounding board."

"I'm not sure I've been very much help. But I'm here for you. Be kind to yourself, Lu. Try to get some sleep. You sound exhausted."

"I am. I'm going to go to bed right now. Thanks. Thank you."

Luella undressed and climbed under the bedcovers. I'm a wreck, she thought, closing her eyes.

7
—

India woke early and soon became aware of an all-pervading silence. She went over to the window and pulled back the drapes. The courtyard was covered with a thick blanket of pristine snow. The air was still. A dusting of flakes was smattering the windowpanes. For a few minutes, she stood transfixed with delight at the picture-perfect scene and then grabbing her phone, she snapped a photograph of the stone fountain against the bare branches of the heavily laden trees.

> Adam – Look what I've woken up to this morning. So wish you were here – you remember that night in St. Petersburg when we drank Schnapps at The Caviar Bar and that guy serenaded us at the table? Do you remember the walk home? I bet you do. Am thinking about that right now...

She pressed 'send.' How could a girl ever forget that night? she thought. The gypsy music, the sledging, the hotel, the way we ran out toward the frozen river and... Snapping out of her reverie, she took in the implications of more bad weather. Today was her museum day. Despite all her careful planning and shopping, she had no suitable clothes for an outing in snow, yet the thought of being marooned indoors was totally depressing.

Maybe it isn't so bad outside the front of the building, she thought. They've probably cleared the main roads by now. It's nine o'clock already.

Not bothering to shower or brush her hair, she pulled on a warm cardigan over leggings and hurried to the foyer, where guests were sitting in disgruntled groups, their luggage piled in front of them, shivering from the icy blasts of the lobby doors, which kept swinging open.

"Charles De Gaulle est ferme," the guy standing next to her offered with a shrug.

"Sorry?" India, who was not yet fully awake, responded.

"People can't get out because of the snow, but some of these people did manage to get in. Chaos as usual. It's what the French are good at. They're wasting their time," he said nodding to the couple in front of him who were venting their frustrations on Jean-Paul. "There's not a lot he can do about it."

"Have you already checked out?" India asked.

"Not yet. I was about to, but I get the impression from what he's saying, that all the rooms are booked for tonight. As I've no way of getting to the airport and the airport itself is closed, I am not about to give up that room. Stalemate. They want it. I need it. Tough."

"I'm sorry," India said. "Maybe it'll stop snowing soon. Anyway, they can hardly kick you out onto the street."

"I need coffee. I've been standing here for an hour," he said. "Care to join me?"

"Actually I was about to have some too," she said, noticing that her new companion was rather good-looking in a Jake Gyllenhall kind of way in his black blazer and open-neck shirt. Not that she was interested in him of course, but a girl could be objective couldn't she? Just as this thought struck India, she looked down aghast at her leggings and oversized hotel terrycloth slippers.

A waitress was clearing off a table as they walked in. Assuming they were together, she quickly set two places opposite one another.

"Henry, by the way."

"India," she replied. "So are you here on business?"

"Yes. You?"

"Visiting," she said. "I live in London."

"Me too," he said, pausing to look up to where the waitress was hovering with a coffeepot. She placed it down between them.

"Cafe au lait s'il vous plait," India said. "C'est tout." It's bad enough to be in public and not showered, without spraying him with a mouthful of croissant, she thought as Henry rattled off his order.

"Les oeufs brouilles et bacon, un petit jus d'orange et les champignons, merci beaucoup. Il neige dure la bas."

"Merci Monsieur. Oui, il m'a fallu un certain temps pour arriver ici ce matin."

"Your French is very good," India said.

"It's okay. Having a French mother helps."

"I'm struggling. They say immersion is the only way to learn. I think you need to be here for a couple of years. Everyone speaks so fast."

"I thought you were French when I saw you yesterday," he said, pouring them each a cup of coffee. "You have the look."

Secretly thrilled, India coughed a little. "I'm barely dressed but rather pleased to hear you can look French when you've just gotten out of bed."

"That's the secret, don't you know." He smiled and India couldn't be certain, but she felt that he was flirting with her.

"All French women want to look like they've just had sex."

India laughed. "Well maybe most of them have but as I said, I'm traveling alone."

"Well that hardly stops you from having sex," he answered, a little too quickly for her comfort.

India twirled her spoon in her coffee cup.

"You're blushing," he said. "How sweet."

"Well, I think a change of subject is called for here," she said.

"Absolutely." He grinned. "By the way, did anyone ever tell you, you look a whole lot like that film actress, Annabelle Butler?"

"Well there'd be a reason for that," India answered. "She's my sister. We're fraternal twins."

"Really?" Henry said. "So, are you close? I hear twins have a special connection, but maybe that's just spin."

"We're as close as you can be when there are thousands of miles between us," she said. "We Skype, I visit, sometimes she comes to London."

Henry put down his fork. "I hear she's great to work with."

"How did you hear that? Are you in the business?"

"Kind of," he said. "So what about you?"

"I'm a drama teacher."

"Did you ever want to be an actress?"

"Never. I'm more into process. I love putting on shows. I like to think of myself as a producer. I'm more into being backstage than in front of the camera. So what do you do?"

Before he could answer, Henry's cell rang and he picked up.

"Sorry," he mouthed to her, "I have to take this."

India pointed toward the door to indicate she was going, slid her chair back and then left with as much dignity as her slippers would allow. Going back to her room, she checked her phone, then remembering the time difference, she sighed. Of course Adam will still be asleep, she thought.

India spent the rest of the morning practicing French online. Her course involved parrot repetition of sentences spoken by a French woman at conversational speed. By lunchtime she had mastered a series of phrases that might be useful in the unlikely event she were ever searching for eggs in a supermarket where nobody spoke English. The irony of interacting with a computer while being in Paris struck India all at once, and she realized she was ravenously hungry. Before venturing out of her room this time, she would shower and dress properly. She wasn't getting caught out again.

Just as well, she thought, a little while later, turning the corner into the sitting room where Henry and Luella were chatting by the fire. They both looked up as she came in.

"Hey there, good to see you again," Henry said, gesturing to the armchair across from him. "Care to join us?"

"Do they serve food in here? I'm starving," India said, hesitating. He's moved in on her fast even though she's wearing a wedding ring, she thought.

"Yes. We've just ordered soup," Luella said. "Do you two know each other?"

"We met earlier," Henry said. "India. Right?"

"Yes," she answered, sitting down in the red velour chair opposite him as an elderly waiter cleared the table in front of them and set out silverware.

"Et vous Madame?" he asked.

"Moi aussi Monsieur. Le potage du jour s'il vous plait," India said, feeling rather delighted at her ability to order soup in French without hesitating. "It's still snowing hard out there."

"Yes. We're marooned like in an Agatha Christie play," Luella sighed. "I hope nobody gets bumped off."

"I'll probably be the first to go if that happens." Henry laughed. "I've not made any friends around here this morning."

"Have you resolved the accommodation issue then?" India asked.

"Yes. I won. I suspect they just wanted the drama. I bet they always have free rooms in case one of their celebrity guests calls in on a whim. I hear Diane Keaton's very fond of the place."

India looked around her. She could see that it would be the kind of hotel for a discreet stay – the chairs arranged in cozy groups, the family feel – well, if your family were fabulously wealthy and French she supposed.

"I love how intimate this hotel is. Do you usually stay here when you're in Paris?" she asked Luella.

"Pretty much. They always give me the room on the ground floor with the conservatory. I can write there – well, I usually can. Oh good. Here's our soup. So what brings you here?"

Henry appeared to have lost interest and was texting furiously on his iPhone.

"It was spur of the moment. I was supposed to be here with a friend, but his plans changed last minute. I decided to come anyway, but I wasn't planning on snow. It's a trick to know what to do with yourself. I suppose you'll spend the time writing," she said. "Is your novel set here?"

"Yes, my next one. It's why I'm here."

"Lulu's written ten books," Henry chimed in. "All best-sellers."

"Ten books?" India gasped. "I wrote one and it nearly killed me."

"You did? Well done, you. What was it about?" Luella asked, pouring herself another glass of wine.

"Un verre de vin blanc merci," India said to the waiter, then turned back to her. "It was a guidebook for parents of teenagers."

"How did you come to write that? You don't look old enough to have teenage kids."

"I don't have kids, but I've taught that age group for years. I was staying in Los Angeles a few summers back with my sister. I worked with some of her friends who were struggling with all these issues. Anyway, I ran some workshops for them and turned the workshop materials into a book. It did quite well actually, but not well enough to give me a living. I came back to London."

"Yes. It's tough to make a living from writing. I've been really lucky. I made a name for myself before the industry changed. The market's flooded now."

Luella sat back in her chair and took another sip of wine.

"God, I could kill for a cigarette. Do you mind?" she said, standing up and grabbing her purse. "I'll be back."

"Did you get your work done?" India asked Henry, who had pushed away his bowl and was leaning back into the cushions contentedly. He rested his arms behind his head.

"Some," he said. "Then I bumped into Luella again. We had meetings earlier in the week. My company represents her. She's an old friend."

"Are you a book agent?"

"No. Our agency, Lichtenstein and Cowan, does her PR and promotions. I'm the Cowan by the way. We've represented Lu for about seven years now."

"I feel a bit foolish not having read any of her novels, I mean, given she's so successful I should have I suppose."

"You've probably got better taste," Luella said, appearing behind India's chair and then sitting back down next to her again. "Frigging freezing out there. I changed my mind."

"You should try the patch," India offered.

"I like to smoke," Luella said. "Especially with a good glass of wine. God, I miss the old days when you didn't feel like a pariah. What now then, Henry? Are we done for the day? Can I clock off and get another drink?"

"Your call, Lu. Sounds like a splendid idea to me. More white for you India?"

Why not? India thought. If what happens in Vegas stays in Vegas, what happens in Paris stays in Paris, thinking of which... She checked her phone and smiled when she saw the text from Adam.

Miss you too. Stay warm, xxoo.

By seven o'clock, India and her new companions had moved into the dining room, and India was negotiating her way around a plate of steaming mussels in a white wine and garlic sauce.

"I think the idea of a link with the Paris Fashion Institute has legs, but we may not be able to pull it off given the time constraints," Henry said, through a mouthful of bœuf bourguignon. The London Institute of Fashion and Technology is on board, and I'm getting very nice noises from a couple of potential sponsors."

Luella forked a piece of Dover sole. "Sorry India. We're talking shop again," she said.

"Let's talk about something else," Henry agreed.

"Well I've got some news then," Luella interjected, clearly buzzed. "Henry, did I tell you Peter's having an affair..."

"No, you didn't, but maybe we should talk about this later," Henry said.

"Possibly, but you might not want to wait to hear the punch line. He's having an affair with another man." She paused and turned toward India. "Peter's my husband of some twenty years."

Omigod and I think I have problems, India thought.

"Hey Lu, steady on," Henry said taking Luella's hand. "Let's talk about this later."

Feeling increasingly awkward, India smiled sympathetically.

"So where do you teach, India?" Henry said, breaking the uncomfortable silence that followed.

"Currently unemployed," she said, grateful for the change of subject. "I just came to the end of a temporary teaching contract in Hackney and decided not to renew it. I'm ready for a change of direction."

"If you do not change direction, you may end up where you are heading," Luella murmured. "I used that Lau Tzu quote in my last book. Changing direction is good I hear. I'm a coward; I don't like change. I like things to float along the way they always have. Henry here on the other hand is an adrenalin junkie."

India felt sure that Luella would regret these over shares in the morning. She mopped the last of her sauce with a chunk of bread, ate it and then wiped her mouth on her napkin. "That was beyond delicious." She sighed. "Has anyone seen a weather forecast recently?"

"I found a letter from his lover," Luella continued. "Several in fact."

"Do people still write letters these days?" Henry asked.

"It would appear they do – all handwritten and no doubt sealed with a loving kiss." Luella muttered, knocking back her drink.

"I miss getting letters," India said. "I'm addicted to the papeteries here. I've a gorgeous Christian Lacroix notepad too. I collect notepads, mostly the Smythson ones. Currently I'm using *J'Adore,* but my favorite is *Profound Thoughts.* I've a beautiful fountain pen. I'm kind of old-fashioned that way. I suppose it depends on your handwriting. People have always said mine's lovely."

Aware that she was starting to babble and that Luella was looking at her strangely, India pushed back her chair.

"Well, I think I'll turn in. I can see you two have a lot to talk about," she said, glancing at Henry. "Maybe I'll see you tomorrow, Luella. Thanks for adopting me today, guys. I'd have gone mad on my own."

Henry pushed back his chair, leaned toward her and whispered, "Most wise my dear."

India smiled. "Enjoy the rest of your evening," she said.

8
—

India was woken by the constant thuds of the elevator in the corridor outside her room. She stared at the clock, and then realizing she had slept later than planned, leapt out of bed and pulled back the heavy drapes. The sky was gray but the snow had melted, leaving a thin layer of gray slush. A light sleet was splattering the window. She glanced across the room and lifted a note from under the door. She sat on the edge of the bed to read it.

> Hi India,
>
> I have to leave for Lucerne this morning. Back tomorrow. Any chance I can take you to dinner at the Lutetia tomorrow night? I've a business proposition I'd like to run past you. Here's my number. 0208-789-2571. Text me. I can pick you up from the hotel at seven.
>
> Henry

Intriguing, India thought, as she texted her reply. Dinner it is. Maybe I'll let Henry loan me his jacket and get my picture taken in it. Ha.

With the prospect of dinner the following evening, India was content with the thought of spending the day alone.

She would visit Musée Marmottan Monet. She loved Impressionism despite the inverted snobbery around it. It seemed insane to India to dismiss works of art simply because some images had become ubiquitous. The wealthy 16th arrondissement would be a contrast and a little distance. There would be plenty to occupy her all day.

Next evening, India, dressed in her newly acquired black dress and leather jacket, assessed her look in the bathroom mirror. Her Chanel lipstick (*Rouge Coco Paradis*) had been an excellent choice, just the right punch of red for a night out in Paris. Of course, the little tremor she was feeling had absolutely nothing whatsoever to do with Henry did it? Grabbing her quilted purse, she threw the chain over her shoulder, adjusted her underskirt and walked into the foyer.

A driver escorted her to the Mercedes and held the door for her. She slid into the dark leather interior next to Henry.

"Bonsoir, Madame Butler," he said. "You smell good. You don't look that bad either."

"Why thank you, Mr. Cowan." She smiled. "You certainly know how to flatter a girl."

"Touché," he said, relaxing back into the seat as the car picked up speed and drove in the direction of Boulevard Raspail.

Arriving at the grand hotel, India's heart gave a flutter as the door opened into the opulent art nouveau lobby and they went through into the airy brasserie with its monochromatic décor and line of attendant waiters.

The maître d' led them to a corner table. From the welcoming smiles of the bartenders and nods from other diners, it was clear that Henry was no stranger to the place.

"So," he said once they were seated and had their menus, "I have had an idea. I think there's a way you can help me."

India looked at him quizzically. "Don't tell me. You want me to be your mule, smuggle heroin? I'd better warn you, I'm not that kind of girl."

Henry laughed. "Not quite what I was thinking."

"Okay. So? Tell me. I'm intrigued," she said.

"Well, as you know, we represent Luella Marchmont."

"Yes. But I'm not sure I understand what it is you do for her."

"Let me tell you about another writer we represent and you'll see. Ever heard of Sally Grace?"

"Who hasn't? Of course. She's the writer who always has recipes at the end of each chapter. Chick lit, right?"

"Women's commercial fiction. We represent Sally. We came up with that idea for her."

"The idea of including recipes?"

"Yes. It gave us a great hook to promote her book. They're real recipes. They're woven into the stories, so say when a character is ill, their Aunty Joan brings her carrot soufflé to the hospital for them."

"Okay," India said.

"It means we can push her book online and through the media in the cooking blogs and programs as well as through the usual outlets. It's a bonus. People who love baking as well as reading go crazy for her books and the book clubs love it."

"So you get two bites of the cherry...literally as it were?"

"That's funny." He smiled. "And yes. You've got it."

"So how could this involve me?"

"Luella always weaves in a message to her stories. *Sunlight in Winter* was about dealing with grief when you lose someone to cancer. We sold a ton of copies by doing joint promotions with cancer charities."

"That sounds rather cynical if you don't mind me saying," India said, pausing as Henry stopped to give his wine order to the sommelier who was standing to the side of their table waiting for a lull in their conversation.

"Puligny Montrachet s'il vous plait," he told him and then turned back to India. "Not cynical at all. It's about finding your target market. It was a win-win. We sold more copies, they got a percentage of sales and the readers got inspiration. It's cause-related marketing."

"Okay. I can see it now that you've explained it. But how would that kind of promotion involve me?"

"You're a teacher. And by the way, if teachers looked like you when I was younger, I wouldn't have dropped out of school."

"You should know that's not an original line, Mr. Cowan, but I'll take the compliment anyway." India smiled.

"Actually I *didn't* drop out of school," he said.

"Very funny then. So how can I be of assistance?"

"We have a whole new potential market in online education. It's not a market I'm familiar with. I think you could be helpful."

"Go on," India said, with a tilt of her head.

"Merci. Pas encore," Henry said, politely waving away the waiter and then turning back to India. "I want to take a minute with this before we order if that's okay."

"Fine by me," she said. "I'm intrigued."

"We hire consultants with expertise in each market – advisors, experts, muses, whatever you want to call them. I may be wildly off base, but you did say you were at the end of your contract and if we could work something out, of course we'd pay you. If you agree in principle, then we'll sit down and work out a proper basis for it."

"I'm flattered," India said, feeling an unexpected surge of adrenalin at the prospect of something new. "But isn't this a bit sudden? I mean you haven't even seen my resumé."

"I think you may be forgetting a little thing called the Internet." Henry laughed.

"Sorry? I don't..."

"I Googled you of course and your guidebook for parents is an ebook, or have you forgotten that?"

India fiddled with her napkin. "No, but I do try to forget that I have an online profile."

"Yes. Well you have quite the profile, I noticed, and you aren't exactly a stranger to promotional events."

"I assume you mean the Firewalk." India laughed. "So what else do you know about me, Henry?"

"Shall we just say that I had my people make a few gentle probes and on the basis of my research, I am more than happy to discuss offering you a consultancy contract. We're thinking big for this promotion. We're talking about bringing this book alive. It's already been sold into several international markets including the states."

India said nothing for a moment. Play it cool, she told herself. Pretend this kind of offer comes around all the time. "Okay," she said and took a sip of her wine. "This sounds interesting. Tell me more."

"We've commissioned a fashion show in New York with one of the leading fashion colleges in the world. It's accredited by FIDM. The students brainstormed and came up with the idea of exchanging research and creative ideas with LIFT – The London Institute of Fashion and Technology."

"Oh yes. I know about LIFT. I sometimes wish I'd gone there myself. I'm a bit of a fashion junky. Tell me about the show."

"It will profile the work of both colleges. We'll be linking by satellite to compères here in Paris and also to Los Angeles."

Henry's voice faded into the background as India's head teamed with possibilities – fashion, New York, Paris, international, muse. She was watching Henry's lips move, but already she could see the runways and the flashing screens. Inès de la Fressange in the front row, pad in hand, taking notes. Georgia Jagger and Fifi Geldof cruising down the catwalk. Lady Gaga making a speech about creativity and then bringing home the finale with *Born This Way*, wearing a plastic bikini and a college cap and gown made from trash bags.

"How long are you staying in Paris?"

Henry's face swam back into focus and India became aware that he had been waiting for an answer from her.

"I leave next Tuesday."

"I have to get back to London in the morning. Tomorrow is Saturday right? I lose track of the days. Tell you what. Why don't you talk to Luella and read her book. Then call me next week when you're back. Here's my card," he said, reaching into his jacket pocket.

"Okay. Sure," she said. "Thanks."

"So now let's enjoy what Paris has to offer," he said, lifting the menu. "They do wonderful scallops here and the oysters are by far the best in Paris."

~ ~ ~

An altogether beautiful Sunday morning, India thought, setting off down the Rue Cassette to meet Luella for lunch. She was early but planned on taking her time. As she turned off the side street her phone buzzed and she fished it out of her pocket.

"Got your e-mail. Honestly India, I leave you on your own for a couple of days and the next thing you know you trip over one of the biggest selling authors of all time and get a job offer. I swear if you fell into a bucket of shit you'd come out smelling of roses."

"Sarah, did you ever consider a career penning greeting card messages? You have such a lovely turn of phrase," India quipped.

"That's what hoisting old-age pensioners onto commodes all day long does for a girl. You get such a romantic perspective on life."

India laughed. She knew her friend loved her new job at the nursing home. She doted on her elderly patients and from all the note cards and little presents, it was clear that their families appreciated Sarah too.

"Seriously though, it does sound like this job would be right up your alley. I've read quite a few of Luella Marchmont's books. The last one was really moving, all about euthanasia. I'm looking after an old lady right now who's begging me to give her an extra shot of morphine and put her out of her misery. We should be able to choose when we die."

"I'll put you out of your misery whenever you like. Would you rather die by asphyxiation or be drowned in the bath? Both can be arranged." India laughed.

"I think I'd like to be found fully clothed. Leave a girl some dignity. Okay so here's one for you. Would you rather be the richest person on the planet or immortal?"

"I'll get back to you on that one."

"Anyway," Sarah said, "while you're working that out, it does sound like you're having a great time. I'm really happy for you."

"Yes. Going away has been the right thing to do. I mean I only think about Adam every ten minutes or so, which is progress, don't you think?"

"And you almost managed a whole conversation without mentioning his name. Did you talk to him yet?"

"Yes. We're back on track, but I'm trying to play it cool."

"Ha! I've seen your version of playing it cool." Sarah laughed. "Anyway, great. Gotta go. I'm needed. See you next week. Enjoy the rest of the trip. Love you."

Sarah clicked off and as India threw her phone into her purse, she became aware of the swell of an organ recital filling the Place Saint Sulpice. Almost involuntarily, she joined the crowd walking toward the entrance to the baroque cathedral and was drawn into the cavernous interior by the sheer power and strength of the music. It had been more than twenty years since India had been inside a Catholic church. She walked slowly past the Delacroix frescoes and paused at a side altar lit by flickering votives.

Ah! St. Jude, she thought, gazing at the statue of the monk. The patron saint of lost causes. I thought they'd abolished him, but maybe that was the patron saint of lost things, the one that used to help me find my car keys. Hard to keep up.

The organ reached a thunderous crescendo as India left the darkness of the church and came out blinking into the sunshine. She wandered in the direction of the Café de Flore.

Luella was already squashed into a red leather banquette in front of the large mahogany mirrors when she arrived.

"Hey India," she said, standing up briefly to greet her with a peck on both cheeks. "I've sacrificed my right to a cigarette for you, but I didn't think you'd appreciate sitting at an outside table in the cold."

"Thanks," India said, pulling out a chair opposite her. "It's busy here."

"It is. It's become a bit of a tourist trap. The toilet downstairs is in all the guidebooks for some reason I've never fathomed, but I still think they do the best croque madame in Paris. Deux Maggots is overrated don't you think?"

"I have to admit I don't know Paris all that well," India said taking off her coat. "But this is lovely."

"Let's decide what we want quickly. They'll be ages getting the order. Let's have a nice glass of wine and we can talk properly."

India glanced at the menu, delighted to see that unlike her hotel, they served Sancerre here by the glass.

"I hear you had a good old chat with Henry the other night," Luella began after they had ordered their drinks. "By the way, I must apologize for my mood at dinner. I had one hell of a shock just before leaving London and between that, the weather and the fact that I have writer's block about the new book...well...it hasn't happened to me before. I usually spew them out, but for some reason I'm totally blocked, and the publishers are breathing down my neck for a synopsis. Anyway, it's no excuse. I was rude to be so self-indulgent."

"Not at all," India said. "You were fine."

"That's kind of you to say. Either way I do want to thank you for taking an interest in my work, and I'd love for you to read it and see if it appeals to you."

"I would be honored." India smiled. "Henry told me the gist of it."

"That's good. This is my own copy. I won't tell you which of the endings I used. I wrote three as you'll see."

"I like the sound of that. I often make up happy endings for books and films that are miserable."

"Funny to think that Hemingway sat here in the Café de Flore and struggled with thirty-seven endings," Luella mused. "Mind you, don't get too excited. *Faux Fashion* is hardly the stuff of great literature, and it's certainly not *A Farewell to Arms.*"

"I can't wait to read it," India said. "And no, don't tell me which ending you favor. No spoilers. I think Hemingway was prone to excess. Three endings sound like more than enough to me."

"I welcome your feedback," Luella said, handing India the manuscript. "And now let's get you something to eat. I'm actually not all that hungry, but you go ahead."

"Are you sure?" India said putting the folder into her bag carefully. "I do rather fancy the croque monsieur."

"Be my guest." Luella smiled. "I'm not very high energy today, but I'm glad of your company. Go ahead."

"My French isn't so great, but I think I can manage to order croque monsieur," India said, catching the waiter's eye. "How about I get a side order of fries and you help me with them."

"Bien sûr," Luella answered.

India finished her meal quickly, sensing from Luella's air of distraction that she needed to be alone.

"I'm going in that direction," Luella told her as they were leaving the café. "Thanks so much, India. When are you going back to London?"

"Tomorrow evening, sadly. I can't believe how quickly these last few days have gone."

"Well I'll see you there if we miss each other tomorrow." She smiled. "À bientôt."

Unsure what to do with the rest of the afternoon, India wandered down the street and spent some time in Librairie la Hune admiring the art books before taking tea at the downstairs café in Monoprix. A few hours later she strolled back to Hotel de l'Abbaye looking forward to settling down in front of the fire with Luella's book. I have all the company I need for tonight's *digestif*, she thought.

~ ~ ~

Luella walked along the stone-arched passageways of Rue de Rivoli slowly. At Le Meurice Hotel, she hesitated a moment before entering the foyer and taking in the opulent splendor of the reception area with its glistening Art Nouveau mirrors marble-tiled floor and gilt furniture. I would never stay in a place like this, she thought. It's far too ostentatious.

"Bonsoir Madame. May I help you?"

A manager was at her side.

"Non Monsieur," she answered. "Merci."

What on earth am I doing here? she wondered, turning quickly to leave. Racing down the steps, she dashed across the street, heedless of the blaring horns as she dodged between cars. She steadied herself against the garden railings and caught her breath. I think I might be going mad, she thought. What on earth did I think I would achieve by going there?

~ ~ ~

It was so much warmer in Paris than here, India thought, pulling her collar around her face against the bitterly cold wind whipping up Shaftsbury Avenue and walking quickly towards Wardour Street. There was something about Soho London that always excited her. She loved the eclectic mix of bars and cafes, sex stores and offices, the warren of tiny side streets barely wide enough to take the cabs and cars that were constantly teeming with office workers and tourists, the pubs spilling patrons outdoors onto every corner in all kinds of weather, and the discreet hotel entrances tucked away down alleys.

And today, India felt not only her usual quickening of pace, but a flutter of excitement at the possibility that she might be about to join the throngs of executives at Pâtisserie Valerie for lunches or grabbing sandwiches to go from Prêt à Manger before meetings.

She took a deep breath before pressing the intercom to the offices of Lichtenstein and Cowan, a tall Georgian building incongruously set opposite a sex shop with its cheap window displays of mannequins in bondage gear. The door buzzed open and India went toward the lift to the second floor, where she was greeted by a young woman she judged to be in her mid-twenties, wearing an immaculately tailored gray skirt and a camel cashmere sweater. Her long blonde hair was pulled back in a neat ponytail, and when she smiled, her teeth had that preternaturally white sheen India had only previously seen in California.

"Mr. Cowan will be with you in a moment. May I take your coat? Would you like a glass of water?" she said, gesturing toward one of the two easy chairs next to a coffee table set out with dozens of international glossy magazines.

"No thank you," India answered, unwrapping her scarf and taking off her raincoat, instantly grateful that she had worn the gray Agnes B shift dress. Shopping in Paris certainly gave a girl added confidence, even if her dress was from a chain that was also in London. A week studying Parisian style had not been wasted on India. Inès was right with her advice to keep things simple – good tailoring, neutral hues and then all you needed was a unique piece of jewelry, preferably inherited from your grandmother. In the absence of a grandmother, India had made a trip to Links and was sporting a delicate necklace with tiny pink pearls.

Henry appeared not long after she sat down. She stood up to meet him and for a moment felt butterflies. Had he been that tall in Paris? Had his eyes been so molasses brown, his shoulders so broad? She felt something close to an electric shock run down her spine.

"Great to see you, India. Come on in," he said, holding the door to his office open wide with his arm and leaving an arc for her to enter through.

"Thanks," she mumbled, ducking into the room and waiting while he closed the door behind them both.

"Here, have a seat if you can find one," he said, lifting a pile of magazines and then gesturing to two leather bucket chairs facing one another.

Henry's office was not at all what she had been expecting. For some reason India had imagined a modern, streamlined minimalist space with stripped wood furnishings and modern art. Instead, every conceivable wall space was filled with shelves straining under the weight of books and manuscripts. Henry's desk was buried under a mountain of files and papers, magazines and folders.

"I'm a hoarder," he said, reading her mind. "Out of chaos comes clarity."

"I love it," India said. "I can't understand how people can be the least bit creative in a sterile workspace. Those cubicle things are the worst."

"Ah. Yes, hot-desking would definitely not work for me." He laughed. "So have you thought about my offer?"

"Well, since we spoke on the phone I've read the book and I have to admit it isn't the kind of book I would usually read, but I couldn't put it down."

"Yes, with Luella there's always a great hook. She's totally commercial. If I could ever persuade her to write more sex scenes she'd probably outsell EL James."

"So have you had a chance to set out how you think I can help?"

"I have," Henry said, picking up a magazine, then tossing it across a coffee table where it landed precariously on top of his briefcase. He stood up, went across to his desk and lifted a phone.

"Samantha, can you bring me the Luella Marchmont file? Thanks, and can you pick up the draft contract for Miss Butler from the legal people? I meant to collect it on my way in."

Turning back to India, he continued. "I think our arrangement will work best on a contracted retainer and an hourly rate, travel expenses to be costed separately. Standard consultancy fixed six-month contract to take us to the end of October, to be reviewed at the end of the strategic planning stage. That's the time allocation to do the build out, production and follow up. I'm assuming you can commit to the time frame. We're already way behind schedule."

Henry was talking so rapidly that India was having difficulty keeping up with him. Samantha was in the room now and handing Henry a manila folder.

"Here you go," he said, handing India a wad of papers. "Have your lawyer check it out, but I think you'll find it's all pretty straightforward. Let me know if you think we've been generous enough." He smiled. "I am pretty sure we're well ahead of a teacher's salary, but equally I want you to be happy. Let me see. We're Wednesday right now. If you could sign it and let me have it by Friday that'd be great. Let's schedule a meeting for early next week and in the meantime take this with you and get up to speed on the promotion and give me your thoughts."

Henry didn't sit down again and it was clear to India the meeting was over. "Er, thank you. Yes. I think Friday will be fine," she managed to say. Thank god for Annie and her team of lawyers, she thought. I'm way out of my depth here.

"Great. Don't go, Samantha; we need to run through the campaign for *Morning in Manhattan* – shouldn't take long." He grimaced. "Same old, same old."

"Let me show you out, Miss Butler," Samantha said graciously.

~ ~ ~

India stood outside on the steps of the building. The entire meeting had taken fewer than ten minutes. Pumped with adrenalin, she set off in the direction of Regent Street unsure what to do with the rest of her afternoon and kicking herself for not asking any of the questions she should have asked Henry.

What exactly did this job entail? Would there be regular hours? Would she be traveling a lot? Would she be working from home? Had she misled him? She'd ended up in a mess that way once before. She wasn't in a rush to mislead anyone again.

India glanced up as the clock outside Fortnum and Mason chimed the hour and realized this would be a good time to call her sister in LA. She turned into the nearby Le Pain Quotidien, ordered a cup of Earl Grey tea and settled into a corner seat. Annabelle picked up quickly.

"Hey sis. How's chilly London? Are you sure I can't tempt you back to LA? It's a glorious day here."

"Hi Annie. I have some news."

"Is everything okay?" Annabelle sounded alarmed.

"Everything's fine. It's just that I need some advice. I've had a job offer. It's all happened a bit fast and you'll probably think I'm insane, but something happened in Paris..."

"Sounds like the opening to a novel."

"Well, funny you should say that," India said. "Okay. I'm not quite sure where to start, but the bottom line is that I've been offered a job in promotions and Annie, I think I may be in over my head."

"Well, I'll avoid saying the obvious." Annabelle laughed. "Just start at the beginning and tell me everything. Just give me a minute to grab a coconut water...okay, I'm sitting down. You have my full attention."

India talked at breakneck speed, filling her sister in on the trip to Paris and the meetings with Luella and Henry. Realizing she was attracting attention from an adjoining table, she lowered her voice and whispered, "So what do you think?"

"I think you'd be mad not to take it."

"But can I do it? Surely that's the more important issue."

"Of course you can. Think of all you've done."

"Like what exactly?"

"Darling, EVERYTHING. Think about it – your teaching, the events you've produced, the workshops you designed, your guidebook, to say nothing of your somewhat unhealthy interest in fashion. You recognize designer labels I've never heard of; you're obsessed. This is made for you."

"You always make things sound so simple," India said, but she was listening hard.

"Go for it, darling. And of course, I'm being selfish. It'd be wonderful. I could meet you in New York; we could catch a show. Why not?"

Henry, India thought. Henry would be the only reason.

"So have you and Adam sorted things out yet?"

"I think so. We've talked a few times and we text. I think I believe he was telling the truth, though I do wonder if he'd have taken that girl out for dinner if she'd been flat-chested and wearing Birkenstocks."

Annabelle laughed. "Probably not," she agreed.

"Anyway, he's promising to take me to Cannes when he's there on location."

"That sounds wonderful, darling. Great. That should make up for not going to Paris."

"It's funny to think of it, but if he'd been with me last week, I probably wouldn't have met Henry and Luella and all this wouldn't be happening."

"True. So it's meant to be; everything's working out. You see? Take the job. Go for it, darling."

India said her goodbyes and clicked off. She stared at the dregs in her teacup. Her sister was always so upbeat. She didn't know what it felt like to fail. Everything she touched turned to gold dust – her amazing career, her wonderful marriage, great kids. She never seemed to doubt herself. Annie was the one who got the confidence genes, that was for sure.

Standing up and pushing her way through the crowded café doorway, India emerged onto a street heaving with tourists. She made her way to the tube station, reflecting on their conversation.

9

—

Luella leaned back in the chintz-covered armchair and sighed heavily. The high-ceilinged room she had decorated with such loving care all those years ago seemed to echo around her. Each possession held a memory: the watercolor she and Peter had picked out on their honeymoon, the coffee table discovered in a junk shop when they were students, the outrageously expensive Waterford crystal chandelier Peter had splurged on to celebrate his promotion to company vice president.

Maybe she should have arranged to be out tonight after all. She'd run the possible scenarios in her head many times and eventually decided to be at home when he left. It would be cowardly to avoid him. She sat up quickly startled by a thump in the hallway as Peter put down his suitcases.

He walked into the drawing room staring around as if he were lost. He looked ragged from lack of sleep, his clothes a crumpled mess. The stress was clearly taking its toll on him. He cut such a pathetic figure that for a split second Luella had the urge to leap up and hug him, but then instantly remembered why he was there.

"How was the flight?" she asked, putting her wine glass onto the coffee table with trembling hands.

"Long."

There was an awkward silence.

"Look Lu..." he began, running his hands through his hair awkwardly. "I never wanted you to find those letters..."

"Stop Peter. I can't do this right now. I can't talk about it. Please just get your things and go. We can talk when I've had more time."

Hesitating for a moment, Peter turned and left the room. Luella switched on the television and sat staring mindlessly at the screen. A while later, she heard the front door close gently and soon after, the revving of an engine.

How can twenty years be over in the space of an hour? she wondered, closing her eyes and blinking back tears.

~ ~ ~

India threw her coat on the back of a chair and spread out Henry's papers across the kitchen table. She sat down to read the contract and gasped.

There must be something wrong with my math, she thought. He can't possibly be offering me more in a week than I've ever earned in a month.

She read the first two pages slowly again. The line for travel and accommodation clearly indicated she would not be expected to stay at a Holiday Inn or to travel coach. There was some legal jargon but it didn't get in the way of her understanding that Lichtenstein and Cowan LLC was hiring Miss India Butler as a consultant and that Lichtenstein and Cowan LLC was offering to pay her very well indeed.

But for what exactly? she thought. What did consulting actually involve? Whatever...Annie was right. She would be insane not to grab this opportunity. What could be the worst that could happen? It was just a job. Why this paralyzing fear of failure? Had she really failed before? Running her workshops in LA and getting published had been a great achievement, but one excruciatingly embarrassing incident (that she sickened even to think about) had knocked so much of her confidence.

Yes, she had written her book and had even overcome the terrors of appearing on primetime television to promote it, but someone who was really driven would have gone on to write another, learned how to promote herself better through the media. There were enough classes out there on that. Something had stopped her. She had come back to London, to her comfort zone, to a job she could do with her eyes shut.

India stood up and went over to the sink. Filling the kettle, she popped a teabag into a pot and stood waiting for the water to boil. What exactly did she want? Of course she knew deep down that all she wanted was for Adam to move their relationship on, ask her to live with him or at least make a long-term plan with her. Clearly, he was still terrified of commitment. Roger was right. It was time to take control and make some plans of her own. She grabbed a teacup and saucer, some skim milk, brought the tea tray back to the table and sat down.

Okay, she thought, shaking off the image she had dreamed about so often: a house overlooking the ocean in Malibu and a bassinet in a bedroom she shared with Adam. Okay. Enough. This really is ENOUGH. What was that Leonard Cohen quote? *Act the way you want to be and soon you'll be the way you act.* "Okay, okay," she said to her cat, asleep and curled under her feet. "I will act like an independent woman of the twenty-first century."

Pushing the tea things away, she reached across the stack of bills and magazines and lifted a well-thumbed book. I wonder what an overpaid consultant type person should wear for meetings, she thought. I shall consult the oracle that is Inès de la Fressange.

~ ~ ~

Luella showered and dressed quickly, relieved to have appointments all day that would get her out of her home office and out of the house. It was unseasonably cold and she was regretting her choice of a linen jacket as she stepped out of the cab in front of Henry's office.

"Hi, Miss Marchmont. Great to see you. How was Paris?"

"Thanks, Samantha. You look lovely as ever. Paris went well. Is India here yet?"

"Yes. She and Henry are in the boardroom already. Can I get you anything? There's water in there but I'll run across the street if you fancy a latte."

"Water will be fine thanks, and I don't think you could run very far in those shoes." She laughed, looking down at Samantha's platform heels.

Henry and India both stood up to greet Luella.

"India, I am absolutely thrilled you liked the book," Luella beamed.

"I *loved* it," she enthused. "Tod's character has stayed with me. I can see him so clearly. I'm interested to know if any of it was based on your own life," she added, hoping the question sounded spontaneous and not as prepared as it was.

"No. My nephew. He's been a vegetarian since he was a teenager, became a vegan after a while and then ran into all the ethical issues once he was at LIFT. He refused to use leather and in his attempt to be purist about it, he avoids even wool and silk. He's broken new ground. He works with ethically sourced fabrics and with scientists. Of course, the actual story is fiction, but his real life experience was the inspiration."

"That's so interesting. Isn't Stella McCartney into all that too?" India asked.

"Absolutely. Many of the new wave of designers are as well. What was your favorite ending?"

"I picked the happy one of course." India laughed. "I loved how everything was still possible with that one."

"I thought you would." Luella smiled. "And so you know, that's the one I picked too."

"Great. It really works. You feel like there's a whole new beginning, that there may even be a sequel."

"Exactly."

"Right. So now let's get on," Henry said, handing them each a press pack. "This is incomplete but will get us started. The London Institute of Fashion and Technology will be partnering with the Fashion Institute in New York. We're talking to the networks to get some televised coverage, although the revenue for the colleges will mostly come from the build-out: online subscriptions, YouTube, websites, standalones. We need to agree on percentages for the book sales. I have your agents working on that."

Henry rattled this off like a tobacco auctioneer. He may as well be speaking Swahili for all I understand, India thought, but she nodded sagely.

"Who's the main sponsor?" Luella asked over the top of her glasses.

Henry leaned back in his chair and threw his arms behind his head. "*Beauty Without Cruelty* will hopefully be in by the end of the week. I'll keep you up to speed on that as soon as we know for sure."

"What do you need from me at this point, Henry?" Luella asked.

"We need to set up some prerecorded interviews, usual thing. What was the inspiration behind writing the book, what was your own education like, are you a vegan, what's the next book? Maybe India can suggest more questions for the online magazines. Get them in the bag early and they're off your plate."

"Okay. I'll fit around your schedule. Just let Margaret know. Margaret is my assistant..." Luella said, turning to India and lifting her purse from the table. "You'll meet her when you come over to the house. She's worked for me for years, and she'll be able to fill you in more. See you soon."

"India," Henry said, putting back the top on his roller pen and getting to his feet. "You might want to lead on how we can maximize the link with Otis College in LA. Stay behind and let's talk about that in a minute."

India froze. Lead? She was having great difficulty following.

"Thanks for popping by Lu," Henry said, walking her toward the door, then sitting down again and facing India across the table.

India shifted in her chair. She was sure he knew how magnetic he was. He was enjoying the effect he was having on her, wasn't he? She fumbled around in her purse by way of distraction.

"Lost something?" He grinned.

"Er, no. Just checking," she mumbled, sitting back straight and avoiding his eyes.

"Okay. So now," he continued "we need a couple of hosts for the show. I *had* been thinking Demi and Ashton a while back, but that obviously won't work anymore. Any suggestions? You don't have to tell me right now. Give me a list by tomorrow. Oh! And you need to get Samantha to set up a meeting for you with the dean at LIFT, ASAP. Get a sense of the project."

"Okay," India said. "I'll get right on it." That was the thing to say, she was sure. Very Olivia Pope.

Henry was sliding back his chair and clearly expecting her to leave. Gathering her papers into the pink leather Smythson folio case she had bought earlier in the week, India hesitated for a moment and then left the room, unsure where she was headed. She was still hovering in the reception area when Samantha appeared again.

"Henry just remembered you might need a desk here from time to time. We haven't a lot of space, but I've cleared a corner of the room the accountant uses when he comes in. Second door on the left. Make a list of anything you need."

India, resisting the urge to grab her coat and run out of the building, smiled and went down the corridor.

What on earth have I got myself into? she wondered, looking at the bleak room with its mismatched battered furniture and peeling paintwork. I don't think I can spend more than five minutes in here.

Glancing at her phone, she saw a text from Sarah.

Can be at your place at 6, India typed quickly. Coming back out to reception, she thanked Samantha, then ran down the stairs onto the street and made for the tube station.

~ ~ ~

India's mind was racing as the train hurtled through the darkness of the underground tunnel and out into the fading sunlight of the suburbs. She leapt up quickly, almost missing her stop. She raced across the platform, onto the street teeming with commuters. Dashing up the path of Sarah's Victorian terraced house, she stood on the step catching her breath and taking in the gentle scent of the lavender hedge. Spring has finally sprung, she thought.

Sarah pulled open the door and gave her a hug. "So how'd it go? Perfect timing, I've made Spaghetti Bolognese – coming right up."

India threw her jacket across the back of the couch.

"Help yourself," Sarah shouted, waving toward a bottle of Pinot Grigio. "Opener's somewhere around. Try the drawer on the left."

"Voila!" she announced, setting a bowl of steaming pasta in the center of her pine kitchen table and wiping her hands on her apron.

"Thanks. That looks delicious," India said, struggling to uncork the bottle. "Where's your glass or have you made an early start? God Sarah, what have I got myself into with this new job? You know I was thinking on the way over that maybe Henry's only hired me to get Annie and Joss to be hosts for the fashion show. He's asking me to lead on that. I think he's under the impression I can just pick up the phone to Brad Pitt or someone."

India stopped speaking abruptly, her train of thought interrupted by Sarah's look of distraction. "Are you okay?"

Sarah put down the serving spoon and leaned back. "Indie, I have news. I hope you're going to be pleased for me."

"Omigod. Sarah! Sarah!" India screamed jumping up. "You're getting married. Right? I knew it. Sarah, you can't keep a secret from me."

"Not exactly, but close," Sarah replied looking decidedly sheepish. She hesitated for a moment. "I'm pregnant," she said.

India sat back down in her chair with a thud. "But I don't understand. You're so sensible. This kind of accident happens to people like me, not you," she said. "When did you find out? How many weeks? Do you know what you're going to do?"

"This isn't an accident," Sarah said quietly, taking a sip of water.

India's jaw dropped. "It's not?"

"No."

"So, okay. How many weeks are you?" India asked, struggling to take in the enormity of what she was hearing.

"Twelve," Sarah answered.

'That's three months. Sarah, you can't possibly be telling me you got pregnant deliberately. You were planning something as big as THIS and you didn't share it with me and you've known for THREE MONTHS." India pushed her plate away from her across the table.

"You know India, everything isn't always about you," Sarah answered quietly.

"I'm sorry, I didn't mean it to come out that way. I just thought, well think, that if the roles were reversed I would've talked something as huge as this through with you. I mean you're my closest friend. I share stuff with you that I don't even talk to Annie about."

"Yes. Well the truth is I've been nervous about telling you. I know things haven't been going well with Adam."

"That's the understatement of the year," India muttered.

"And you and Damien haven't ever gelled."

"I suppose that's true," she said.

"There. You see. Do you honestly believe that if I had

told you I was planning on getting pregnant with him you wouldn't have tried to persuade me out of it?"

India felt cornered. "I'm not sure," she said slowly. "I never really thought about it. I do like Damien well enough. It's just we don't have much in common. I'm just surprised that's all. Did you plan it together?"

"Sort of. We have an agreement. I know you've never really understood my broodiness, but I felt time was running out for me. I didn't deliberately try – I just didn't especially *not* try if you get what I mean."

"So are you planning on getting married?"

"The subject hasn't even come up. If things work out between us, then maybe at some point, but that's not important right now. Whatever happens with us, I'll be fine. I really will. I own this house, even if it is tiny. I can afford childcare. Don't worry, Indie. Look, all I want is for you to be pleased for me."

India leapt up and ran around the table to give her friend a hug. "I am. Of course I'm pleased. I am just so surprised, that's all. Of course I'm thrilled for you if it's what you want. Congratulations. I am so very sorry I didn't start off with that."

"It's okay. I overreacted. It's the hormones. It's been really hard to keep this from you, but I needed to know there was no turning back before I told you."

"So all that stuff about too much fattening hospital food and planning on going to Weight Watchers was just camouflage?"

"I feel bad about that, but I had to throw you off the scent a bit," Sarah said. "Indie, I needed to hug this to myself for a while, and the last few months haven't been as easy as I thought they would be. I wasn't expecting all the mood swings and feeling like maybe I'd done the wrong thing after all, and I've been nauseous and exhausted. Oh, I don't know. Look. You know now. Can we please move forward?"

"Absolutely. I have no idea why I had such a strong reaction either. I do understand."

"Here. Get started before this goes cold." Sarah smiled, pushing the dish of spaghetti toward India. "There's an apple pie in the oven too. I seem to be coming over all domesticated. Bon appetit."

Later that evening, as she was getting ready for bed in an apartment that felt emptier than usual, India was struggling to work out why she had responded to Sarah's news with such intensity. Was it really that Sarah had taken so long to share her news with her or did it go deeper than that? Could it possibly be that she was feeling envious? That would be the last thing she would want to feel about Sarah. She would hate herself for that.

She poured scalding water into a hot water bottle and cradled it to herself as she dragged up the stairs. Glancing up at the moon as she closed the drapes, she heaved a deep sigh. The street below was bathed in silvery moonlight, the trees heavy with blossom.

A night for romance, she thought wistfully before climbing under the covers and curling into a ball. Why did I have to fall in love with someone who lives on the other side of the world?

～～～

It surprised Luella that her house didn't feel especially empty with Peter gone. They had kept separate bedrooms for some time. Ostensibly, he had become irritated by her propensity for switching on the bedside light in the middle of the night to jot down a thought before it escaped her. It had been a gradual transition, pillows and duvets carried across the landing in the middle of the night, his increasingly regular decision to 'sleep in the spare room if you're going to come up late.' Of course, now Luella understood that her erratic hours had given him the perfect excuse to avoid intimacy.

The arrangement had suited her. She worked from her laptop nowadays, not the sturdy computer that had served her so well over the years. Gradually her bedroom had become her oasis. The tea maker she installed meant she didn't even have to go downstairs in the morning until Peter had left for the office. They had both been burrowing into their own lairs, coming together occasionally to eat or watch television.

Luella wandered into the spare room, anxious for clues about the husband she had never really known. A faint trace of cinnamon lingered in the air from Peter's Aramis cologne. She swung open the double doors of the antique mirrored wardrobe. It was empty apart from a line of cedar hangers. The bed had been stripped, the shelves cleared. It was as if the room had been host to a phantom.

10

——

❝Thank god for whoever invented twenty-four hour room service, India thought, pressing down hard on the lid of the French press and pouring herself a large mug of coffee. Slathering a piece of toast with butter and orange marmalade, she climbed back into the crumpled sheets of her bed at The Warwick Hotel.

India had been in New York for four days and the jetlag (possibly a hangover but she was too tired to be sure) was hitting her badly now that she was no longer running on adrenalin.

She checked the clock. Four-fifty in the morning! A five-hour time difference between London and New York meant this was an insane hour for a conference call.

But at least I can stay in my pajamas, she thought, punching in the numbers on the hotel phone. Exhilarating and all as it was to be an international jetsetter, a woman of the twenty-first century, an executive no less, she was pretty sure she had nothing to show for her efforts that could not have been achieved by Skyping from England.

She was here on Henry's instructions to 'build relationships.' Unsure quite what this entailed, she had thrown herself (and the company Amex card) into hyperdrive. The previous days had been one long continuum of coffees, lunches, drinks and dinners interspersed with visits to a Korean nail salon and a blow dry hair bar, emerging coiffed and polished at speeds that would challenge a prong-horned antelope. The City That Never Sleeps never seemed to slow down either.

She had wined and dined uptown at Town, midtown at Kitty Chi and downtown in Tribeca at Mr. Chow. She had sipped champagne at the Mandarin Oriental on Columbus Circle, shared afternoon tea at The Plaza and espressos at The Mercer.

Each appointment had been scheduled and set out in meticulously detailed itineraries prepared by Samantha. She schmoozed with potential sponsors, met the publicist from Lush and the marketing director of Jeffrey Campbell. She went with Henry to meet the vice president of Luella's publishing house and back to her hotel in Manhattan, courtesy of cabs reeking of kebabs and stale cigar smoke. Maybe one day she would use the subway here – after all, millions of people survived it without getting mugged – but in the meantime, foul odors and a lack of air conditioning was the price she was prepared to pay for her lack of courage.

She pressed the pound key and stated her name as instructed by the automated voice on the conference call. She listened to a few minutes of background music and then heard, "Henry has joined the call," and finally, "Corrie has joined the call."

A pause before, "Hello. Is everybody here?"

It was reminding India of a séance.

"Is that you, Corrie?" Henry said. "I'm here and so is India. We're waiting for Luella."

Another few minutes went by before Luella announced herself. "Luella. Sorry I'm late. Hello, is everyone else here?"

A chorus of 'hellos' was followed by another long gap.

"Can everyone hear me?"

As the only male voice, Henry was easy for India to identify.

A round of "Yesses" was followed by an echoing silence.

"Thanks everyone. So Corrie, I wanted you to meet India and Luella."

"Hello, Corrie." India's and Luella's voices crashed into each other.

"Hello," Corrie responded.

"Corrie, as you know, is the events coordinator," Henry continued. "Corrie, would you like to lead on where we're up to now?"

There was a long silence, during which India sank back into the pillows. She was seriously in danger of dozing off. Maybe she needed more coffee.

"I think we lost Luella," Henry said.

"No. I'm still here, Henry, but I can't hear so well. I'm going to dial in again."

I've an even better idea, India thought. Why don't I go back to sleep and you and Corrie can have an old-fashioned chat, one to one and tell us all how it went in an e-mail?

The line crackled.

"Okay. I'm back but it's still a terrible line. Corrie, can you hear me better now?"

"Not really. Can you hear ME?"

"India. Are you still there?"

Barely, she thought. "Yes. I'm still here." She sighed, glancing at the digital clock on the nightstand. It was five-thirty.

"This isn't working, people. Sorry," Henry said. "India, can you hear me?"

"Yes. I'm still here."

"I'll see you at The Greenwich at one o'clock to meet Rebecca. I may be running..." Henry had been cut off.

India, forgetting Corrie was still on the line, dropped the phone and was asleep within minutes. She woke with a start to a loud knocking.

"Housekeeping. Hello...housekeeping."

"Later," she yelled. "Later. Thank you. Not NOW." What time was this to be servicing a room? She glanced at the clock and then jumped up realizing it was twelve fifteen. Running over to the window and stubbing her toe on a jutting low-level coffee table, she cursed and hopped as she yanked back the drapes. The street below was flooded. Cars were sloshing through the water. Pedestrians were running for cover in all directions. A jagged bolt of lightening streaked the sky and the inevitable thunderclap was so loud it made her jump back into the offending coffee table, sending the early morning tray crashing to the floor.

India cursed and then took a deep breath. She needed to slow down. She had plenty of time to get to The Greenwich, and if she was a bit late, she could blame the weather. Right? Henry would be there ahead of her to greet Rebecca. This need to be punctual was old conditioning from years teaching school and racing for the bell. It wasn't as if she still had thirty kids waiting outside on a playground for her or a full assembly to take. This was a whole new world where you were allowed to run as late as you liked as long as you arrived looking fabulous, your lipstick intact and your hair immaculately blown out. Clearly, the women she was meeting had absorbed too many episodes of *Sex and the City*.

The thing was, even when you got to the meetings, you didn't have to give people your full attention. You could check your texts every five minutes, step out of rooms to take calls, leave early because you had yet another (implication, more important) meeting to go to. Imagine if you behaved like that when you were giving a lesson, she mused. You'd be fired – wouldn't last a day.

After showering and quickly putting on her makeup, India rifled through her half-unpacked suitcase in search of a pair of black tights. A frantic race around the room failed to locate them. She was running out of time to be even fashionably 'consultant late' she realized. Damn it, she would have to abandon the skirt and wear those Agnes B black pants yet again. She was already experiencing suitcase fatigue – absolutely sick to death of the clothes she had packed.

How were you supposed to anticipate freak weather in June? The humidity alone was already doing terrible things to her hair. Did Inès de la Fressange ever find herself on day four of a work trip down to her last clean pair of knickers? Somehow, India doubted it. There were glaring omissions in that style guidebook and absolutely no advice on how to get out of the Warwick Hotel in the absence of a rowing boat or an ark.

Minutes later, standing under the awning at the entrance to the hotel, help came in the form of a doorman who flagged down a cab with a shrill ear-piercing whistle. India climbed into it under the protection of his supersized hotel umbrella.

Her phone rang as the cab lurched forward. Fishing it out of her pocket, she saw from the caller ID it was Adam. She let it ring a few times before picking up. It had been days since she'd heard from him; she could wait another few seconds.

"Hello."

"Hey. Where are you?" Adam said, his gravelly voice sending shivers down her spine.

"New York," she said.

"Really? How come you didn't tell me?"

"It was arranged quickly. I worked out you were probably on your way to Marrakech." (Read, *'You never bother telling me your plans; see how you like it...'*) "So where are you? Are you there now?"

"No. I'm in Cannes," he said.

India went pale. He was in Cannes. He was in the south of France. He was in *le sud de la France* WITHOUT HER. How could he do this? He'd absolutely promised to take her. That had been the trade off for letting her down about the Paris trip.

"So why aren't you in Morocco?" she managed.

"We couldn't get the right permits so here we are. Cannes is super busy. I thought it all went quiet after the Film Festival, who knew? I'm at Eden-Roc. It's really warm out here today. So what are you up to in New York?"

"Oh. You know," India said, "meetings. Absolutely tons of meetings. You should see my schedule – it's insane." (Read, *Am international business-woman; meetings are in my DNA.*)

"Who are you meeting with?"

"Adam, I'm in a cab right now. I can't really talk." Read, *Am international business-type person who cannot risk being overheard by a driver.*

"Oh! Sorry, okay."

"How long are you in France for?"

"Not sure yet. I was thinking maybe we could meet up in London on my way back?"

"Absolutely," she said and then concerned she might have sounded too available. "Though best give me some notice. I may not be in town." (Read, *Am international traveler who may well pop down to Cannes herself.*)

"Will do. Miss you."

"Okay," she said. "Enjoy Cannes. I have to go."

And she did have to go. She had to stop the conversation right there while she still had the strength to keep up this air of cool detachment. It was killing her. She *had* managed an air of cool detachment though, hadn't she?

It took a while for India to find the discreet entrance to The Greenwich Hotel. For a moment she was surprised that Henry had chosen to stay at such a low-key location. This was downtown; wasn't he an uptown kind of a guy? Once inside the doors, she remembered his fondness for boutique hotels. She gave her name to the concierge.

"Mr. Cowan is expecting you." He smiled, nodding toward a short hallway.

Shaking off her raincoat, India made her way into the dark interior of a large sitting room. The place had the feel of a gentlemen's club; the stout leather armchairs, worn oriental rugs and the mahogany bar leant a decidedly masculine ambience, where the Hotel de l'Abbaye in Saint Germain had been chintzy and feminine. Nevertheless, it was a similar vibe – a calm oasis in a frantically busy city. She could not help but think it would be the perfect place for a tryst.

Henry was sitting on a low camel back couch by the fireplace. The woman opposite him looked up as India walked over.

"Sorry I'm so late," India said. "I misjudged the time it'd take me to get here in this weather."

"No problem," Henry said. "We'll bring you up to speed. Rebecca, this is India Butler, our education consultant.

Do all the women Henry works with look like this? India thought, as a willowy airbrushed blonde reached out an extended hand. I wouldn't be able to pick any one of them out in a lineup.

Henry gestured to the armchair next to him. India shook hands, then sank down in the gently worn tapestry cushions.

"We've ordered Crostini for starters to keep us going," Henry said, indicating the plates of olives and fava beans, ricotta and pita bread spread out on the low table in front of them. "What would you like to drink?"

India, resisting the urge for a Bloody Mary, took her cue from Rebecca, who was nursing a Diet Coke. "Pellegrino," she said. God it was so cozy in here; all she wanted to do was curl up and go to sleep.

After ordering her drink, Henry turned to her. "Let me fill you in on where we've gotten to. Rebecca, as you know, is dean of one of the leading fashion institutions in the world. She's been responsible for some of the most experiential industry collaborations of the last decade."

Rebecca lowered her eyes coquettishly. "Thank you. That's very kind, Henry. We do like to feel that we're ahead of the curve in testing the boundaries of creativity and innovation."

Very smooth, Henry, India thought. You're good.

"Rebecca, tell India, if you wouldn't mind, about *Time is a Gift.* It's a great model for *Faux Fashion.*"

"Sure. Absolutely, Henry. Happy to."

Crossing one gazelle-like leg across the other and displaying what India recognized as the appropriate amount of thigh for an informal New York meeting (skirt just below hip level), Rebecca continued.

"For that project there were five cross-disciplinary teams of students of music, dance, design, theater and photography. They came together to present live performances...all original choreography, music scores and conceptual garments of course. The deconstruction and reconstruction in their respective fields was their interpretation of the theme of *Time is a Gift*, which was inspired by Baume Mercier's Heritage."

India was mesmerized. How was it possible for a human being to speak written English so fluently and in an American accent too! She lost concentration for a few moments, watching Rebecca's coral pink mouth open and close. Snapping back into the moment, she tried desperately hard to make sense of what she was hearing.

"With project-based work we put a heavy emphasis on the tangibility of outcomes. Our educational outreach stresses the importance of design approaches that are grounded in well-researched collaborations and rooted in an environmentally sustainable ethos. Our students have the opportunity to base their work in sound methodological theory."

"Absolutely," Henry interjected.

"And Henry," Rebecca continued, "the commercial implications for designs that result from project work like this are immeasurable. Two of our students won contracts with Bloomingdales on the strength of their analogue fabric designs and one alumnus is currently head of product design at Cartier. He's only twenty-four."

"That's impressive," India said, delighted that she at last had something concrete to hang onto; everything Rebecca said seemed so abstract.

"So for *Faux Fashion* the potential for innovative outcomes is huge." Henry was speaking fluent Rebeccan and India was beginning to feel frustrated.

"Henry, I have to thank you and Luella for this amazing opportunity. Her book is a validation for every Arts and Design student who's had to claw their way through academia to get to the place where they could find their voice.

My students have been so inspired by the themes in her book. India, I am so happy you are coming to the college to see what we're doing."

"I'm really looking forward to it." India smiled. "Tomorrow. Yes?"

"I can meet you at ten then. Does that work for you?"

India nodded. "Perfect," she said.

Then Henry adjusted the belt on his jeans, ran the flat of his hands down the inside of his thighs and stretched out his extremely toned arms on his knees before levering himself into a standing position. The action disturbed India in ways she didn't want to think about right now.

"Great. Well let's go through to Locanda Verde. They have a table waiting for us," he said, guiding them both toward the doorway and through the Victorian engraved glass doors of the adjoining restaurant.

11
—

A few days later India was on her way back to London, her suitcase heavier from the frantic yet fruitful dash around the boutiques in Soho. The exchange rate meant her English pounds had gone a long way and of course, it was important to have a closet appropriate for an international consultant. It made sound financial sense to shop in the states. How could anyone have resisted the summer cashmere in Cottonier and the dresses in Club Monaco?

She had been surprisingly quick getting through security, and it left her plenty of time to pick up a few essential purchases from Duty Free: Guerlain perfume, Chanel nail polish, Clarins moisturizer, a Longchamp travel tote (which on refection might probably have been cheaper in Paris), a Swarovski crystal iPhone case and a compact. After showing her passport and paying, she made her way to the Club Lounge feeling very much the world traveler.

Going through to the shower stalls, she changed into a comfortable pair of pajama bottoms and a worn Gap T-shirt, aware she was breaking one of Inès's golden rules, but comfort at this point was more important than looking tres chic. She planned on sleeping her way back to London.

After helping herself to an array of snacks and drinks from a counter, she sat for a while watching CNN news until, seeing from the monitor that her flight had been delayed, she decided to call her friend.

"Hey Sarah. How's it going? I'm at JFK on my way back. How're you feeling?"

"Wonderful! Absolutely wonderful. It's starting to feel very real."

"I just saw the ultrasound picture you posted on Facebook," India said pushing away her plate of nachos and salsa and finishing her glass of Pinot Grigio.

"Yes, I thought it was time to share. It was quite a moment. Damien came with me and went all glassy eyed when he saw her."

India inhaled, unable to quite place the emotion she was feeling. Why hadn't Sarah shared the picture with her privately – as in *in an e-mail* – before posting online for those hundreds of so-called 'friends' to see?

"So you know it's a girl?" she said.

"Yes, well I've known that for a while."

"Oh!" India managed. "Oh...great...Well, I'm sure you must both be delighted."

"I've never been happier," she said. There was an awkward pause. "So. What are you up to? How did the meetings go?"

"I'll tell you all about it when I see you. It went really well," India said. "Actually, sorry Sarah. I don't think I'm in the cell phone area of the lounge. I've got to go. Catch up later. Bye."

India clicked off, leaned back awkwardly in the circular plastic chair and closed her eyes. Somehow, she seemed to have lost the connection with Sarah. Maybe she'd neglected her friend recently. Had she been too preoccupied with the dramas over Adam or the stage production at the end of the school semester? Maybe she was imagining things, maybe not. Either way, right now with Adam in France, her sister in California and Sarah nesting in London with Damien, India felt unmoored.

The tinny announcement of another hour's delay did nothing to help her mood. She refilled her wine glass and then gathering together her pashmina and purse, dragged her carry-on suitcase into the business area of the lounge and went into a cubby where she sat down and pulled out some of the papers the students had given her the day before.

The college visit had been exhilarating. Rebecca had escorted India around brick-walled, open-plan studios to workstations with draped mannequins and cutting tables spilling over with fabric. India had marveled at the standard of the illustrations displayed on the oversized pin boards and at the precision of the technical drawings laid out on drafting machines. The students barely broke their fierce concentration until Rebecca approached them directly, at which point they jumped up to share whatever they were creating, explaining their process with infectious enthusiasm, even at one point letting India try out a state-of-the-art sewing machine.

India had toured the art department and seen handbags being fashioned from papier-mache and learned how eco-friendly canvas could be woven into biodegradable dresses. What really blew her mind were the scarf designs that had been innovated from the genetic printout of DNA macro-molecules.

By the end of that day, the shows were no longer an abstraction to her. She had the visuals and was deeply impressed. She'd also warmed to Rebecca who'd been at pains to explain everything in detail and spoken to her in plain English. She was clearly idolized and respected by her students.

India opened one of the portfolios:

> The illustrator produces unique images
> offering an original red and indigo cre-
> ation, making a break away from her usual
> monochrome world. The audience will be
> delighted to find the designer's complex
> motifs bursting in a panoply of color. This
> collaboration between the biotechnology

laboratory and the design department will create a unique evening dress printed with original designs conceived by Julie Levine, Year 3.

The idea of scientists of molecular and synthetic biology working with design students was intriguing. Even though India was unsure what synthetic biology was, she was certain it must be fascinating. She had much to learn. She turned page after page for a while, so engrossed that she barely registered the loudspeaker announcement.

"Passenger India Butler please make your way to Gate Two-K immediately. This gate will be closing in five minutes. Repeat. Passenger India Butler..."

"That's ME! I'm India Butler!" she yelped, scrambling to collect her things, dashing through the terminal building and careening down a ramp where she was escorted onto the plane by a highly irritated flight attendant who yanked the cabin doors closed behind her. Left struggling to cram her case and bags of Duty Free into the overhead locker, India finally managed to slam the bin shut, before collapsing into her seat. A few seconds later, she saw Henry sitting across from her, an expression of high amusement on his face.

What on earth is he doing here? she thought. He's supposed to be coming back tomorrow.

India brushed a damp strand of hair and a bead of sweat from her cheek and attempted a smile. In that moment she desperately wanted to press rewind – to have been there ahead of him, flicking through a copy of *Vanity Fair*, her hair in a smooth chignon, a Pucci scarf around her neck, a glass of sparkling wine in hand.

There would be no escaping him. The cramped love-seat arrangement of the seats meant he was going to be diagonally across from her for the next seven hours. India wasn't entirely sure why this was bothering her so much.

"Hello, Miss Butler." He grinned.

"Hello, Mr. Cowan," she answered, snapping shut her seatbelt and gripping the armrest as the plane taxied down the runway. She could sense Henry looking at her as she stared fixedly out of the window.

"I didn't know you were scared of flying." He laughed shortly after takeoff.

"I'm not," she said, letting out a squeal as the plane suddenly dropped altitude and there came a crash of metal from the nearby galley. "Omigod."

"It's only a bit of turbulence. We'll be okay once we get higher," Henry reassured her.

"I'm fine." India grimaced, clenching her fists in terror, as the plane hit another bump. "Actually I'm not," she muttered.

"Here," he said, stretching his hand across the screen divider. "Hold my hand."

~ ~ ~

Luella carried her iPad into the sitting room, flopped on the couch and zipped open the case. She stared at the accumulation of unopened e-mails from Peter. These last few weeks he had been relentless in his attempts to contact her - turning up on the doorstep at all hours of the night, filling her answering machines with emotionally charged messages. This morning, having slept for a merciful seven hours, Luella braced herself. She would have to respond sooner or later. It may as well be now.

Setting down her coffee mug, she shook a cigarette out of a pack of Marlboro Lights and flicked her thumb furiously on a disposable lighter. It refused to work. Frustrated in the attempt, she aimed the thing, with its tacky image of the Eiffel Tower at the trash basket and threw down the unlit cigarette.

Okay, she thought, opening his latest e-mail. It's time.

Lu, we must talk. We must. Maybe when
you hear what I have to say, you'll understand. I never set out to hurt you or to
deceive you. I would probably have come
out sooner if things were different. It's
complicated in all directions and when
you're ready to hear it, I'll tell you. All I
want you to know and believe is that there
have been no others. None. I have been in
agony for the longest time. I can't put this
in an e-mail. I need to talk to you. Please.
Please Lu, let me see you.

Luella read the open page several times.

Okay. Tomorrow. She typed and then paused. Where? They
needed to meet some place she could walk away from if she
lost control. Their house or local pub was out of the question. She stood up and rifled through a dresser in search of
matches. Coming back to the couch, she lit a cigarette and
sat watching the smoke curl into the air. She took a couple
of drags and then stuffed it into the overspilling ashtray.
The park would be best she decided, firing off the rest of the
e-mail and pressing 'send' before she could change her mind.

After a restless night, Luella showered quickly and sat
at her desk dealing with the press requests she had been
sent the previous week. She plowed through the mountain of
household bills that Peter usually handled.

Funny, she thought, it's the little things you miss the
most.

Just before twelve o'clock, she dragged a comb through
her hair, grabbed her scarf and bag and left the house. She
walked quickly past the local restaurants and shops at the
end of her street, marveling that life was proceeding nor-
mally all around her – the usual gaggle of teenagers hanging
around the chip shop, the mothers pushing strollers, the
homeless guy curled up in a sleeping bag in a doorway.

As she turned into the park, she looked up through the

sycamore trees at the remarkably blue sky. Nothing around her on this beautiful summer's day reflected her inner turmoil. Surely there should be rain, a threat of thunder, something ominous in the atmosphere, she thought, as a couple of kids whizzed past her on bicycles and an ice cream van pulled up discordantly chiming "Greensleeves." Luella paused by the railings to let a dog walker go past and then, swallowing hard, she approached the bench where Peter stood waiting.

"Hello, Peter," she said after a few awkward moments of silence. "Shall we walk?"

Luella dug her hands deep in her pocket as they past stragglers and skateboarding teens and the picnickers dotted across the lawns. They followed the gravel path along the side of the lake.

"Lu..." Peter started. "Lu, I am so sorry. I don't know where to begin."

Luella felt tears stinging the back of her eyes. "Me either," she said, staring out across the water at the steady pull of a rowing boat. They stood for a while. Eventually Luella broke the heavy silence between them.

"Before you say anything, Pete, I want you to know that I've had time to give this a lot of thought. I'm over the first shock and..." she turned to face him "...and it was a terrible shock, but I am trying to come to terms with it, whatever 'it' is. I'm sufficiently mature to recognize this can't have been easy for you...and, well, I want you to know that I'm not angry anymore. I'm terribly sad if you want to know. Terribly sad."

Peter motioned to interrupt and she put her hand up toward him to stop him. "I suppose what I'm saying," she said slowly, "is that I need to understand. Pete, are you in love with this man?"

Peter stared at the ground. "I wish it were as simple as that, but yes." He sighed.

They reached a park bench near an old wooden summer-house and sat down next to each other awkwardly.

"Do you think it might help for us to see a counselor?" he volunteered, breaking the silence.

"A marriage guidance counselor?" Luella was incredulous. "I think that's hardly appropriate given we can't possibly rescue our marriage."

Peter sighed heavily. "But maybe, if you understood, we could salvage our friendship. I can't imagine my life without you in it, Lu."

Luella's voice shook. "Pete. Do you know how degrading it was for me to walk into Dr. Robert's surgery and ask to be tested for STDs?"

"You didn't need to. I told you. I've only had one lover."

Lover. Luella winced. He could have said 'relationship' or 'experience' but no, he'd said 'lover.' How incredible that one simple word could carry such weight.

"Come on, Pete. Are you trying to tell me this man has been celibate his entire life? Are you screwing the pope? Not that THAT would rule anything out of course," she added bitterly.

"Lu, I'm sorry I put you in that position, but for what it's worth, we've been practicing safe sex and..."

Luella blanched.

"...and it's not about sex. Well, the attraction is, but it's more than that."

"So did you never find me attractive? Did you ever enjoy sex with me?"

Peter stared at the ground kicking at the grass with his shoe. "Lu, of course I found you attractive."

Luella lit a cigarette, inhaled deeply and exhaled the smoke in a loud rush. "Forget that. I suppose I'm asking if our whole life together has been an act for you. Look at me. Answer me," she demanded. "Have you always known you liked other men? If we'd not lost the baby, would that have changed things? For fuck's sake, Peter, did I ever know you?"

An elderly woman walked past flashing Luella a disapproving look. "Fuck. Yes. I said fuck," Luella muttered.

"It's a fucking park not a fucking church...and...if you want to know, this is my husband here and he's been fucking another MAN!"

Luella stamped out her cigarette, trembling uncontrollably. The woman walked on quickly, looking over her shoulder a few times as she went. Luella leapt to her feet.

"I'm not ready to talk, Pete. I have to go."

Peter took her arm gently. "Please, can we meet again soon?"

"Maybe," she said. "Yes. Yes, okay. Just give me a bit more time. I can't think straight right now." She pulled out a Kleenex and blew her nose. "Look at me; I'm a complete mess and I have to go into the office this afternoon."

"I can't find words to tell you how dreadful I feel for putting you through this," he said.

"You know, Peter, some mornings I wake up and I've forgotten for a moment that this is happening. Then the enormity of it floods over me. I feel engulfed. I am trying so desperately to understand and to accept it, but...I think I am still in shock."

"I understand," he said softly. "I really wish I had been brave enough to tell you, rather than you finding out the way you did."

"I have to go," Luella said, turning to walk away. "I really do."

～ ～ ～

Immediately after the seatbelt signs had been turned off, India grabbed her wash bag and went to the bathroom. She freshened up as best she could, scrubbing her teeth and splashing her face in the tiny sink, losing her balance on the way back as she squeezed past the flight attendant serving drinks.

"I'm really sorry," she mumbled, attempting to climb over Henry's outstretched legs, then catching his shoulder to save herself from landing in his lap. God he smells good, she thought as he leaned forward to steady her and she caught a glimpse of dark chest hair under his unbuttoned shirt.

Yes. It's official, she thought. He's hot. Very hot...disturbingly hot and...

Their faces were now inches away from each other and India was stuck straddling him.

"I'm kind of enjoying this." He grinned.

Summoning all her strength to resist the almost overpowering urge to kiss him, India righted herself and stumbled into her own seat.

"I'll have a gin and tonic, not too much ice," Henry told the flight attendant, who had made no attempt to help India and was focusing her attention solely on him. "Care to join me for a cocktail, Miss Butler? We're off the clock now."

"Yes," India said, pulling out her tray. "White wine, please."

Her glass of wine was delivered with a charmless nod. Henry raised his glass in India's direction. "Cheers," he said, holding her gaze for the longest time. "Here's to a bump-free ride."

India registered the double entendre and lowered her eyes. "Are you pleased with how the project's going?" she asked, hoping that the heat rising to her cheeks would not betray her.

"Very. But as I said, we're off the clock. Here, have some warm nuts." He laughed, handing her a dish of hot cashews, then adjusting his headrest and closing his eyes. "I'll see you for dinner. Order me the steak when she comes around again will you?"

India stopped short of telling him to stay awake and order his own food. She pulled the screen divider up between them, reclined her seat so that she couldn't see him and pulled out the airline video player. A few minutes later, she'd settled into a rerun of *Ab Fab* when the flight attendant pushed the divider back down to take her meal order. India unhooked one earpiece.

"Oh. Sorry. I'm not sure yet," she said, lifting the menu from the pocket next to her, very much aware that Henry had one eye open and was looking at her again. She settled on the chicken with green beans and turned back to her program. The system refused to reboot and stayed stuck on Joanna Lumley's freeze-framed image. India pressed her call button and waited.

"I can't get it to play," she told Henry after about fifteen minutes. He yanked out his player.

"Mine's dead too," he said, pressing his call light.

The flight attendant appeared at his side instantly, twiddling buttons, apologizing and offering him another cocktail, a customer feedback form and complimentary air miles.

Next, she'll be offering him a blow job, India thought, as the girl hovered over his seat, untangling his headset. "Mine isn't working either," she told her.

"I'll be with you shortly, Madam," the attendant snapped, turning back to Henry with a flashing smile. "I'm sorry, Mr. Cowan. Please let me know if there is anything more I can do to make your flight more enjoyable."

India packed away her system and extended the seat into a sleeping position. What a man's woman, she thought. You're welcome to him. He's all yours. I shall be having a little snooze. Now where did I put my purse?

~ ~ ~

India woke up with a jolt. She seemed to be moving. What was going on? She eased herself up and looked out of the car window at a line of garages and a wire-fenced playing field she didn't recognize. Scrambling around for a reference point, she came up with a blank.

Omigod, I've been kidnapped, she thought, stifling a scream. Stay calm, say nothing, think. Think. She let out a whimper.

"You're awake."

The voice was coming from the driver's seat.

"Let me out of here," she screeched, trying the door as the car pulled up at a set of traffic lights. "You won't get away with this you know. They'll find you. Let me out NOW."

"Calm down, Miss Butler."

India paled. "Henry?" she said. "Is that you? What on earth are you doing? I don't understand. Where are we? We're supposed to be on a plane."

"We *were* on a plane and now we're in my car."

"I don't understand, Henry. Why am I in my pajamas and in the back of your car?"

"I expect the last hour or so might be a little blurry for you. Yes?"

"What are you talking about and by the way, where are we going? I can't go to a meeting dressed like this," she said, relieved to see that her purse was on the seat next to her and that she still had her wallet and phone. This was all very disturbing; had Henry had some kind of mental breakdown?

"I am taking you home."

"Well that's a relief." She sighed, but what's going on, she wondered. "What happened? Do I have a concussion? Was there an accident? Did the plane crash?"

"I believe the accident was all you." He laughed, grinning at her through the rearview mirror. Don't you remember anything? At one point you seemed to be making sense, then you conked out again."

"Last thing I remember...Oh!"

"Yes?"

"I took an Ambien."

"Didn't anyone ever tell you you're not supposed to drink with those things?"

"Did you have to carry me off the plane or something?" she asked, unsure if she wanted the answer or not.

"You were very sweet," he said. "You offered no resistance. The only tricky bit was getting you through immigration."

"Look. You may be finding this all highly amusing and don't think I'm not grateful for the lift home, but if I haven't committed a crime and I'm not blacklisted by the airline I think I'd like to forget the whole incident if that's okay with you."

"Fine by me." He smirked. "However, I shall treasure the thought of what you would like to do to me when you get my trousers off."

"Very funny." India blushed. "It would appear I was drugged," she said, climbing out of the car unsteadily now that they had reached her house. "I have no intention of taking your trousers off."

"Pity." He grinned, lifting her case up the path for her. "By the way, who's Adam?"

12
—

"Sarah, I'm mortified. I think I'm going to have to resign. I can't remember anything much after the plane took off."

"Resign? Bollocks!" Sarah snorted. "Don't be ridiculous. Anyway, we've come here to relax remember? This place is called *The Sanctuary* for a reason."

"You're right." India smiled, adjusting the towel on her head. "Happy birthday."

"This is so great. Thank you. I love this spa. I can't believe I have the whole day to do nothing. I haven't been here for years." Sarah sighed happily, trailing her hand in the lily pond and watching a woman sway back and forth across the swimming pool on a roped swing.

"I come past here most days. Henry's office is just up the street. That's what made me think of it," India said. "Shall we order lunch soon. I like the sound of the quinoa salad."

"Here, let me look. What time's your next treatment?"

"Not till three," India said, leaning over to catch sight of a shoal of Koi carp. "So you think I should just pretend it never happened?"

"Well from what you've said you can't remember much anyway."

India took a sip of her watermelon juice. "That's the problem. I keep getting awful flashbacks, and apparently I said things I don't remember."

"Like what?"

"You don't want to know."

"That's funny; I DO want to know."

"Okay...well apparently I said something about taking off his trousers. I don't remember. He told me that's what I said."

"What! You said WHAT? He told you that you said that?" Sarah's eyes widened. She gaped at India. "Tell me you're making this up."

"You couldn't make it up!" India said, suppressing a giggle. "That's all I know. I have no recollection of it."

"Mortifying."

"I know..."

They sat for a moment, taking in the implications. Sarah broke the silence.

"Well, maybe it's about time you did see someone else."

"Even if I wanted to see someone else, Henry would be a really bad idea. I have to work with the guy, though I do admit I have a kind of chemical reaction to him. I feel a bit out of control when I'm around him."

"That's pheromones."

"What?"

"Sex hormones; some animals produce pheromones that can attract mates from two miles away. They're rendered helpless in their presence."

"I seem to be okay up until about a three-yard radius." India laughed.

"Stop beating yourself up. It's not like you got blind drunk and slept with him. It could have happened to anyone. I read somewhere that people go on all kinds of insane trips on Ambien. I'm pretty sure if you'd done anything *that* outrageous it would be all over the news."

"I suppose you're right. I thought they were just to relax you. I'd no idea."

"Yes well you know now, that's for sure. Did you see that clip the other week of the woman who wouldn't stop singing that Whitney Houston song 'I Will Always Love You?' They had to make an emergency landing and drag her off the plane."

"That's hysterical. Well, not if you were sitting next to her I suppose." India laughed, admiring her freshly manicured nails.

"Anyway, don't worry Indie. You're just paranoid since that incident a few years back at Annie's. Lightning doesn't strike twice in the same place. You're fine. Just promise me you won't take that stuff again."

"Promise."

They both sat back contentedly. Sarah flicked over a couple of pages of *Mother and Baby* magazine. "By the way, did I tell you we've picked out a name for the baby?" she said, adjusting the top of her polka dot maternity swimsuit.

India put down the copy of Vogue she'd been flicking through. "Go on," she said.

"Alana. What do you think?"

"That's beautiful." India sighed. "*Alana*. Lovely. Sarah, can we clear the air a bit? I know I've seemed a bit off lately but I want you to know that I really am delighted for you." She hesitated. "I hate to admit it, but I'm also a bit envious. You seem so settled and content and..."

"Indie." Sarah sat up and took her friend's hand as India's eyes filled with tears. "Your time will come. I'm sure it will. Hang in there."

"You're right. Tell you what, a day with you here was exactly what I needed to clear my head."

"Me too. It's not been all plain sailing at work since you've been away. Lots going on."

"I want to hear all about it. You have the conch," India said, lolling back in the lounger.

Leaving the spa, India decided to treat herself to a taxi home. It had been such a perfect day; why ruin it jostling for the tube? She sat in the back of the black cab, taking in the city as they edged their way through the snarled traffic past

The Ritz and Green Park's endless railings with displays of art. They cut through Hyde Park and passed Marble Arch with its landmark equestrian statue outlined against the sky. I take this city for granted, she thought. It's as beautiful as Paris if you look at it with fresh eyes. Maybe I'll see if Adam would like to come for a few days. I could take him to so many wonderful places we didn't get to see last time he was here. She pulled out her phone and fired off the text.

> Hey, I'm back from New York. How about you come to London next weekend? Miss you. Xxx000

After happily paying what she knew to be an outrageous amount of money for the ride, she skipped up the path to her house. Yes. I'll plan out a weekend every bit as magical as the one we should have had in Paris.

~ ~ ~

"Sorry I'm late," Luella said, sitting down opposite Henry in the conference room. "I had a stressful morning."

"Peter?"

"Yes. I don't want to talk about it right now. Tell me where we're up to with the show."

Henry opened his laptop. "I have good news," he said. "I think you'll be pleased. I've been trawling around for a fashion designer to host the show, someone uncontroversial who's not going to be targeted by PETA. I thought of the French designer Jean-Luc. He's always at the palace with Elton John or at charity events with Sting and whomever. I dug around a bit to see how we could best contact him."

"I love his work," Luella said. "His designs are kind of 'out there' without being insane like Galliano's. He always uses such beautiful silks."

"We struck lucky." Henry grinned. "Jean-Luc graduated from LIFT."

"Really? I would have thought he'd have trained in Paris."

"He did his post-graduate degree at LIFT. I asked the dean of the college to approach him for us and she reached out to him and...wait for it...he's agreed."

"That's brilliant," Luella said. "Absolutely brilliant. My nephew's in awe of him; he'll be thrilled about this."

"Not only that. She told me he's donating his fee to the college."

"They must be delighted too then."

"They're all over it. Here, watch this video. You're going to love it."

Henry swiveled his Mac toward her and Jean-Luc appeared on the YouTube video wearing an outfit that, to the untrained eye, could be mistaken for a dress. The sheath of fabric, hitting at the knee, was reminiscent of something Gandhi might have worn to lead the Salt March. His toned arms were swathed in tattoos, his head preternaturally shiny, making his eyes glint like buttons on a military jacket.

"There's a revolution happening in fashion," he said, bringing his speech to a climax. "The fundamentals remain the same – the silhouette, the balance, the color, the fabric – but the focus is on innovation, on forging new creative partnerships. It is about defining and redefining a designer's philosophy. In this ever-expanding global market, it is no longer about keeping to a rigid set of rules or the latest trends. It's about individuality, a respect for the environment and collaboration. Thank you. Thank you all."

He smiled graciously at the camera before taking a bow with a flourish of his arm.

"He's a real showman," Luella remarked. "What he's saying is absolutely on target for us. He's absolutely perfect. Congratulations. That's a coup."

"He's exactly what we need to get traffic to the sites," Henry said. "Yes. I'm rather impressed with myself."

"More so than usual?" she quipped. "I can't believe how far we've come in just a few months. India is a real asset isn't she?" She held his gaze for a moment.

"Are you fishing, Lu?" Henry grinned, pushing his seat away from the table. "And in case you ask, no we haven't."

Luella laughed. "Don't tell me you've finally come across a woman who can resist your sexual charisma, Henry. That would be too awful to contemplate."

He raised his eyebrows in mock disdain. "Were ever such a thing to happen I agree, it would be quite awful."

"So what about the female presenter? Do you have any thoughts on that?"

"This is where I'm hoping the lovely Miss Butler will come in handy. I think Annabelle Butler would be perfect, don't you? She's just been promoting her latest movie. She's smoking as they say and she just happens to be India's sister."

"You know Henry, sometimes you still manage to surprise me. That's what you had in mind all along isn't it? That's why you hired her. You had this planned from day one."

"Well that wasn't the only reason, but yes I have to admit it was a factor for sure."

"I've a feeling India will be cool with it. Why wouldn't she be? Shall I ask her tomorrow? We're working from my house in the afternoon."

"No. Leave it with me to talk to her. I need to handle the 'ask' carefully. Don't say anything."

"Okay," Luella said, clicking her reading glasses into their case. "So Henry, if we're all done here, it's five o'clock. I'm not hungry, but I could do with a drink. I don't want to go back to an empty house right now."

"Absolutely," Henry said, pressing the intercom. "All done here for today, Samantha. Miss Marchmont and I are leaving. There are some papers on the desk for you to collect on your way out."

Luella picked up her purse, pulled on her jacket and followed him into the corridor.

"Tell me, Henry," she said as they waited for the elevator.

"Do you ever play it completely straight with anyone?"

"Rarely." He grinned as the door slid open. "But of course, I always do with you my dear."

~~ ~~ ~~

"You're very quiet. What is it?" Luella asked India the next day as they were checking the invitation list in her office.

"Am I? Sorry," India said, snatching up some papers as the breeze caught them. "Nothing to do with work."

"I won't probe, but feel free to talk if it'll help," Luella said, closing over the window.

"I feel pathetic talking about it, especially as I know you have your own problems right now," India answered. "Where do you want the rest of these illustrations to go?"

"Here. Just put them on Margaret's desk. She can sort them in the morning. Look, we've made as much progress as we're going to today," she said, dropping a pile of photographs into a file drawer. "How about we go for a drink? It's far too lovely an evening to be inside."

"You're right," India sighed. "That sounds like a great idea."

"Let me grab my purse. How about Caprice? It's pretty basic, but it's just around the corner."

"Sure. Do you want help putting the rest of this away?"

"Leave it. I'll come to it fresh in the morning. Let's go. You and I need some downtime. Let me get my coat."

"Great news that we've nailed Jean-Luc don't you think?" India said as they turned the corner of the street and grabbed a couple of empty chairs outside the wine bar.

"Yes. Brilliant," Luella agreed.

"I've been researching him," India said. "He's incredible. He started out as a hairdresser. How do you go from working in a salon to becoming a world famous photographer, an art director and fashion designer? That's serious talent."

"And charisma. One hell of a trajectory," Luella agreed. "He was awarded the Order of Arts and Letters last year too."

"The project is coming together well isn't it?"

"It is and you're such a great addition to the team," Luella said, shunting her chair underneath the table. "Will this do, by the way? It's a bit cramped but at least we get to sit outside."

"It's fine. As long as they serve decent wine I'm happy."

"So what are you going to have, red or white?"

"White for me."

"Shall we split a bottle of Pinot Grigio?"

"Perfect," India said. "So, I'm sorry if I've seemed a bit distracted today."

"That's okay. You've just been very quiet that's all. Do you want to talk about it?"

"Well, it's just that I'm in a long-distance relationship. The distance part is getting to be a major problem as in 'no relationship because of the distance.'"

"I understand how that can happen. Sorry to interrupt, but hold on while I get this girl's attention. We need that wine," Luella said with a wave of her arm. She ordered and turned back to India. "Sorry. You were saying. Long distance..."

"Yes. Well, right now he's on location in France, so I thought he could maybe come for the weekend. He says he can't get away. Okay, so I know he's working, but what I'm trying to fathom is if he's making excuses not to see me or if he really *can't* get away. He's an actor. He's always going to be an actor and it's starting to dawn on me that this is never going to change. He was married for a while. I can see maybe why it didn't last."

"So you're not sure if the lifestyle would suit you long term."

"That about sums it up." India nodded.

"In the interest of full disclosure I have to admit that I Googled you a while back," Luella said, as the waitress poured their wine. "I hope you don't think that's awful; it's the writer in me. I can't stop myself. I'm always looking for stories. But anyway the truth is, I can't sit here pretending not to know that this 'long-distance relationship' is with Adam Brooks."

"I really don't mind," India reassured her. "So now you know, you can see my dilemma; I mean he's gorgeous right? And clever and funny and..." She stopped.

"Yes. I have absolutely no difficulty seeing your problem there."

"So. Any advice?"

"A while ago I'd have told you to stick with it, to work it out, that love would conquer all. I'd have told you that marriages last even if there are chunks of time you spend apart. I'm afraid I don't believe that anymore. I don't think you're talking to the right person to give advice."

"I suppose nobody can give you advice you don't want to hear either. I'm sure it'll all work out." India sighed. "So okay. Now you know why I've been a bit preoccupied today. Anyway, going back to what we were talking about, Henry told me Jean-Luc is going to be giving a lecture at The London College of Fashion tomorrow night."

"Yes. I'm glad you can make it. How about we have dinner together afterward? I was hoping to meet him, but as it's a fundraiser, he has a formal dinner with some alumni."

"That sounds like a plan," India said. "Speaking of dinner I'm starting to feel hungry. I haven't eaten all day. Shall we order some food? The tapas look good."

"Sure. Go for it. I'll eat later. I'm not hungry right now," Luella said, taking another sip of her wine. "Mind if I smoke?"

"Go ahead," India said, though I wish you wouldn't, she thought.

"So tell me more about Adam," Luella said, lighting up and wafting the smoke away from the table. "How did you meet him? How long have you been together?"

"That's a hard one to answer. I mean do you count the months we've been apart as 'being together' if you see what I mean? I met him the summer before last at my sister's house. We really hit it off. It was a summer romance, but it was so much more than that. I was having a major crisis about work. I wanted to leave teaching but I'd no clue how to go about it. He really helped me build my confidence. Just being with him and his friends helped so much. There's such a 'can do' culture over there."

"Yes. I agree. I sense that when I'm in America too."

"You feel like anything's possible there, don't you? Of course it wasn't all about work. We just clicked. He makes me laugh. I feel like I can be completely myself around him." She paused. "Anyway, for one reason or another I had to come back to London. He's come to stay a few times, but then he got this huge part in this last movie and the travel just hasn't worked out."

"That's tough." Luella nodded.

"I keep trying to catch that girl's eye. Hang on a minute; it'll be quicker if I go inside to give her my order." India said standing up and squeezing between the tables.

"Okay Luella. That's enough about me," she said a few minutes later coming back to her seat. "I want to hear about the new book you're writing, the one set in Paris. You've written so many; where does the inspiration come from?"

"Ha." Luella laughed. "I'm not so sure inspiration has very much to do with it. As I said earlier, it can be a slog."

"But how do you get the characters? How do you dream them up?"

Luella looked thoughtful.

"Well," she said, "I suppose you could say I audition them. I give them a name and some personality traits and get to know them. Sooner or later, one or two of them start to write their own dialogue. It's hard to explain really. I suppose it must come from my subconscious. They start to take on a life of their own. They become real in my head.

Mind you, I've been wondering lately if I have another book in me."

"I'm sure you have," India said. "You must have. It's probably writer's block."

"Writer's block is a myth," Luella said, pausing while the waitress set down India's plate.

"How so? I thought it's an accepted fact," India asked, dipping her pita bread into the humus.

"You're forgetting about discipline. Talking of which, or the lack of it rather, I need more wine," Luella said, looking up at the server and nodding in the direction of the ice bucket. "You can't call it writer's block if you don't turn up at the computer to write. Writers write. Simple as that."

"I suppose so," India said thoughtfully. "It'd be like a dancer saying they can't dance when they haven't been practicing enough."

"Exactly." Luella smiled. "That's exactly it. I'm not practicing enough. I haven't been able to focus lately. That's all it is. Real life has intervened. Frankly, I couldn't have made up the stuff I'm dealing with right now. But let's not go there. Let's talk about something else. Where shall we go for dinner after Jean-Luc's talk?"

13

—

The students sat with rapt attention in the college lecture hall. Jean-Luc clicked the remote control in his hand and a collage of rapid-fire images accompanied by a retro soundtrack of "Heart of Glass" hit the screen behind him. It abruptly switched to a Stravinsky piece India recognized as Orpheus, a composition she had decided years before, ranked as possibly the most painfully discordant piece of music she had ever heard.

Next, they'll be playing Kate Bush. Take me now Lord, she thought, squirming in her seat. Where are the models, the runway, the CLOTHES? Why this sequence of demolished buildings, metal sculptures and cars erupting into flames? Why all this ugliness. How much longer is this going to go on?

After what seemed like an age, the screen went black. There was a moment's pause before the audience rose to its feet in thunderous appreciation. India struggled to her feet, nonplussed. What? A standing ovation? she thought, peering to see how Henry, who had been sitting next to Luella, was responding. If the way he was clapping were anything to go by, he'd experienced some kind of spiritual epiphany. People sat down again in reverent silence as Jean-Luc walked over to the lectern and thumbed through his notes.

"Thank you. Merci." He smiled. "I do apologize if my English is not so clear. As some of you may know I am not

Eeenglish." There was a ripple of laughter.

"I would like to use a quote from a *leetel* fashion designer that some of you may have heard of. Her Name was Coco Chanel." Another ripple of laughter. "Madame Chanel once said, '*Fashion is not something that exists in dresses only. Fashion is in the sky, in the street, fashion has to do with ideas, the way we live, what is happening.*'

"Let us take a few minutes to think about what is 'appening. What is 'appening now? We have a world that we are abusing by using up all our resources out of greed and corruption. We 'ave 'the Internet' that is changing everything. We 'ave crime, we have poverty, we 'ave war. Our planet is on the road to destruction. We 'ave a moral responsibility as artists to reflect that."

Jean-Luc thumped the lectern with his fist.

"We are the vanguard of a movement. We have inherited this 'brave new world.' We must stand up and be counted. This is a revolution."

The students rose to their feet again, clapping and screaming, punching the air, hooting and whistling.

If I'd known I was coming to a rally, I'd have brought a hard hat, India thought. The idea of working with Jean-Luc just got a whole lot more interesting.

~ ~ ~

Adam Brooks was taking in the afternoon sun, reclining by the seawater infinity swimming pool at Hotel du Cap-Eden-Roc. Lost in thought, he gazed across the expanse of glistening blue ocean to where the oligarchs' sleek yachts were outlined against the horizon.

The woman stretched out next to him rolled onto her back, rearranged her Pucci sarong and adjusted her sunglasses and floppy white sun hat.

"We really should have booked a cabana," she drawled. "I feel totally exposed out here."

"You're such a diva, Diane. Here, this might help." Adam said, topping up her glass of rose Krug champagne and handing it to her.

"It's okay for you. You're clearly only too delighted to have that six-pack of yours on display. I, on the other hand, am an actress of a certain age. One rogue photograph could herald the end of my career."

"You're safe," Adam yawned. "Nobody's taking any notice of you. Relax. I'm going to make a call."

Diane flipped onto her stomach. "Catch you later. Pass me that towel before you go."

Adam hurled the towel at her head. "Thanks a bunch," she grunted.

He threw on a shirt and slid his feet into deck shoes. Taking the stone steps two at a time, he reached the cantilevered Eden Pavilion terrace and pulled out his phone. The call went straight to voice mail. "Hey Indie. It's me. Miss you," he said. "Call when you get a minute. I have an idea to run past you..."

"Damn. Why don't you ever pick up?" he muttered, thumping his fist against the granite pillar. "That woman is the most irritating person I've ever come across."

"Adam. Adam Brooks, I don't believe it." A woman in a diaphanous sundress let out a shriek, leaping up from one of the long oceanfront tables and racing over to him.

Adam raised his hand to shield his eyes from the sun. A crazed fan; that's all I need right now, he thought.

"ADAM! What are you doing here? I don't believe it. It's Natalie," the girl gushed. "Natalie. You remember me?"

It took a moment for him to register. "Natalie. Of course," he said, recovering quickly. "This IS a surprise."

"Here, come and meet some of my new friends," she said. "C'mon."

Adam hesitated and then followed her the few steps to the table.

"Everyone. Meet Adam Brooks, the man who almost literally knocked me off my feet in Vegas a few months back," she said, wobbling slightly on her six-inch espadrilles.

A couple of middle-aged men slid their chairs back and leaned over to shake Adam's hand.

"This is Ross," Natalie gushed, "CEO of Charles Davis Advertising Company and this gentleman here is Tom Waters from Saatchi and Saatchi. This is Sam Goldman, who needs no introduction of course, and Pete here is from Morgan Stanley. We're all in town for the Advertising Festival."

"Pleased to meet you," Adam said, nodding at the guys at the top end of the table and smiling at the two women at the far end whom Natalie had failed to introduce.

"You must have a drink with us," she said, pouting. "This place is awesome isn't it? Come on. Here, sit next to me," she schmoosed, waving to the hovering waiter who took her signal and lifted over another chair.

"I'd like to but I'm with a friend. She's waiting for me," Adam protested, nodding his head in the direction of the line of bleached calico parasols by the pool.

"How about just one glass of bubbles?" Natalie teased. "Tom here just ordered another bottle of champagne. We could use some help with it."

Adam hesitated. Diane had been appalling company all morning; working with her was becoming extremely wearing. He wasn't needed on set now for the next two days. Why not?

"Okay. If you're sure I'm not crashing your business lunch."

They sat down together. Natalie leaned forward, pulled the tiny shoulder strap of her sundress down her arm and crossed one long tan leg over the other. She covered the side of her face, tilted her head in the direction of the man next to her and mouthed, "B-O-R-I-N-G."

Tom handed Adam a glass of pink champagne. "Santé, as they say here. So, what company are you with Adam? Don't I know you from somewhere?"

"Adam's an actor," Natalie said, but Tom wasn't listening.

"There's John Hegarty. I must go talk to him," he said, getting to his feet. "Sir John. Sir John," he yelled. "Great to see you. I was hoping to catch you after your talk tomorrow."

The others around the table were engrossed in conversation. Natalie moved closer to Adam. "So how long are you here for? I can't believe we've run into each other again like this. It must be fate," she said, circling the rim of her glass with her forefinger and then licking the tip of it very slowly with her tongue.

14

India was perched on a cubist stool in the Soho Hotel library, marveling at the eclectic mix of designs, the bold use of color, the luxe fabrics, the vibrant artwork. That's a whole new take on library steps, she thought, admiring a neon-lit ladder resting against shelves of leather-bound vintage books. What an incredible space. Who'd have thought to put those rugs against dark wooden floorboards?

India had agonized for hours over what to wear for this first meeting – it was important to get it right. After all, Jean-Luc was one of the world's foremost designers. She had settled on her Isabel Marant linen jacket, A-line Cottonier skirt and Repetto ballet flats. Surely you couldn't go wrong with a totally French ensemble to meet a *Createur de mode*?

She stood up as Jean-Luc appeared in the doorway wearing a crumpled white linen suit and panama hat. The 'story' he is telling today is more *Last Days of the Raj* than anarchic revolutionary, India thought.

"Enchante," he said, air-kissing her on either cheek. "Please let us sit down. I have ordered afternoon tea. We 'ave the room for the next hour; we will not be disturbed."

"Thank you," India said. "This is such a lovely room."

"Yes. Kit 'as done an exceptional job. It ees a beautiful thing – the power of imagination in the hands of someone who knows what she is doing. Who needs to 'ave their own place in London when you 'ave a room waiting for you 'ere?

And tomorrow I return to Provence to my abandoned house guests."

India had gleaned from a recent spread in *Vanity Fair* that Jean-Luc entertained his house guests in grand style in his renovated farmhouse, a sprawling property nestled in acres of lush French countryside. Artists, musicians, writers, actors and designers, 'dropped in' for weeks at a time during the summer months to horse ride, cycle and swim. Evenings they would come together to dine around a reclaimed wooden trestle in the kitchen, a vast converted barn complete with Adobe walls, exposed ceiling beams, squashy sofas and a roaring fire. She had read that the wine they drank was from his adjoining vineyard, the organic vegetables picked daily by his chef. The milk was from his pedigree cows, eggs from his bantam chickens and herbs from his lavender-hedged kitchen garden. There were photographs of mouthwatering pastries created from ripe fruit from the orchard.

It sounded like heaven, although India was somewhat consoled by the fact that she might not enjoy the company of some of the houseguests. She had no desire to spend time with Sting and from what she knew of her, was in no rush to meet Tracey Emin either. Not that the opportunity was likely to present itself anytime soon, she'd mused.

The article had nevertheless made India ache to live in a rural idyll, forever frozen in time, riding a stallion bareback, a white chiffon dress falling from her shoulders, her windswept hair flying behind her as she galloped in slow motion through fields of barley. She pushed the image away as they were served tea in fragile tea cups from English china pots and a tier of dainty sandwiches and scones were arranged on the low glass table in front of them.

"So, India. I have seen the draft that has been written for me. Of course, I will put it in my own words. I am arrogant enough to believe nobody would have expressed how I feel so well as I feel zees things."

He leaned forward and picked out a cucumber sandwich. "I understand what you need now is some copy for the website, yes? So. We will look at the images and I can tell you the thoughts they provoke in me so that you can use my words."

"Perfect," India said, opening her MacBook Air and sifting through to find the folder that profiled the students' designs and the philosophies behind them. Then, pulling the pictures onto the screen one by one, she switched on her tape recorder.

"This is unique," Jean-Luc said after a few moments. "The aesthetic seems almost accidental...now this one is ambitious...dramatic, unexpected....punk meets burlesque. How I ADORE burlesque. This, now THIS. It is reductionist. I like the form – it challenges – this is an unharmonic melody. Pure poetry...next please...influenced by Mondrian...ah yes, look it says 'ere."

India was mesmerized. Jean-Luc sipped his tea and spoke in a stream of consciousness, reading the copy the students had written with laser-focused attention. As the final image flashed on the screen, he sat back and looked at her intensely.

"This is a very important project. It will have a long life. I am honored to be a part of it."

"Thank you. I know the students will be thrilled. I will have the tape transcribed and edited then we will let you see it before it goes online to be certain you're happy with it."

Jean-Luc glanced at the wall clock. Precisely one hour had passed.

"I must not keep you," he said, getting to his feet. "I am thinking that I would like to reward the most talented of these creative young people by having them work with me in my studio in Paris for a month."

"What a wonderful idea," India said enthusiastically. "The students would be beyond thrilled at the opportunity."

"A month would be the perfect time. A month in Paris will change your life. As Henry Miller once said, 'To know

Paris, is to know a great deal.' I will be honored to make this offer. One month in my studio."

India powered down her computer and put the recorder away in her tote. "Thank you. That is very generous."

"Bien sûr, youth is energy. Creativity thrives on energy and talent."

"Thank you for the tea. It was delicious," India said. "I look forward to seeing you again at the show. If you need anything else in the meantime, you have my e-mail. Merci beaucoup."

"One more thing," Jean-Luc said as she reached the door.

India turned around and waited.

"I will share with you something."

"Yes?" India smiled.

He ran his hand over his head. "I am needing something now. I don't know what it ees, but I am tired. I have used up the energy that has been around me. This project, these students – they are the life-blood – they feed my creativity. I am doing this project for myself also, not just for them. I need inspiration. I need them maybe even more than they need me."

"Thank you for telling me., India said, somewhat surprised by his intensity, his apparent vulnerability.

She waited a few minutes before leaving the room. That was quite an interview, she thought, wandering up Wardour Street to Henry's offices. I am so loving this job.

The air was muggy and the streets crowded with people racing for the subway. It was getting close to four o'clock. Samantha was packing things away at the reception desk when she got there.

How does she manage to stay that groomed all day long?' India wondered, admiring the girl's sleek ponytail and her flawless complexion. She looks airbrushed.

"Hi India." Samantha smiled. "I'll be with you in a moment. I have to take these papers through to be signed by Mr. Lichtenstein."

India masked her surprise. She had assumed 'Lichtenstein' to be a sleeping partner as she had yet to meet him.

"If I can have the transcript by Wednesday that'd be great," she said, handing the tape to Samantha a few minutes later.

"Not a problem. Did the meeting go well?"

"Very."

Just then a door swung open and a wiry guy wearing the London city 'uniform' of a white shirt, pinstripe suit and tortoise-shell glasses appeared in the foyer.

"You must be India," he said, extending his hand. "At last we meet. Joel. Joel Lichtenstein. Henry's told me all about you."

"Mr. Lichtenstein, your car for the airport is waiting for you," Samantha said, hovering with his coat and scarf.

"Thanks," he said, checking his watch. "I have to dash, India. I'm running late as it is. It has been lovely meeting you." With that, the elevator pinged and he was gone.

India turned to Samantha. "Where's he off to?"

"Cannes. The Advertising Festival," she said.

"That's such a coincidence. I have a friend in Cannes right now."

"Is he in advertising?"

"No. He's an actor. He's on location there."

"Would I know him?" Samantha asked.

"Probably. Adam Brooks?"

"Adam Brooks. Adam Brooks!" Samantha exclaimed. "That is SO weird."

"What is?" India said. "I met him through my sister when I was staying in LA a few years ago."

"No. It's not weird you know him, but I was looking at his photograph only an hour ago."

"You were? How come?"

"I was checking hotel availability for Mr. Lichtenstein. He's booked at The Carlton, where he always stays. He goes to the festival every year for the week. Last year he came back saying it was so crazy busy – like a bun fight was how he put it – so he's only going for the final three days this time and at the last minute he asked me to see if I could get him into Hotel du Cap-Eden-Roc instead."

That's where Adam's staying, India thought mournfully, where I should be too.

"So I was checking it out and then it all looked so amazing I started noodling around on the gossip from the week. They like to call it The Creativity Festival and hype it up. Mr. Lichtenstein gets great coverage for his clients there. He won two awards last year. Anyway, there was Adam Brooks. How funny is that? What a coincidence. Here look, I'll show you."

Samantha had the page from the *New York Post* up within seconds and swiveled her computer toward India.

Cannes: The Hottest Photos and
Gossip from the Ad World's Top Festival.

Stars on Eden-Roc Terrace

India skimmed the article, the predictable journalese: drinks at sunset, hottest party of Cannes Lion Festival, Michael Bublé performing, followed by a list of names, most of which meant nothing. She scrolled down to a photograph of Adam framed against an expanse of ocean with a girl and not just *any* girl. There was no mistaking this one, with her cleavage and stack heels and her trout pout. Her image was burned into India's memory. This was the girl who had been in Vegas with him – the girl who had the so-called 'accident,' the girl he took out for dinner – and now here she was in Cannes. Cannes of all places.

"Are you okay?" Samantha asked as India clamped her hand over her mouth.

"Er. Yes. Yes I'm fine, absolutely fine," India answered unsteadily.

Samantha strained to get another look at the picture.

"She's pretty. They make a cute couple."

"They certainly look like a couple," India managed to say.

Gathering every ounce of her strength, she smiled. "Thank you. Have a great weekend, Samantha."

"You too. Oh! I nearly forgot. Henry said he and a couple of people he'd like you to meet are at the corner wine bar if you'd care to join them for a drink."

"Thanks," India replied over her shoulder, before racing down the stairs and out of the building onto the dusty street, narrowly avoiding a line of stationary bikes. She leapt back onto the crowded pavement to escape a speeding cyclist. Jostling her way past the teenagers clustered outside the neighboring pub, she turned down a cobbled side street to get away from the crowds and away from the stench of grease coming from a fast food truck.

She stopped for a moment trying to steady the pounding in her chest, craving a wide-open space where she could run, punch the air and scream. Everything around her was suddenly alien: the sex shops, tattoo parlors, the garbage and graffiti, the endless stream of commuters, the hotel workers smoking cigarettes around kitchen dumpsters. Turning in the opposite direction, unsure where to go next, she walked aimlessly for a while and then hesitated at the street corner by the Gielgud Theater. It was showing *Les Misérables*. How appropriate, she thought. Adam Brooks, you are dead to me.

Opening her purse, she checked her mascara in a tiny mirror, touched up her lipstick and took a deep breath. Turning back in the direction of Henry's office, she paced up and down the block several times before pushing open the double doors to the wine bar.

Henry was jostling to get served. She shoved her way through to him unapologetically and managed to catch his eye.

"What can I get you?" he yelled.

"Vodka tonic please," she yelled back.

It felt like everyone who worked in Soho had picked this place tonight. India stood there irritated by everything and everyone around her. Henry relayed the drinks to the couple hovering behind him and handed India hers.

"Before you drink that," he said, nodding toward her glass and raising his eyebrows, "you're certain you haven't taken any medication?"

"Funny. Ha!" India snapped. "No I haven't. Could we agree to drop the subject?"

"Pity. I was rather looking forward to continuing our conversation."

India felt a shock of contact as he held her gaze for the longest time. Right now I hate you, you smug bastard, she thought.

"Whatever conversation you'd like to continue, you'd better be prepared to work very hard for it," she said.

"Believe me, I am prepared to get as hard as you would like me to," he said under his breath, and then turning to the couple next to him he said, "Here, let me introduce you. Mike, Paula, meet India Butler. Hey. Grab that table; those people are leaving."

They squeezed their way across the room to the window table and sat down. India went through the motions, smiling politely, doing her best to feign interest as she became increasingly aware of Henry's Bulgari cologne.

"Another round?" Mike said. "My shout."

"Yes please," India said. "Vodka and tonic. Same again."

India sat still with great difficulty. She wanted to push back the table and scream. She knocked back her drink.

Will they ever leave? This is excruciating, she thought. She felt the electricity between herself and Henry was so palpable she couldn't believe his friends hadn't picked up on it. She felt as if 'fuck off' must be written in large letters across her forehead.

"So, how long have you two been working together?" Paula asked. "Henry and I go way back. We were at university together."

"A couple of months now. It gets more interesting every day," India said. And it's about to get way more interesting, she thought.

"Cheers," Henry said, as yet more drinks arrived. "Thanks Mike. Aren't you having another?"

"We've gotta go," Paula said. "Hopefully miss the traffic; we're heading down to Chichester for the weekend."

India downed her second vodka fast.

At last, the couple said their goodbyes with many promises to get together for longer next time, catch a game of squash, a round of golf. Finally, they were gone. There was the longest pause. Henry looked at India.

"Shall we go?" he said.

"Do you have some place in mind?"

"I do," he said.

She followed him out of the bar and across the street. He pushed open the door to his building and grabbed her by the hand. They raced up the two flights of stairs and into his office, where he closed the door behind him and loosened off his tie. He began unbuttoning her shirt as he kissed her. She pulled her hands through his hair as he swiped the papers off his desk and leaned her back onto it. As his hand began working its way up her thigh India heard the click of the door.

"There's someone there," she whispered.

"It's just the cleaner. She'll go away. She usually does."

India snapped to her senses. Pushing Henry away. "SHE USUALLY DOES? What the hell am I doing?" she thought.

Leaping up and grabbing her purse, she flew from the room. Racing down the stairs onto the street, she managed to flag down a black cab as it came around the corner of Broome Street.

"Queens Park," India panted, climbing inside.

"You're in a hurry, luv. Robbed a bank or something?" the cabbie quipped as she clanked the door shut.

"Just need to get home fast. Bad day. VERY bad day."

"Boyfriend problems is it?"

"Actually, yes. Are you some kind of clairvoyant or something?"

"See it all in this business, luv. My missus reckons I should write a book – had that actress, what's her name, the one in *Coronation Street*, in the back last week. Could make a fortune off of the *Daily Mail* if I wanted to, the stories I hear. Don't you worry about him, kiddo. He's not worth it," he said, switching on the meter and waiting for the traffic lights to change. He looked at her through his rearview mirror as she fought back tears. "Cheer up, luv."

India sighed, leaning back in the seat, closing her eyes and catching her breath as she waited for her heart to stop pounding. The cab wound its way slowly through the city and picked up speed as it headed toward the suburbs.

Thank god it's the weekend. At least I won't have to see Henry until next week, that's if I still have a job to go to of course. Shit. What if I've wounded his pride? Wasn't there something in the contract about a review? Can you get fired for NOT screwing your boss? Is that legal?

"Next on the left thanks," she yelled to the driver, realizing they'd overshot her house. He pulled up abruptly.

"Cheers, luv." He smiled, handing her a receipt. "Don't let the buggers grind you down."

India wearily climbed the stairs to her apartment. She opened the front door and her cat greeted her padding down the hallway and fussing around her ankles.

"I almost did something really reckless this evening, Countess," she murmured, lifting and cradling the purring ball of fur. "But I *didn't*. Well I *almost* didn't. That's the good news. I'll tell you the bad news when you've had your dinner and I've had another drink."

Throwing her purse onto the couch, India pulled open a packet of Whiskas and scattered the biscuits into a dish in front of the cat. She opened the freezer and grabbed a bottle of vodka, bought for Sarah and left untouched for reasons India now understood. Filling a tumbler with ice and pouring a generous measure, she added tonic water and went into the sitting room. She rifled through her collection of CDs and found her favorite Edith Piaf album. Then, flopping into an armchair, she took several large gulps and began singing along mournfully. *Quand il me prend dans ses bras, il me parle tous bas, je vois la vie en rose...*

As the track reached its crescendo, she drained the glass, refilled it clumsily, then belted out the next song. *Non, rien de rien, non je ne regrette rien...*

She poured a straight shot, knocked it back and then hurling the remaining ice cubes at the wall, leapt onto the couch and karaoked her way through the reprise. *Non, rien de rien...*she yelled, fist thumping the air. After a few minutes, she collapsed flat on her back into the cushions. Sitting up again, tears streaking her face, she blubbered the final chorus. *Avec mes souvenirs...J'ai allumé le feu...Mes chagrins, mes plaisirs...Je n'ai plus besoin d'eux...*

"Counteshh," she slurred, "you are a cat. I am a conshultant. You are my besht friend and I am yours...letsh have a little sleep now..."

15

Luella made her way to the Charlotte Street Hotel, where she settled at a table by the window. She was about to pull out her iPad when she saw Peter scanning the room for her.

"Over here." She waved to him.

"Hi," he said, pulling out the chair across from her. "Sorry I'm late. Traffic."

"It's fine. I walked from Henry's office," she said. "Sorry, you had to cross town. I forgot it's the holiday weekend."

"No problem. I was just happy you wanted to talk to me," he said. "Peroni please." He nodded to the barman. "The usual, Lu?"

She nodded.

"And a vodka martini thanks. So how're the plans for the show coming along?"

"Really well. Henry has worked his magic. Jean-Luc has agreed to be the host. I can hardly believe it, can you? Jean-Luc. We're all thrilled. It's such a coup don't you think? Tod will be so excited to meet him." She paused, noticing Peter's hands were trembling. "Okay. I'm talking too much."

Peter eventually broke the long silence that followed. "Lu, I want you to understand that I never wanted this. I didn't choose it. I never wanted to be different. I don't. I've fought against it for years, dealt with these feelings, suppressed them. It's why I've always been such a workaholic I suppose. I've been trying to fill up the spaces, not give myself time to think."

Luella said nothing.

"The other day, you wanted to know if being with you was good for me. It was. I mean sleeping with you, Lu. It was okay."

"Okay?"

"Lu, you're the only woman I've ever slept with. We were kids when we met. I told myself I had these feelings under control. I thought, well, I tried to believe this was something I could handle. It's not like I had these strong urges to go out looking for sex for the sake of it. I suppose I tuned it out, tried to turn the volume down on the noise in my head."

"Peter. Peter look at me."

He looked up.

"I feel bad that you've lived like this all these years. The other day you said you wanted us to stay in each other's lives. You've been my best friend for so long that I want to understand. I need to understand for my own sanity."

Peter went to speak and she put up her hand to stop him.

"Let me finish what I have to say. Please. It's taken me so many sleepless nights to feel strong enough to talk. When I found the letter it felt like a hammer blow, but in a weird way it's been easier than if I'd found a letter from another woman."

Peter looked at her in astonishment.

"I know you find that surprising, but I think if it had been another woman I'd have tried to get you back. With this, well, there's no competition. It's so, well, final, I suppose."

Luella felt a catch in her throat. Her cough attracted the attention of the couple at the neighboring table. She lowered her voice.

"This is useless. We can't talk here, Peter. Let's fix a time for you to come to the house. Are you around this weekend?"

"Yes. I'm here on my own all week. Maisie's out of town and I'm minding the dog."

"Come over tomorrow, lunchtime."

"Okay." He nodded.

"Just tell me one thing before then. How long have you been seeing him?"

Peter hesitated. "A while...it's been a while."

Luella leaned in closer. "Years? Months? Tell me, Peter. I think you owe it to me to tell me."

"I can't. Not now, Lu. Not here."

Luella put down her martini glass and pushed back her chair.

"Okay. Let's take things one step at a time then," she said, getting to her feet. "I've waited this long. I can wait a little longer. We'll talk tomorrow. I'll see you at the house at one. Okay?"

"I'll be there," he answered quietly.

Luella left the hotel lobby and walked down the street past the crowded wine bars and al fresco cafés. The air was heavy with the scent of cooking spices and cigarette smoke, and throbbing with the buzz of conversation and music. She felt unutterably alone.

Frustrated in her attempts to get a taxi, she cut through Soho Square Gardens. Then realizing she was in no rush to go home, she decided to call Susie and see if she was around for a drink. Susie had been a rock these last few months; the adage about old friends being the best was so true.

~ ~ ~

Late Saturday afternoon India took the train over to Sarah's place.

"You look like shit," Sarah said, greeting her at the door with a warm hug. "Come in. What's going on? Tell me the whole sad saga."

"You are blooming," India said. "It suits you. You look beautiful."

"I feel great, thanks." Sarah grinned. "So, sit yourself down and tell me all."

"Here you go. Isn't a picture worth a thousand words?" India said, pulling her iPad from her purse and opening it on the kitchen table.

Sarah looked at the image of Adam with Natalie in Cannes. "I'm sorry. I'm really sorry. She looks like a right piece of work. Eew," she said. "Do you want a cup of tea? Happens an aspirin?"

"Both thanks," India said, sinking deeper into the chair and putting her head into her hands.

"Well, cheer up. There's still Henry," Sarah said across her shoulder as she filled the kettle with water.

"About Henry," India sighed. "There's been a development."

"Oh?"

India filled her in on the previous evening. "It's going to be even more awkward at work I suppose," she said, "if such a thing were possible. I love this job, Sarah. Why does everything always get so complicated?"

"C'est la vie. Remember? Look. Henry needs you. You said he's asked you to see if Annabelle will be a presenter at the fashion show, yes?"

"True," India said, swallowing the aspirin with a shudder and taking a sip of tea. "He was kind of cautious around it, like he didn't feel comfortable asking me to ask her or something. I told him. It's no big deal but I might have to go out to LA to persuade her."

"Really? I mean, can't you just call her?"

"I was joking," India said. "Though I *was* kind of hoping he'd send me to LA to meet the students at Otis College. But as I never want to see Adam Brooks again..." Her thoughts trailed off.

"Have you spoken to him? Does he know you've seen this?"

"He keeps leaving me texts like everything is normal. I haven't answered them. I don't intend to either."

"So, assuming everything blows over with Henry, you

know, you explain you're not used to vodka or better still you pretend nothing happened and nothing much DID happen, so you march in there on Monday, business as usual. I've never seen you so happy in a job. You're not going to lose it. Henry will get over it. From what you've told me he probably found it very funny. He'll respect you for not going there."

"Do you really think so?" India looked up hopefully. "You're not just saying that to cheer me up?"

"Really. I mean it. Sounds like Henry's a big boy. He'll get over it. Do you want the advice of a pregnant woman?"

"Go on."

"Well I don't think you'll have closure until you talk to Adam properly. Don't get your hopes up, but there may still be an explanation. Maybe he's not sleeping with her. Maybe they're just friends."

India shook her head.

"Listen. I'm just saying. Give him a chance to explain. Talk to him. End it properly if it is the end. You'll feel better. You'll be able to move on, meet someone else."

"Maybe." India sounded doubtful. "I'll think about it. In the meantime, can I go and lie down? I feel really bad."

"Sure." Sarah smiled. "Mi casa. Su casa. I'll wake you up when the pasta's ready. We'll eat when Damien gets here. He's coming over around seven. Then you'll get to listen to nothing but baby talk. It'll make you delighted to get back to work on Monday. I'm even boring myself these days."

India laughed. She gave her friend a grateful smile. "Thanks," she murmured. "Never again. I'm NEVER drinking vodka again."

16
—

"Good weekend?" Luella asked India the following Monday morning, taking off her blue suede jacket and folding it carefully over a chair in the meeting room.

"Pretty low-key. My friend's expecting a baby soon," India said. "I had dinner at her place. You?"

Henry walked in before Luella could answer.

Okay, so the moment of truth. How is he going to handle this I wonder? India thought.

"Good morning. Thanks for coming in so early," he said briskly, addressing them both as he sat down and throwing a sheath of papers onto the committee desk. "I have to be out of here in ten minutes, but I want to get things fast out of the gate this week. Here's my summary of where we're up to and what we need to pin down in the next two weeks."

Samantha popped her head around the corner. India noticed she had a fresh head of highlights and that her skin was glowing and dewy. She must have spent all weekend pampering herself, she thought.

"Would anyone like tea, coffee, more water, or anything else before I leave you to get on?" Samantha smiled.

"I think we're fine, thanks," Henry said, taking his seat across from Luella.

He's come over all inscrutable and professional this morning, India thought. I really hope Sarah's right and I haven't blown this.

"Okay." He ran his hands through his hair. "Reprise. *Faux Fashion* will be released in hardback two weeks before the show. India, you also have a copy there of Luella's book signing events and media interviews to date. We've created some serious media buzz and that's before we add the celeb factor for the show. Time is getting tight. India, we need to take stock of where we're up to."

India sat up startled. He's not going to fire me in front of Luella is he? she thought, adjusting the collar of her shirt.

"Thank you for your report on the New York visits. I'll need the breakdown and timings from LIFT by the end of the week. Is that doable with everything else you've got going on?"

"Yes," she said. "There are a few loose ends they still had to sign off on, but I'll chase them." Phew. Looks like I still have a job, she thought.

"Did you reach out to your sister to see if she's available to be a presenter with Jean-Luc? I don't mean to pressure you, but if she's not up for it we need to get back to the drawing board and lock down an alternative."

Reach out?' Sounds like she needs some kind of rescuing, India thought, unavoidably catching Henry's eye and looking away quickly. You're locking up, reaching out and getting out of that gate fast this morning Henry, she thought.

"Er. No, not yet," she said. "I will. She's been on vacation in Hawaii, coming back at the weekend."

"Great. Great, India. So now Lu, are you happy with how things are developing so far?"

"Yes," Luella said. "The percentage deal with the publishers looks good. Not that I can get my head around all the mechanics of the online build out, but I understand that the students will get to promote and sell their designs online by linking to their own websites. That's great."

"I'm still not sure how it all works exactly," India said. Shit, she thought, I should have pretended I understand what's going on.

"In principle it's straightforward," Luella said, "By

'mechanics,' I mean how it will work technically. All you really need to understand is that for each copy of the book that's bought through the online college websites, a percentage of the profit goes to the college. The students can maximize the connections for their own work by linking to their own websites and connecting to each other to market their work internationally."

"Great. And isn't it exciting that the student with the best, I mean of course, 'most innovative' designs, will get to intern with Jean-Luc for a whole month in Paris?"

"That's the first I've heard of that," Luella said. "How wonderful. What a great opportunity." She beamed, turning to Henry. "You didn't tell me you'd persuaded him to do that on top of everything else. Well done."

Henry pulled at the neck of his sweater looking decidedly uncomfortable and then quickly recovered his equilibrium. "Have you pinned it down, India?"

"Sorry?" India said.

"Will Jean-Luc pay for the flights and accommodation and basic living expenses? When will we get that in the contract, do you know? Will the student have ownership of their intellectual property if they produce work in Paris or will that go to Jean-Luc? Did you tie up all the loose ends?"

"I didn't actually think to ask him the details; I got rather caught up in the excitement of the moment," she said. "He was really charged."

"It'll be perfect," Luella chimed in. "I'm sure you'll be able to firm up the details with him, Henry. Well done you."

"I'm going to Paris tomorrow," Henry said. "Probably talk it through with him when I'm there."

"He's not going to be in Paris. He left for Provence," India volunteered.

"Whatever. I'll call him," Henry said, pushing back his chair.

"When are you back from France?" Luella asked, gathering her papers from the desk.

"Thursday."

She stood up. "Have a good trip. I'll be in touch India," she said. "Let me know how you get on at the LIFT meeting."

"India. A word before you leave?" Henry was standing in the doorway. He closed the door and lowered his voice.

"In future I'd appreciate it if you'd keep me informed of all developments before sharing them with the client. Okay?"

"Sure," India mumbled. "I had planned to tell you first thing this morning, but Luella was here ahead of you."

"No big deal. Let's move on shall we?" he said, running his hands through his hair and looking at her intensely. "New rules, hey? Professional protocol and all that...you understand I am not only talking about Jean-Luc. About Friday...too much drink on the job, water under the bridge?"

"Of course," India said. "Absolutely. New rules. Water under the bridge."

Henry opened the door for her and India caught her breath as she walked past him. He's still going to be hard to resist, she thought. Damn his pheromones.

~ ~ ~

India's skirt flew up as the wind from the river whipped around the corner of The Embankment. Holding it down with one hand, she struggled to read directions with the other. The London Institute of Fashion and Technology was inconveniently spread out across the city on several separate campuses. Finding each one this week had presented her with something of a challenge. The Technology and Manufacturing Center had been all the way out at Shoreditch and it had taken her hours to get to the Footwear and Accessories Department meeting that morning in Hackney. Eventually using Google maps, she located an ugly building incongruously squashed between two red brick edifices. In the absence of an elevator, she climbed several flights of stone stairs to the fourth floor and pushed open a steel door.

Who says the fashion industry is glamorous? she thought,

catching her breath and looking for signs for the reception area.

"You must be India."

India spun around. The voice was coming from a girl in her early twenties with spiked purple hair, a selection of predictable piercings and arms festooned with vibrant tattoos. "Victoria asked me to find you."

How come 'creatives' aren't more creative? India wondered. They all look so alike. "Yes." She smiled before following her down a bleak corridor to a room with a single window overlooking the scaffolding of a nearby building site.

"Come on in. I'm Victoria. Lovely to meet you, India."

An exceptionally thin woman stood up from behind a white melamine desk. India noticed that she bore an uncanny resemblance to Tilda Swinton. Her blonde hair had been chopped into a severely masculine cut and she was wearing an asymmetrical sheath dress split wide at the neck. An arm shot out from some mysterious side opening as she went to shake India's hand.

"Here, grab a seat next to that console. I'll be able to talk you through the images more easily from there. Would you like a drink? I can offer you green tea, mint tea or water."

"Thanks," India said, sitting down on the steel chair beside her. "Just water."

"So you're the educational consultant to this project. What does that mean exactly?"

Good question, India thought. I ask myself that quite a lot. "I'm working as a consultant with Lichtenstein and Cowen to maximize the education outreach." She hesitated and then added, "They consult me a lot...about all sorts of things."

"Fascinating. Well, may I just say that as a vegan, I am personally happier than you can possibly imagine to be part of this project," Victoria said, sitting down in front of the computer screen and tucking one improbably long leg behind her ankle. "Many of the garments you are going to see here have been designed using organic cotton and recycled fibers. We aim to leave a low carbon footprint. No wool, sheepskin, silk or fur of course, but I think the students have even pushed the boundaries beyond the usual limitations."

India nodded and watched as Victoria set up the slideshow on her flat screen and they waited for the images to download.

"We have stayed away from slogans and propaganda. This project is about education, not alienation. We want people to see that being cruelty free doesn't mean fashion can't be fun or sexy."

"Are all of the students vegan?"

"Of course not." Victoria laughed, looking at her curiously. "When we took the theme of desolation last year we didn't expect the students to all be depressives."

"Of course. How silly of me," India said. She concentrated hard as Victoria talked her through the montage on the screen and then pulled out specific designs by way of more detailed explanation.

"Oh! Look, it's hard to believe those trousers aren't leather," India exclaimed, spotting a pair of skinny jeans similar to the ones she had coveted from a Kate Moss advert recently. "Does the fabric breathe like leather or does it smell a bit off?"

"Vegan 'leather' can be made from many materials. These trousers, as you can see from the notes, are made from acrylic and polyamide felt fibers."

"Isn't acrylic made from petrochemicals?" India asked, confused.

"Well observed, India. Yes, it's the perpetual dilemma. The environment versus the animal rights issue. The line we have taken with this project is to use only recycled materials. The fabric for these pants comes from man-made fibers that are damaging to the environment, both in the dying as well as in the manufacturing process. In this case, the 'pleather,' as it is sometimes known, has been recycled and refashioned to make the garment, thus being both ethically sound, animal-free and still protective of the environment."

India shuddered. The idea of wearing recycled plastic trousers was altogether gross. "Tell me more about the shirt," she said, attempting to switch Victoria's focus. "It looks exactly like silk."

"It's called 'Soysilk.' As the name suggests it's made from soybean residue and is fully biodegradable."

"Who knew?" India murmured. "I thought soy was just tofu and milk."

"I have a particular issue around silk garments," Victoria continued. "The idea of all those mulberry worms being bred and harvested for human vanity breaks my heart. The thought of pupae or caterpillars being tortured knocks me sick. The cocoons are dropped into boiling water, as I'm sure you know. It makes me shudder. It's criminal. Brutal."

"Horrible," India agreed, adjusting the buttons on her cotton blouse. I wonder if old Joe's still pickin' cotton, she thought, remembering the line from a Leonard Cohen song.

"If they lived as nature intended," Victoria continued, "the worms would turn into moths and chew their way out of their cocoons to escape."

And then go on to chew great big holes in my cashmere sweaters in karmic revenge, India thought.

Victoria, still glassy-eyed with emotion, took India through the remainder of the presentation, finally hitting the 'off' button and turning to her with a deep sigh. "So what do you think of our attempts to change the world through fashion?"

"I've learned so much. The collection is wonderful and you and the students are to be congratulated. As an ex-teacher, I know only too well how hard you must have worked to produce this."

"Thank you." Victoria smiled. "I very much appreciate you saying that, although this is a labor of love as I'm sure it is for you. Let me give you the stills, and I understand you're coming to our main campus to meet the students next week."

"That's right. We have some exciting news to share with them, but I can't tell you right now. Mr. Cowan wants to tell them himself. He'll be coming with me next Tuesday."

"How exciting. I look forward to it."

Victoria stood up and strode over to her desk. India noticed her 'pleather' Birkenstocks. Every bit as ugly as the regular kind, she thought.

"Here's the schedule. Sorry you had to wait for it. I'll call Tara now and she'll show you out. This place is a maze. I don't want you to get lost."

17

———

Luella threw down a tea towel on the kitchen worktop and checked her hair in the hall mirror before going to open her front door. Peter was framed in the archway wearing his weekend uniform of beige khakis and a Ralph Lauren polo shirt. He handed her the mail. She took the envelopes from him and walked briskly down the hallway into the kitchen.

"It's such a lovely day I thought we'd eat in the garden," she said, gesturing to the wrought iron circular table on the patio set out with two places.

"Good idea," he said as he stepped outside onto the verandah. "The wisteria's doing well."

"Kind of," Luella answered. "It still hasn't flowered even after all this time. It must be at least ten years old, don't you think?"

She handed him a serving dish piled with olives, heirloom tomatoes and mozzarella. "Can you manage the arugula too?"

"Sure," he said, taking the salad bowl from her. "We planted it the year we went to Cyprus. I remember because that's when we bought the olive trees."

"They didn't survive long did they? Too much rain here I suppose," she shouted opening the fridge. "Would you like a glass of Prosecco?"

"Yes. Please," he said, stepping back indoors and taking the bottle from her. "Anything else to carry out?"

"Over there," she said, pulling warm ciabatta from the Aga. "Grab the olive oil and the balsamic and we're good to go."

Taking off her oven gloves, Luella untied her apron and joined him under the shade of a beech tree as he pried open the cork.

"Here," she said, lifting two long-stemmed glasses from the table and holding them toward the bottle.

"Cin Cin," he said, raising his glass.

"Cheers," she said without raising hers. "Let's eat. You look like you've not had a meal in months."

"This is so civilized." Peter sighed, pulling out the ornate garden chair and shaking out a floral napkin. He speared a tomato and layered a slice of cheese curd onto the warm crusty bread. "I miss you, Lu. I miss this."

Luella didn't respond. She sat down looking into the middle distance, avoiding eye contact with him.

"How's the new book coming on?" he asked through a mouthful of salad.

"Not so well. I'm collecting content right now," she said pouring iced lemon water from a jug into their tumblers. "Planning the fashion show and preparing for the media promotion is taking up so much of my time it's impossible to get into a writing rhythm."

"I'm so proud of you, Lu. I think *Faux Fashion* is your best book yet."

"I've given you a good acknowledgement for all the research you helped me with," she said. "I felt so close to you when I was writing this book. You were such a big part of the process...it's hard to imagine that when I was running all that by you and you were taking such an interest, you were..."

Peter refilled their glasses. "I know. I know," he murmured. "Tell me what I can do to make things any better."

Luella sighed heavily, put down her silverware and pushed her plate away. She shook out a cigarette and tapped it on the table, twisting it between her finger and thumb.

"I've been to see a counselor," she said. "I've been going every week. It's helping. It's why I'm able to sit here with you, like this."

"A counselor? I thought you didn't want that."

"Well, turns out I do. Having you here today, meeting you yesterday was all part of how I'm supposed to, and I quote, 'begin to understand what's happened and not blame you or blame myself.' Apparently and somewhat obviously, if we aren't communicating I won't get answers to all my questions and I have SO many questions."

Peter looked at her intensely. "Do you want me to come to the sessions? I told you ages ago that I would if you'd like me to."

"No," she said, more forcefully than she intended. "At least not yet. Maybe not at all." She struck at the side of a card of matchsticks and lit her cigarette. "Peter, I'm not going to pretend that sitting here like this and being all civilized and grown up isn't difficult." She blew the smoke away from him over her shoulder and flicked the ash into the grass. "It's excruciating if you want to know."

"So what can I say or do now?"

"I have questions. You owe it to me to answer them truthfully."

"Okay. Absolutely. I promise."

"Are you still seeing this man?"

Peter pushed away his plate. "Yes," he said.

"When did you meet him?"

"Five years ago, when Société Générale was extending its asset management and mutual funds business. You remember I stayed in Paris for a month."

"And then went back there virtually every week for a while," Luella said. "Yes. I remember. Ironically, I was writing *Synchronized Secrets* at the time."

"Yes. That wasn't lost on me. Life imitating art as they say."

"I was chasing a deadline. I was grateful to have the time to myself to work while you were away."

"That's when it started," he said quietly.

"Peter, how long would you have gone on deceiving me if I hadn't found the letters?"

"Lu, I'd have told you years ago if I hadn't been so torn. I've been in denial. You have no idea how many times I've wanted to break it off with him. Nobody wants to be different. I didn't. I really don't, but now that you know, it has forced me to take a hard look at myself and accept that this is *what*, I mean, *who* I am."

He looked at her, his face creased with pain. "There's more I have to tell you," he said.

"Go on."

"It's about my job."

"Peter, you aren't telling me you'd lose your job for coming out as gay. That's ridiculous, surely?"

"No. Not for being gay, but there could be insider-trading issues here if I do – if they find out about us. He's wealthy. He's well known. He invested strongly in shares that, well...look, it could be construed that he had access to information that he might only have known about through me if they find out we are..." he hesitated, "...having an affair. He's being investigated."

Luella's mouth dropped open. She leapt up and looked at him in horror. "What the flying fuck? Are you telling me that not only do I have to come to terms with your homosexuality and infidelity now I also have to get my head around the fact that you're a crook? What the fuck, Peter? Do I even know you at all?"

Throwing down her cigarette and squashing it hard into the gravel path with her foot, she turned and faced him, her voice exploding with rage. "You're involved in some kind of Martha Stewart insider-trading thing? You could go to fucking jail. We have joint accounts. We have investments. Are they at risk? What's going on?"

"I can't talk to you when you're like this, Luella," Peter said quietly. "I haven't done anything wrong. It's just how it might look. I will be investigated no doubt, but they won't find anything. What they will find out is that we have had an affair and I didn't want you finding that out before I explained everything, and I haven't had the courage to tell you."

Luella sat down and lit another cigarette. She felt spent. Her head throbbed and her throat felt so raw she could barely swallow. Leaning back, she put her hand on her chest to stop the palpitations.

"Peter, I can't think straight. Please leave now. Please. I'll call you."

"Okay," he said. "I'm making this harder than it needs to be. Maybe I'll put it in writing. That way we can talk more calmly."

Luella watched him walk away. Pushing away the remains of her half-eaten lunch plate she remembered how badly Peter had always responded to confrontation, how frustrated she had always been by his inability to show emotion. In the early days of their marriage whenever they would disagree, she would fly into a rage, becoming more articulate the angrier she became and whipping things up into a more furious row. Peter would simmer silently, retreat into his personal space and freeze her out for hours, sometimes days.

Now as she began to calm down, she could see how futile and extreme her response had been. As the red mists of anger lifted, she felt saddened. She had done everything within her power to behave with civility, with dignity and maturity. She had been to see a counselor every week for months, called help-lines, talked endlessly to Susie, scoured books and followed blogs for hours on end, reading heart-wrenching stories of other women who had discovered their husbands were gay.

Taking deep drags of her cigarette, Luella understood how badly the months of agony, self-reproach and shock had affected her. Something had to give. After all, she had been functioning for all intents and purposes as if nothing had happened, going to meetings, writing, preparing guest blogs and traveling, while her life was crumbling around her. She had been feeling the intense pain of grieving. It was as if she had been numb up to this point. Now she felt the searing pain of abandonment.

Luella looked up. Peter was standing in the kitchen doorway.

"There's something else you should know," he said.

"I thought you'd left." She sighed, getting to her feet and lifting a couple of their lunch plates. "Peter, I'm exhausted. I thought I made it abundantly clear I need some space right now."

"Sit down, Lu. Please. I have to tell you something," he said.

Hearing the urgency in his voice, Luella put down the dishes and sank back in the chair. "Okay...what do I need to know that can't wait?" she said, wincing at the grating sound of metal as Peter dragged out the chair opposite her.

"The man I've been seeing..." he began tentatively.

Luella inhaled sharply. "Yes?"

"The man is Jean-Luc."

Luella stared at him. "Jean-Luc?" she whispered. "Jean-Luc?"

"Yes."

She closed her eyes for a few moments then opened them again. "You and Jean-Luc. Jean-Luc?" she said. "What the fuck? What the fuck, Peter?"

She stopped speaking for a moment, choking on her words. Peter said nothing. "Not only have you managed to screw up my personal life..." she said, "...managed to destroy everything I thought we had. Not only that, but now you've managed to fuck with my professional life too."

"Lu...I...it wasn't deliberate. I promise, this isn't..."

"You know what. I'm done. Get out, Peter. I mean it. I really do." She stood up and faced him, her eyes flashing dangerously. "If you stay here a minute longer, I will not be accountable for my actions. Get out, Peter. Get out right now before I lose it completely."

~ ~ ~

Returning to her apartment after a full day of meetings, India was buzzing with adrenalin and at a loss as to how to fill her Friday evening. She needed a distraction, a project, anything to take her mind off of Adam Brooks this weekend. The day had given her much to consider. She had experienced an epiphany on the subway home, had come to understand that fashion was not simply about wearing beautiful things. Fashion was an art form in and of itself. The fashion industry was a fundamental force to be reckoned with politically and ethically.

Fashion involved so much more than the shallow merchandising of clothes or labels. It was not all about *Vogue* shoots and Italian designers peddling impossible lifestyle aspirations, encouraging greed and ostentation. Sure, an obsession with fashion could lead to eating disorders and overspending, but it turned out that an interest in fashion, such as the one she indeed herself possessed, was more a form of social responsibility.

No longer would India see fashion as simply a form of self-expression or retail therapy. From this day forward, she would approach all purchases with an understanding of the vital contribution she was making to the survival of the planet. What had once been simply an absorbing pastime, which admittedly bordered on obsession, would now be a contribution to a cause, a responsibility to the earth. Bolstered by this very thought, India went through to her bedroom, a woman on a mission.

Two hours later, she was regretting her decision to conduct an appraisal of her closet in order to assess the political correctness of its contents. Clearly her shoes were, without exception, unsustainable. She surveyed the Louboutins bought in LA, the Prada sandals from New York, the Repetto ballet slippers from Paris, her nude pumps from LK Bennett as well as several pairs of All Saints boots, K Jacques sandals, Uggs and Lanvin flats that were heaped on her bed. This area had been designated the 'Dead animals – footwear section' and she was running out of space.

A bedside chair, an area designated 'More dead animals section' was covered in coats. Unsure where to file it, she placed her Arthur and Fox cashmere jacket lovingly on top of her Cottonier leather biker jacket, pretty sure that cashmere involved the exploitation of a protected species of Himalayan mountain goat.

Her shirts could remain on their hangers while she tallied them. Silk should never be thrown around, she thought, especially now I know what those worms have sacrificed. Stacking her merino wool and cashmere sweaters on a storage trunk in their protective moth repellant plastic zipper bags, she stopped to think.

Clearly there was no need to pull out any of her purses. They would never pass muster – Longchamp and Mulberry were not prone to the use of plastic even if given a fancy new name like 'pleather.'

She appraised the remaining woolen skirts and silk dresses, 'garments' as Victoria would call them.

Many have died that you might live. She sighed, closing the mirrored doors.

Opening her underwear drawer and banishing an image of caterpillars in scalding water, India sighed at the memory of the many evenings she had spent with Adam in Los Angeles in her Agent Provocateur negligees, satin corsets and silk stockings.

Why does everything I do always bring me back to a memory of you? she thought mournfully as she began returning things to their place. There's the shirt I wore for our very first date, the shoes from that magical night in Malibu, the pashmina you wrapped around me coming out of Chateau

Marmont, and the little black dress of Annie's that I should probably give back to her sometime.

When she was done, India showered and put on her Gap pajamas, made herself a hot chocolate and climbed into bed. Sipping on the comforting drink, she checked her phone and saw the text from Adam.

> Will be in Saint-Paul de Vence next Tuesday and Wednesday... want to join me at La Colombe d'Or? Can send car to collect from Nice airport.

India stared at the screen for a moment, then put down her mug and lay back gazing at the ceiling. Suddenly wide-awake, she sat bolt upright and dialed Los Angeles.

"Hey sis," Annabelle answered. "How's it going? What time is it there?"

India glanced at the bedside clock. "Ten thirty. Is this a good time? Are you still jetlagged from Hawaii? Were you taking a nap?"

"I'm fine. Wonderful *vacay* as they say here. The girls have just come back from surf camp in Malibu. That's the racket you can hear in the background."

"Say hello to them for me," India said, climbing out of bed and hunting under it for her Uggs.

"Hey girls. Keep it down. Put Clooney outside; he's making too much noise. India, hold on a second while I let the dog out and get the kids sorted."

India could visualize the scene clearly. How she longed right now to be with them all, flopped on one of Annie's cozy sofas, the afternoon California sunshine streaming through the French windows. She listened to her sister talking to her nieces. "Sandwiches in the fridge...juice usual place, where else? Give me a minute, Bella, can't you see I'm on the phone? Maria, there you are. Puede terminar la fijacion del almverzo de chicas?"

"Sorry, India, I've just asked Maria to sort the girls out – they're famished. I'm going to take the phone outside so we can talk properly. Okay, shoot," she said a few minutes later. "How's the job? How's Sarah? What's going on with Adam?"

"I was calling about Adam mostly, but now that I think about it and I have you on the phone, let me tell you where we're up to with the fashion show."

India fired her sister a synopsis of the last few weeks and her meetings with the deans of the colleges, avoiding all mention of Henry.

"I told you you'd be brilliant at this job, didn't I? See how talented you are? Jean-Luc will definitely pull the crowd and get the media attention," Annabelle enthused.

"So Annie," India took a deep breath, "we need a female presenter too, so..."

"Don't tell me, you want me to ask Rihanna for you."

"Very funny. Of course not. You know what I'm asking. Will you?"

"Of course, darling. Text me the date and the details. If I'm free, I'd be delighted. I'm so flattered to be asked. I'll check the minute Tess gets in tomorrow and get straight back to you."

"Wonderful, Annie. That's brilliant."

"So what else has been going on since I've been away?"

"It's a sad saga."

"Adam?"

"Yes," India said, fighting back tears as she described the photograph of Adam in Cannes.

"Thing is, Annie, he's still texting me as if nothing's going on. I've not answered him for a week or so but now he's suggesting I just fly out to Nice and stay with him at La Colombe D'Or."

"It's beyond beautiful and the artwork will blow your mind," Annabelle said.

"I can't possibly go, not now that I know he's seeing someone else or at least that he has been with someone else in all probability. I have to hang onto some sense of pride, don't I?"

"Darling, I've told you how hard it is to keep a relationship going in this business. I think you may be being unrealistic. I mean, you haven't agreed on monogamy have you? You're not living together. Maybe you need to see him if only to try to establish some ground rules. But let's face it..." she lowered her voice, "I keep Joss as close as I can with all those groupies. They're stalkers, predators. He's only a man. You've heard me say often enough that absence doesn't always make the heart grow fonder."

India remembered how Annabelle stressed about her husband whenever he was on tour with his band. How she would call him frequently, fly out to be with him whenever she could.

"Adam has always seemed more grounded than most of them," Annabelle continued, "but maybe it IS time to move on. I don't think you can do that unless you have a frank conversation with him. You owe it to both of you to do that I think."

"That's what Sarah thinks too."

"Talk to him, darling. If it's over, you'll have your work to distract you, and if you're wrong and this girl is just someone he knows, then you'll have thrown it all away for no good reason."

"You're right," India said hesitantly. "I've had a long week and I'm tired and I'm not thinking straight. I needed this conversation. You always talk such sense, Annie."

"So now. How's Sarah? How many weeks to go?"

"About six. She's got it all down: home delivery, maternity leave, childcare. She's so organized. I don't know when that happened – being with Damien I suppose."

"Uh-oh! Gotta go, darling. I'm needed back on the farm. Bella's friend and her mother just arrived."

India sank back onto the bed and leaned against the pillows, staring at her phone. Finally, she started to key in a text to Adam. *Would love to.* No, too eager, she thought hitting the delete key. She tried again. *Maybe.* She stared at the single word and grimaced. Now I sound like I'm dithering.

Starting over one more time, she typed, *Will check with Henry to see if I can get the time off.*

Shit, that's actually a factor, she thought, leaping up. I'm supposed to be helping send the invitations out for the show. I have a full week of meetings too. Going into the kitchen, she fired up her computer and checked her diary for the coming week.

Skype with New York, call with Jean-Luc, student presentation, producer's update, conference call with Entertainment Manager and Director...the list went on.

That's going to be hard to unravel, she thought. Where exactly is La Colombe d'Or anyway? Googling the boutique hotel, India sat back with an overwhelming sense of longing. The historic building was set high up in a medieval walled town and each picture threw up the promise of something more inviting than the next. Paintings lined the walls, from Miro to Chagall, each image so evocative. Only thirteen bedrooms, a garden restaurant, a swimming pool discreetly curtained with established hedges, the mahogany-lined dining room, the antique rustic tables, the fig trees, the views. India could barely breathe; how she longed to be there in France and with Adam.

Going back to her calendar, she felt a drop in her spirit as she looked at all of her commitments. "Thing is, Countess, I'm really loving this job," she said to the cat curled up at her feet. "It doesn't even feel like work. I can't just abandon it now for anyone, not even Adam."

India sank back in the chair with a deep sigh. She had a sense of responsibility, didn't she? You don't take off for several days without warning just when things are getting busy. "India Butler, for once in your life you're going to have to be a grown-up," she said, then fired off a text and pressed 'send' before she could change her mind.

Looked at diary. Too much going on at
work. Sorry, can't make it.

The reply came in fast.

Really? Are you sure?

Yes.

That sucks.

..
⌢

India didn't reply.

18

———

Sitting in Henry's office the following Monday afternoon waiting for the Skype from New York to begin, India knew that as difficult as it had been, she had made the right call not to go to France. It was as if everything had ramped up several gears now that the show was only a few weeks away. The phones in the office had been ringing off the hook all morning and Samantha had hired an assistant, Patricia, to be her runner.

India was relieved to be back at work. The weekend had been interminable. The thing is, she'd decided through a fistful of Kleenex, Adam needs to realize I can't just drop everything to be with him even if things are okay with us and he isn't seeing someone else.

Much of Sunday morning had been a pity party on the phone to Sarah and Annabelle followed by an afternoon movie marathon of the most miserable films she could find on Netflix. She had sobbed through three hours of *Gone With the Wind* followed by *Love Story, Sophie's Choice, The Notebook,* and *Bambi.*

Samantha jolted her out of her thoughts." Can I get you anything?" she asked.

"I'm fine, thanks," India said. "I have a coffee already." Henry looks like he could do with a tranquilizer though, she thought, but didn't say.

Henry was standing by a wall-mounted screen with a

technician and cursing the many attempts it was taking to connect with New York. Finally, a face became visible, and after a few minutes of mime, the sound connected and they were on broadcast.

A disembodied voice boomed in the room. "Good morning or rather should I say good afternoon?"

"He looks like he's at the fairground in the hall of mirrors," India whispered to Samantha, who smiled back politely and then stared at the screen intently.

I'm not certain Samantha's human, India thought. I wonder if she ever gets a fit of the giggles; she's always so proper.

Once the technician had realigned the screen, the face became recognizable. Ron Glasser, the producer, was only visible from the waist up. India could see a bald guy in his mid-thirties wearing black horn-rimmed glasses, a starched white shirt and a black jacket.

I wonder if he's still in his pajama bottoms, India mused.

"Hey, good to see you all." Ron grinned.

"Hi, Ron. We're all here. Luella, India, Samantha, Patricia, and myself," Henry replied.

"Great. Okay guys, we're running late and I only have the studio booked for another thirty minutes, so let me bring you up to speed."

"Sure," Henry said. "Fire away."

"My job has been to translate and enhance what the students have produced. I hope I've captured the spirit and the emotion of their collections. The title 'Faux Fashion' is wonderfully obtuse, so I've been able to interpret freely. We have here a multidimensional futuristic aesthetic inspired in part by Lagerfield's *Derelicte* and also by the interior of the theater."

Images of the historic Harvey Theater in Brooklyn appeared on the screen.

"We chose the venue in part because it is very unique."

There are no degrees of unique, India thought, reminded of how she would correct her students on this.

"The original twentieth century architectural elements have been preserved as you can see. It's reminiscent of the faded glory of Venice, a deconstructed timeless ruin. It is so purposefully distressed it fired my imagination to think in terms of both the past and the future."

India was taken back to a trip to Italy when she was a student. The theater looked for all the world like the Teatro La Fenice, where she had first seen *Carmen*.

"This means that we have been able to keep within budget and will be using the existing proscenium and house as is without the expense of added staging. The models will enter through the tiered seating to the right and down the raked seating on both sides and across the front of the stage to become part of the montage of onscreen images. This has cut the audience down to six hundred from a potential eight hundred seventy-four, but we have room for roving cameras as well as fixed ones. This is vitally important for streaming live on video."

Ron then talked them through 3D mock-ups of the staging. "The backdrop is the Steinberg movie screen with digital projection and a seven-point-one Dolby digital sound with forty-two surround speakers."

"And the music?" Henry asked, taking a sip of iced tea.

"It's on the CD. Do you have it?"

"We do," Samantha told him.

"Okay. Henry will you be joining us for the tech rehearsal and run-through on that Wednesday?"

"One of us will for sure, Ron."

"Okay. Cool. Just let my office know. If you have any more questions you know where to find me."

"Great work, Ron. Thank you," Henry said, bringing Skype to a close when the presentation was over and many more of their questions had been answered.

"You're welcome. Look forward to meeting you all. Have a great day."

"So what do you think?" Henry said, swiveling his chair to face the assembled team.

"I'm blown away," Luella said, visibly animated for the first time that day.

"It's so creative," India agreed. "I was imagining a traditional runway with a T-shape and models strutting up and down, but this is pure theater. It's absolutely mind blowing."

"I agree." Henry grinned. "It's going to create exactly the buzz we want. So to bring you up to speed, we have almost a full house for the show. The VIP after-party is set. I can let you have the full acceptance list by the end of the week."

He's in his element, India thought. He just loves all this.

"Thanks to Samantha here, we have goodie bags groaning with politically correct cosmetics: Burt's Bees, The Body Shop and Beauty Without Cruelty have all come through." He continued. "Well done, Samantha, for sourcing the ethical faux pearls and getting Mango Bay to donate the soy soaps."

"My pleasure." Samantha smiled. "I'm working on some Stella McCartney perfume too."

"Luella, you'll need to personalize a hundred signed copies of *Faux Fashion* for the VIPs, but that's easily done in New York when you're there," Henry said, checking off his list.

"Not a problem; just let me have the names," she answered, getting to her feet. "Love the sound of those gifts. So no hemp or patchouli oil, Samantha?"

"Not my style, Luella." Samantha smiled.

"Perish the thought," Henry agreed.

"Great job everyone," Luella said, making her way to the door. "Have to dash; I'm meeting a friend for dinner."

India's phone buzzed as she was gathering her papers from the table. She picked up.

"Hey, do you have a minute? We need to talk."

"Just give me a second. I'm at work," she said. "Henry, I've got to take this. I'll be back in a moment."

Going quickly down the corridor to the accountant's office, she shut the door behind her. "Okay. I can talk now," she said.

"So. What's going on, India? Why aren't you answering my texts? What's with the big freeze?"

"Nothing, er, nothing. I'm just busy," she said.

"Don't give me that. I know something's up. I know you too well."

India paced the tiny room. "You're right, actually. Yes. I need to ask you something." She paused. "You remember that girl, the one in Vegas in the photograph with you?" she said.

"Yep."

"The one you ran over or nearly ran over. Whatever, you know the one I mean?"

"Yep."

"Well, clearly you've, how can I put it, *run* into her again. I saw another photograph of you together."

"Yep?"

"Will you please say something more than 'yep?' It's very irritating."

"Let me tell you what's irritating, India," Adam answered. "Having you jump to conclusions every time my picture appears in some fucking tabloid. Try getting a life. Read a decent newspaper."

"I can assure you I don't go looking for pictures," she said stiffly, "but when I have one shoved in my face I can hardly ignore it. Henry's assistant showed it to me. It was online. Can't you see why I might think something is going on? I mean, two pictures with the same girl in two different cities. The media is certainly making a connection."

"Yes. I saw that, so I kind of get it, but what I can't see is why you would immediately always jump to the same conclusion. Do you not trust me at all?"

India went over to the window. She ran her fingers across the dusty pane and gazed through the rain down at the street. "So what was she doing in Cannes with you?" she said.

"She wasn't with me. Pure coincidence. She was with other people. I ran into her on the way back to my room. We had drinks. She was there for business. So, is that why you didn't come out to La Colombe d'Or?"

"No. I really do have to work."

There was a long silence. "India this might not be the best time to say it, but I don't think this is working between us anymore."

India inhaled sharply. "What are you saying?" she said.

"You don't trust me, and I don't think that's ever going to change no matter what I do."

"I'm sorry," she murmured.

"So am I."

She hesitated. "So what now? What do we do about it?"

"I think we have to go our separate ways and move on," he said.

There was a long pause. "You're probably right." She sighed. "I'm sorry. I don't think I can do this anymore either."

"Okay. Okay then."

"Okay," she said.

"Right," he said, clicking off.

India stood for a while in the fading light feeling strangely calm. Something had shifted. She could sense it. It really doesn't matter if he's telling the truth or not. It's over, she thought.

She flicked on the light and made her way back to the conference room. Straightening her back and smoothing down her hair, she took a deep breath before opening the door.

~ ~ ~

Luella crossed the street to Quo Vadis restaurant. She shook off her raincoat and handed it to the cloakroom attendant. Susie was waiting for her in the dining room. She stood up and gave her a hug. The waiter pulled out a chair and unfolded her napkin.

"May I offer you a drink, Madam?" he said as they sat down.

"Dry martini." She smiled. "Kettel One, thanks."

"Sorry I started ahead of you," her friend said, taking a sip of her cocktail. "You've lost quite a bit of weight, Lu. You need to be careful."

"I can't do much about it," Luella said, pulling her cardigan around her. "I'm stressed to the eyeballs, Susie. Things have gotten a whole lot worse. I need to tell you the latest but let's order first."

She looked at the menu. "Oh my goodness, just look at this. It's like going back to the Middle Ages. Grilled ox tongue, salt duck...Guinea fowl. Don't they have anything less literal?"

"They have plaice too. That should be okay for you." Susie said. "I picked here as it was so close to the office. I forgot you're not a big meat eater."

"It's fine, honestly. Plaice with horseradish sounds weird, but it might be good. What about you?"

"I'm thinking steak and mashed potatoes. Let's share a salad to start with. Caesar?"

"Go for it. You pick the wine."

Susie signaled the waiter and gave him their order. Turning back to her friend, she lowered her voice. "So tell me, what's happened? What's going on?"

"Okay." Luella took a deep breath. "Peter's told me who he is. I know who the letters are from."

"So who is it? Do we know him?"

"Sort of...I guess in a way. Susie, Peter's having an affair with Jean-Luc."

"The fashion designer? THAT Jean-Luc?" Susie gasped.

"Yes. Yes, him."

Susie's jaw dropped open. She sat gaping at Luella. "Wait. What – are you serious? Are you sure?" she managed eventually. "Omigod. I am finding this really hard to take in."

"Yes. Yes, I'm sure. But that's not the full story. It's not just that. It's much worse than that."

"Really? How?"

Luella leaned back as the waiter placed a fish knife in front of her. She waited for him to move away.

"In two weeks' time, I am supposed to be sharing a platform with him in New York at the fashion show." She leaned forward again. "He's the host of my show."

"He's the host? The host?"

"Yes. Jean-Luc is presenting the awards at *Faux Fashion*. How the hell can I be in the same room, let alone share a stage with him? How am I supposed to do that?"

"Omigod, Lu. Does Jean-Luc know who you are?"

"I have no idea. None at all. I didn't think to ask him."

"How did this happen?"

"It was Henry's idea. I haven't actually met him, but I did go to see him speak at the London College of Fashion."

"I remember that now. You told me about it."

"You know, I find it almost impossible to imagine him with Peter. He's so flamboyant. He's so 'out there.' God, Susie. I really don't know Peter at all, do I? I mean he's always seemed so...well...boring if I'm being honest. I've been living with a stranger all these years. What's going on? Is all this really happening? What's wrong with me?"

"There's nothing wrong with you. It's not you. Think about it. We're all fooled a lot of the time. I mean, that guy two tables down is probably a spy. Obviously our waiter's in the Mafia, and I'm pretty sure that woman over there in the red dress is really a man. Take a look. We are the only people in this room who are not leading double lives."

Luella let her napkin drop and swiveled around as she bent down to pick it up. "I think you might be right." She laughed. "Susie, you crack me up. You really do."

"It's great to see you laughing again, Lu. It's been a while. Ah, here's our starter. I think we need something stronger than wine, don't you?"

"Urgently," Luella agreed, draining her glass.

"Could we have a refill on the cocktails please?" Susie told the waiter.

"See, Lu? The ring on his little finger," she whispered. "Cosa Nostra."

"Shhh." Luella giggled.

"Cheers," Susie said, raising her glass. "Who's better than us?"

"NO-ONE," they chimed in unison.

19

W hy don't they teach pilots how to land planes properly? India thought, clinging to the armrest as the wheels of the airbus touched down bumpily in the crosswind before tearing along the landing strip. A voice came across the loudspeaker welcoming them to Kennedy airport as she jostled with the nearby passengers to gather her belongings from the overhead locker before making a dash through the arrivals terminal for immigration.

An hour later, sitting in the backseat of a town car, India dozed off. The journey to Manhattan was taking forever. She woke up an hour later to learn they were locked in bumper-to-bumper traffic on the Triborough Bridge. At last, the car broke free of the traffic and weaved its way through a maze of crowded side streets, finally arriving onto East Fifty-Fifth Street and pulling up at the St. Regis Hotel.

A liveried bellman opened the car door, took her suitcase and showed her through the revolving doors of the grand marbled entrance to reception, where she was greeted by an immaculately coiffed young woman in a gray tailored suit speaking Cantonese to the couple checking in ahead of her.

"Welcome, Miss Butler. Sorry to keep you waiting. How was your trip?" she said with a welcoming smile.

"Long," India answered, returning the smile. "The traffic was awful."

"That's New York for you. Well, you're here now, and if there is anything at all we can do to make your stay more comfortable just let us know," she said as she checked her computer. "The Imperial Suite is ready for you. You are the first to arrive. The other...excuse me but I seem to have two Miss Butlers."

"Yes. My twin sister," India explained.

"Ah! Lovely. Well then please give me a moment to prepare your keys, and I will show you to the elevator. Your butler will greet you as you come out on the floor."

Butler? Welcome to Annie's world, India thought, her excitement mounting as they walked through the elegant Edwardian foyer. Admiring the silk wall coverings and spectacular displays of fresh flowers arranged on carved columns, she waited for the doors to open and then checked her watch. She'll have landed by now, she thought.

India gasped as she walked into the hallway of the suite. She attempted to appear unfazed as the uniformed butler, a guy no older than herself, toured her around the rooms. He pointed out the two luxurious bedrooms with foot-high duvets, the dining room with carved walnut panels, the oyster blue silk wallpaper, the sitting room, the oriental rugs, the kitchen, the bathrooms, the powder room and finally, the magnificent views across Central Park.

After the bellman had delivered her cases, the butler left the suite looking somewhat confused that India had not allowed him to unpack and hang her clothes. She pulled her silk Muji dress from the case, laid it on the bed, and ran a bath. She soaked in the deep tub, her toes playing with the gold-plated faucets as she struggled to find the music channel on the wall-mounted flat-screen TV. Then pouring the full contents of a bottle of rich scented bath oil, she lay back and luxuriated.

After a while, conscious of the time, she dripped her way across the Italian marble floor and wrapped herself in an oversized towel. Then after slathering on a generous helping of body lotion, she padded across the thick oriental carpet and searched her case for underwear.

A thump in the hallway announced the arrival of her

sister, and India squealed and raced to give her a hug.

"Look at you. You look so well, you international consultant you." Annie smiled.

"And you look amazing as ever," India said, admiring her sister's red leather Balenciaga biker jacket, black skinny jeans and what she instantly recognized as a Proenza Schouler shawl.

"I assume you won't be wearing that jacket to the rehearsal tomorrow." India laughed.

"Oops," Annabelle said, resting her tan Hermes tote on the hall console table. "This is my 'go to' uniform when I fly commercial. I suppose if they were insisting on a vegan presenter they'd have asked Natalie Portman."

"True." India laughed. "Anyway, it's just a theme not a religion. Even so."

"Don't worry. I've done my homework. I shall be all Stella tomorrow, darling."

A knock on the door announced the return of the butler, humming now as he went into the master bedroom, clearly delighted at the prospect of unpacking Annabelle's Louis Vuitton suitcases and hanging her designer clothes on silk padded hangers.

"Tess has booked us dinner at the restaurant here tonight," Annabelle said. "I hope the food's okay. I thought we wouldn't feel like venturing out, but now I learn Alain Ducasse has taken his bat and ball and abandoned the place."

"It'll be fine if the rest of the hotel is anything to go by," India assured her. "We need an intercom to communicate in this suite, Annie," she whispered. "Isn't it amazing? Thank you so much for doing this. Henry has me on a budget obviously. I stayed at The Warwick last time. It was fine but I wasn't in a rush to go back."

"Of course, don't be silly," Annabelle said, giving her a peck on the cheek. "What's mine is yours, with the exception of the Balenciaga jacket you have your eye on. Now, give me ten minutes to shower and turn around and then I think it's martini time, don't you?"

20

I ndia anxiously checked her watch. She was unprepared for how long it was taking the town car to get them to Brooklyn the next morning. She'd somehow imagined the Harvey Theater to be closer to the hotel. Traveling by subway would have been quicker, but of course that was out of the question, not only because of her own dread of underground transport but because Annabelle would be mobbed. You'd be more likely to see Angelina Jolie on a commuter train than Annie, she'd thought.

Annie always seemed so normal, so down to earth, that even India would sometimes forget her sister was an A-list celebrity and that there were adjustments to be made. She glanced over at her. She looked exquisite in her black Stella McCartney jewel-embellished jacket and black pants, her long blonde hair pulled back in a chic chignon, and her faux leather gold-chained purse resting on her lap.

India had chosen carefully too. She was wearing her Isabel Marant jacket with a long tee, blue jeans, and Converse sneakers. It had been a no-brainer. She was the consultant, Annabelle the superstar. No contest. India was proud of her sister and delighted at the prospect of showing her off and basking in reflected glory.

The car pulled up outside the theater and they made their way to a side entrance, where they were greeted by Joanne, the stage manager, who took them backstage past lighting and sound technicians to the green room where Henry was waiting. He stood up, tucking his shirt into his denim jeans and running his hand through his hair.

"Henry. Meet my sister, Annabelle," India said.

"Hello, Annabelle," he said, extending his hand and giving her his widest smile. "This is such a pleasure. I'm your biggest fan."

Mr. Smooth or what? India thought.

"How was your flight?"

Annabelle smiled graciously. "It was fine."

"I can't tell you how delighted we are you're able to do this," Henry said, pulling around a battered chair. "Please. Sit down for a few moments. Alex, the entertainment's manager, and the producer, Ron, should be with us in a minute."

India looked around for another chair and pulled one over for herself.

"Can I get you anything in the meantime?" Henry asked, nodding in the direction of a table piled high with drinks, wrapped sandwiches, protein bars, and chips.

"I'm fine right now," she said, looking up as a bald guy India recognized from the Skype meeting as Ron, marched into the room, picked up a bottle of water, and took a slug.

"Student models. How come they've got attitude? They're fucking students for Chrissake," he said, wiping his mouth. "You could get two-year-olds to walk straighter."

"Ron, meet Annabelle Butler," Henry said.

Ron nodded at Annabelle. "Great to meet you. It'll be a relief to work with at least one professional."

"And I'm India."

Ron nodded in India's direction. "Hi. Great to see you," he said. "Can't stay, Henry. Annabelle, I'll see you out there in about ten minutes. Joanne will come for you. We won't need you for too long this afternoon – just a walk-through."

"As long as I get a sense of the stage and you spot me, I'll be fine," Annabelle said.

"We've another run-through in the morning with Jean-Luc, but you won't be needed until tomorrow evening. Alex will confirm, but I think five will be time enough for makeup and hair. See you out there in a minute. Sorry Alex," he said, careening into the entertainment manager, who was coming through the door at the same moment.

"Alex. This is India; she's here to help," Henry said. "She'll be looking after Luella Marchmont tomorrow."

What happened to 'This is India, our education consultant?' India thought, standing up to greet him. "Hello," she said.

"Shall we?" Alex answered, with a charmless nod, gesturing to the doorway.

India followed him down a labyrinth of backstage corridors into a spacious room with high ceilings and exposed brickwork. The place was buzzing with energy. Cocktail tables were being dragged into place, screens and scaffolding hauled onto a makeshift platform, and students were setting out pamphlets and exhibits for the silent auction.

"Let's start with the red carpet area," Alex said, steering her to the foyer where the sponsors' company logos were displayed on step and repeat boards and lighting engineers were assembling cables.

"I thought you said 'red' carpet." India laughed with a tilt of her head. "It may just be me, but that looks green."

"The students voted to keep with the environmental awareness theme," he answered humorlessly.

"Right." India nodded.

"Entrance over there." Alex pointed.

"Okay." India nodded again.

"Ron and I will be looking after Annabelle Butler and Jean-Luc when you get here. We'll get them on and off the carpet, a few autographs, plenty of shots, a couple of interviews and then backstage the way we've just come to the green room. They'll put in a brief appearance at the end of the VIP reception, and then I'll get them behind the curtain for the opening. After the show – that'll be around nine thirty – I'll give them five minutes backstage with students, ten minutes for comfort breaks, then through there for the after-party, more photographs, drinks and schmoozing. I'll make sure the sponsors get plenty of one on one. We aim to have them both out of there by ten thirty at the latest."

Alex checked his watch. "Any questions?" he asked, looking over her shoulder as a technician came toward him.

"What time do you need Luella?" she asked.

"You can get her here around seven twenty. Ron doesn't want her first on the carpet. It'll be good to have a bit of a buzz going."

"Okay," India said, "and then where?"

"You'll take her through to the reception to meet and greet and then sit in the two reserved front-row seats at the right-hand side of the stage. I'll show you. Let's walk it through now."

He turned and led India backstage and into the auditorium. "After Annabelle gives her closing speech, she'll invite Luella up from here and introduce her," he said pointing out the seats. "Luella will make her speech, then Annabelle will hand her the LIFT award to present to the winning student. Annabelle will thank her. She'll stay onstage until Jean-Luc has given his award. Applause and then all exit stage left."

"Okay. So, let me get this straight. Red...sorry, green carpet, backstage, seated, speech, then she hands out the LIFT award, stays onstage until they all get signal to leave stage left."

"Yes. Are we done?" he asked, pulling out his phone. "I have a gazillion things to be doing."

We're SO done, India thought. She nodded.

Alex walked away as if India had suddenly become invisible.

India spotted Annabelle sitting in the back row of the theater talking with a group of students and went across. "Ready?" she said. "Are you needed for anything more?"

"Not sure, darling."

India ran over to Ron and signaled to him. He jumped down from a plinth where he had been adjusting an installation and wiped a line of sweat off his forehead with the back of his hand.

"Do you have Luella's call sheet?" he asked.

"Yes. I just walked it through with Alex. It's all pretty straightforward."

"Great," he said.

"Do you need Annabelle for anything else?"

"No. Let me check in with her to see if she needs anything more."

Taking the steps two at a time, he reached Annabelle. "Thanks for your patience just now," he said.

"Always." Annabelle smiled graciously. "Be gentle with them. Remember, they're kids. Am I free to go?"

"Yes. You are. Thanks again. See you tomorrow."

Settling back in the car on the way from the theater, Annie turned to India. "That was fun. Where shall we go for dinner? I hear there are some great restaurants in Brooklyn; shall I ask Tess to find us one?"

"How about we go to The Greenwich?" India said. "Luella's arriving there tonight, and I could leave her schedule at the desk."

"Okay. Let me call Tess and have her reserve us a couch. We'll eat in the sitting room; it'll be more private."

India checked her makeup in a hand mirror as they drew up to the hotel. "I feel like a toe rag," she said. "The time difference is catching up with me."

"You'll feel better when you've had something to eat," Annabelle answered, taking the mirror from her and touching up her lipstick. "We'll make it an early night. We've a long day tomorrow. I'm so proud of you, darling. This is going to be such a great event."

~ ~ ~

Waking up early the morning of the show, India crept out of their suite and left Annabelle to sleep on. After a quick breakfast of scrambled eggs and coffee in the gloriously elegant hotel dining room, she moved into a quiet sitting area to a sofa and pulled out her computer and cell phone. She called Samantha and Patricia, had a long conversation with Rebecca, and double-checked with Henry that everything was on track at his end. She was relieved to hear that Jean-Luc was already in town. He was staying at the Soho House.

How much simpler is all this? India thought, remembering the many school productions she had directed virtually single-handed. Now, with hours to spare, she even had time to get a manicure and have her hair blown out. She was planning on wearing her little black dress and the black patent Louboutins she hadn't worn since she was in LA.

Making sure that Annabelle had all she needed and that her driver was booked, India headed downtown to wait to meet and brief Luella at The Greenwich. Two hours later, she was still waiting.

Damn it. I knew she was cutting it close, but where is she? she thought, drumming her hand against a chair, then turning and walking back through the sitting room and pacing up and down the adjoining courtyard for a few more minutes before calling Henry again.

"The plane's landed; it was on time but Luella's still not picking up," she told him.

"Have you tried calling the driver?" he said.

"He's not answering either. Henry, I've been waiting here for hours. If we don't leave soon we're going to miss the red carpet."

"This isn't at all like her," Henry said, his voice tight with strain.

"All I have is the text last night saying she was getting the later flight," India said, sitting down on a wicker chair.

"This is not Luella's style. What time is it now?"

"Ten past six."

"Shit. Okay. You keep trying the car. I'll have Samantha check to see if she got on the plane. If she's still not there by six thirty, text her to come straight to the theater and you jump in a cab and get here."

Half an hour later India sat in the back of a yellow cab checking her cell repeatedly and then gazing out of the window at a loss for a plan. There was still no word from Luella. She leapt out of the cab when they reached the theater, dashed through the backstage door and flew up the stairs in search of Henry, who was nowhere to be seen. She ran back downstairs onto the street past the crowd waiting in line.

"Let me through, please," she said, pushing her way through the doorway and waving to Joanne who escorted her through to the red carpet area. At that moment, a flurry of whirring lights signaled the arrival of Jean-Luc. India watched him stride forward and pose theatrically. He was bare-chested under a faux fur vest, his arm muscles glistening with his signature tattoos. His hands were thrust into black harem pants cut several inches above his black canvas sandals. Photographers leaned into the crash barriers yelling for him to face them as they fired off their cameras. "Over Here Jean-Luc."

"Jean-Luc."

"Jean-Luc."

There was a riot of excitement as Annabelle strolled down to join him wearing a Stella McCartney lace evening gown, the iridescent red bouncing in the Chimera lighting. India caught her breath. Her sister was transcendentally beautiful, her skin translucent, her back a sinuous curve as she turned and posed. Then after checking her phone yet again, India watched as the other VIPs were shepherded onto the carpet.

At last, she spotted Henry sidestepping through the crowd, coming toward her.

"Where the fuck IS she?" he whispered.

India shook her head. "No idea."

"Well, keep trying. We have another couple of hours before this gets serious. I've told Joanne not to move from the backstage entrance. You stay here. I'll go sweet talk the sponsors at the reception."

"Okay," she said. "If she isn't here by the time the show starts, what shall I do?"

"I'll text you. Let's hope she makes it by then. What the fuck?" he muttered. "I'm starting to get really worried. It's so out of character."

This is such a drag, India thought. I could slaughter a glass of wine. Fat chance now. She stood waiting as the last of the students were photographed and the carpet area stood eerily empty. She leaned against the wall as the foyer filled up with people jostling at will-call and watched as the last of the guests filed into the auditorium and the doors finally closed.

She texted Henry. *No sign of her.*

His reply came back seconds later. *She didn't get on the plane. Come to the green room. We need to talk.*

India made her way backstage, whispering her apologies as she squeezed past the models crushed together waiting nervously for the opening signal. She reached the green room as the house lights went down.

"Close the door," Henry said.

"What's going on? Do you know where she is? Is she okay?" India whispered.

"She's okay," he said. "It's Peter, her husband."

"What about him?"

Henry lowered his voice. "He tried to commit suicide."

India's mouth fell open in horror. "How awful. Is he okay?"

"I can't say. India, we mustn't breathe a word of this to anyone."

"Of course. I won't say anything, even to Annie."

"Good. Luella was on her way to the airport when she

got the call. She changed for a later flight. When she got to the hospital and found out how serious things were, she couldn't leave."

"So why didn't she tell us sooner?"

"India, I don't think she's thinking straight."

"Of course. Of course not. How stupid of me. Sorry, I'm still a bit shocked myself. What an awful thing. I do hope he's okay."

"I haven't had any more news through yet."

"So what do we do?"

"This is what's going to happen. You are going to make the speech and give the award on Luella's behalf."

India looked at him, stunned. "I'm what?" she gasped. "No way. Why me? There must be someone else. Why not YOU?"

"I've talked to Ron and he agrees. You know what Luella was going to say. You helped her draft the speech. We've adapted it here," he said, handing her a sheet of paper from the table next to him.

India began to feel queasy. Henry continued. "Annabelle will explain why you're standing in and introduce you. Ron has already given her the wire. She'll be there with you. You won't be on your own onstage."

"Henry, there are almost seven hundred people out there. I am terrified of public speaking. I've not had a rehearsal. I couldn't possibly."

"Come on, India. It's only a student fashion show. It's not the Oscars."

"But it's being filmed. It's being streamed to LA and to Paris and London."

"So?"

"Apart from anything else, I'm not dressed for it."

"That's easily fixed," he said. "I'm taking you through to wardrobe right now. Come on, India. You can do it. You haven't any choice. We need you, I need you," he said pulling her out of the chair and leading her by the hand down the corridor.

India felt distinctly-light headed. This can't be happening, she thought. Please tell me this isn't happening.

Jean-Luc was holding the microphone and still speaking as India slid into Luella's seat at the end of the front row a little while later.

"As you know, this event...to promote the innovation of young fashion students is the culmination of months of...and the collaboration...with...the students who produced that last incredibly creative collection. Please give them another round of applause...Now welcome the..."

India barely heard his remarks. She was feeling decidedly uncomfortable. The whalebone corset in her gown was cutting into her ribs and was altogether too tight around her middle. Her hair had been caught up in a tight topknot with tendrils and her toes were squashed into wrongly sized pumps.

Aiming her cell phone light at the crumpled piece of paper on her lap, she blew on a ringlet and attempted to familiarize herself with what had been written for her. This is agony. I'd rather do another fire-walk, a bungee jump, anything other than stand up there and make a speech. I think I'm going to die, she thought as the electronic dance music heralded the eveningwear collection.

India watched the students stomping to the rhythmic beat of Paul Van Dyke's *Purple Haze* modeling asymmetric designs, biker boots and balloon gowns made from recycled wood fibers. I can't see these at a Beverly-Wilshire gala anytime soon, she thought. What's next?

Scrutinizing her program, she saw that it was the men's collection...the men's collection...men's collection? Why did that ring a bell? Shit, she thought. Ah! Yes. Luella was supposed to be onstage right after the men's collection.

The pulsing rhythm gave way to a solitary Indian flute and six male students, their faces invisible behind Native American war paint, walked across the stage against images of the Appalachian mountain range.

Okay. What did Alex tell me? she thought, gripping the sides of her seat. Okay...carpet, backstage, seated...speech, then she hands out LIFT award, stays onstage until they all get signal to leave stage left.

India saw Ron crouched down and coming toward her from the side aisle. I can't do this. I can't do this, she thought. "India," he whispered. "Come with me. Annabelle is going to introduce you in about five minutes."

These are going to be the worst five minutes of my life, she thought struggling to stand up and then smoothing down her gown.

Standing in the wings, Annabelle caught her eye. "You'll be great," she mouthed.

I will, won't I? she thought. India Butler, you walked on fire, you went on *The View*...shit, you froze on *The View*. You died...but you DID walk on fire.

India took a deep breath. She could feel an elbow steadying her and then suddenly she was onstage, blinded for a moment by the Klieg lights, her heart pounding in her chest. Where was the audience? She couldn't see anything beyond the edge of the stage.

Annabelle smiled at her. "Take a breath, darling. Smile. You'll be fine," she whispered as the measured beat of *Mon Legionnaire* filled the room and the models began to cross the stage and strut up the central aisle of the theater. Black and white images of a chain-smoking Serge Gainsbourg flashed up on the screens as half- clothed male dancers performed a stylized routine against the backdrop of a derelict warehouse. The audience rose to its feet and began clapping along to the music and, after a rousing applause, took their seats again as the house lights went up.

India saw the sea of expectant faces in front of her. I think I preferred the dark, she thought.

Annabelle stepped forward. "I think you will all agree with me that this has been a spectacular evening."

This was greeted by thunderous applause.

"As you know, this design work has been inspired by a novel written by the much loved writer Luella Marchmont. Sadly Miss Marchmont is unable to be with us tonight to give the LIFT Award."

India was trembling now. She leaned on the side of the podium, clinging onto her script.

"Stepping in for her tonight is the education consultant to the project. She is Luella's friend and most important of all, she is my sister." She paused. "Ladies and gentlemen, please welcome the beautiful India Butler."

Annabelle hugged India and kissed her on the cheek. "You'll be great," she whispered.

India stepped forward as the applause died down.

"Thank you," she said, her voice aquiver. "Miss Marchmont is extremely sorry she can't be with us tonight. She was honored to have been asked to present the LIFT award and delighted that *Faux Fashion* has inspired this stunning show."

She hesitated and looked around her, reminded of the many presentations she had made at school productions. I can do this, she thought, putting her notes down on the podium and looking at the tense faces of the students assembled at the foot of the stage waiting to hear the name of the winner. She smiled.

"Over the last few months it has been my privilege to get to know many of you and to see the incredible work you have all produced." Her voice was steady now.

"Your discipline, innovation, and creativity have inspired me. I salute your talent. I am looking at design through new eyes. We have all learned so much about ethical, cruelty-free fashion. All the work here tonight deserves the utmost praise. Let me read Luella's message of congratulations to you all."

India picked up her notes again and read Luella's closing remarks. Pausing, she looked up. "And now, I would like to announce the winner."

She opened the envelope, pulled out the card, and waited. The room was deathly silent, tense with expectation.

India paused again, deliberately extending the suspense of the moment.

"Georgia Pullman."

A whoop of delight and a shriek came from the stalls.

"Well, that must be Georgia," India quipped. "Please give it up for Georgia Pullman. Congratulations, Georgia. Come on up."

There was much stomping applause from the students as Georgia accepted the figurine. Annabelle took India's arm and they stepped back a few paces as Jean-Luc returned to the stage.

"Well done, darling. That was perfect," Annabelle whispered under her breath.

Jean-Luc bowed to the audience. "Thank you. And so to close, I will announce zee name of the student who will intern with me next spring in Paris," he said. The room fell silent again.

"Before that I would like to address all of the students here." He looked at the assembled group with fierce intensity. "Winning awards is wonderful. I have been fortunate to win many. But awards are not the lifeblood of an artist. If any of you thought that a career in fashion would be an easy ride, think again. Leave now unless you are prepared to tunnel the depths of your soul, to take risks for your creativity, to carve a unique path. As Martha Graham once said..."

Here he flicked through his notes and read, "'*There is a vitality, a life force, an energy, a quickening that is translated through you into action, and because there is only one of you in all of time, this expression is unique. And if you block it, it will never exist through any other medium and it will be lost. The world will not have it.*'

"Get a copy of that and paste it to your workstations. Never forget – *if you block it, the world will not have it.*" He paused. "You have chosen this creative path; make sure you give your work every fiber of your being."

The room was enthralled.

"And now," he continued, "for outstanding innovation and design, would Evan Johns please step up?"

India heard very little of Jean-Luc's speech. Pumped with adrenalin, she was looking forward to the after party and to the very large glass of wine she would be having. Within minutes of curtain-down, the backstage area was crowded with students and models hugging and high-fiving each other and making plans for the rest of the evening. India lost sight of Annabelle, whom she had last seen chatting with the student assigned to look after her. She was making her way toward the green room when Annabelle appeared at her side.

"Quick. My dressing room," she said. "This way. Now."

India ran behind, trying to keep up. "What's the rush, Annie?"

"I'll tell you when we're somewhere quiet and you can hear yourself think."

"Is everything okay?"

"In a minute," she muttered, squeezing behind a rack of clothes and opening the door of her dressing room.

"Okay," she said once they were inside. "Damien's been trying to reach you. Sarah gave him my number. She's gone into labor early and there are some complications but right now, she's stable. They're on their way to the hospital. He said she keeps asking for you."

"She's not due for another two weeks," India said. "Ron has my phone. Where is he? I have to get back to London. What time is it?"

"Nine thirty. I'll call Tess, see if she can get you on a red eye," Annabelle said. "Here, use mine. Call Damien."

"God, I hope she's going to be okay," India mumbled pressing the keys. "Hello. Hello. Is that you Damien?"

"India?"

"Yes. What's going on? I'm in New York. What's happened?"

"We're at Ealing Hospital."

"Is Sarah okay?"

"I think so. I hope so. They've taken her into surgery. They're giving her an emergency caesarian. The baby has the cord wrapped around its neck. I'm outside the ER."

"Oh Damien, I'm sorry. I'm sure she'll be okay. I'll get there as soon as I possibly can. This must be so awful for you. I'll text in a minute, when I know when I can get there."

She gave the phone back to Annabelle to call her assistant.

"I'll hold," Annabelle said, then mouthing to India. "She's checking now. Oh. Okay. Tess says the first direct flight is at seven twenty tomorrow morning."

"Tomorrow? There's got to be something sooner. I need to get there NOW."

"You've missed the last flight tonight. You have to be there two hours ahead. Next one leaves at seven twenty; shall she book it?"

India looked defeated. "Okay. If she's sure that's the only option. What time does it get in?"

"With the time difference, seven fifteen tomorrow evening."

"Shit. Okay."

"Go ahead and book. Yes, first class. Thanks, Tess. One way. Yes."

"I'll text Damien and let him know. I feel so sorry for him. He sounds awful," India said taking the phone from her sister.

"I'm sure. Okay let's go and get you a drink," Annabelle said, putting her arm around her. "Here, let me fix your hair. You look like Helena Bonham Carter in a wind tunnel. Those are some sad ringlets."

India felt surreal as she walked into the crush of the after-party a while later. The room throbbed with the vibration of electronic music. A sea of fashionistas, photographers, and guests were crammed into one heaving space.

"Hey India, come and meet some people. Have a drink,"

Henry yelled, appearing at her side and lifting a glass of sparkling wine from a passing waiter. "Great job, India. Where's Annabelle?"

"She's over with the *Vanity Fair* photographers," India yelled back, taking a large sip from the glass. "Henry, how's Peter? How's Luella?"

"Not sure. She's still not picking up. I'll try her again later. Come and charm the sponsors."

"Henry. Before we do, I have to tell you I'm leaving for London first thing in the morning. I won't be able to go to the college tomorrow as planned."

Henry looked startled. "You can't," he said. "There's a PR issue with Luella not here and we have all the interviews to tape with the winners for the video, and you're the best at schmoozing Jean-Luc. We're all booked for dinner at the Mandarin tomorrow night, remember?"

"Henry I know. I know, but I have to go home. My best friend has just been taken to the ER. She's having an emergency caesarian right now and I don't know if she's going to be okay or if the baby is going to..." She welled up. "Whatever...I need to be there. I have to get back. I'm already booked on a flight first thing in the morning."

"Let me think," Henry said, taking her elbow. "Let's move over there away from this crowd." He leaned against the wall to let a group of photographers pass by.

"All right. Okay," he said. "We'll have to manage. I'll have Samantha reschedule things. I owe you one after tonight. You were great."

"Thanks Henry. Thanks for understanding. It means a lot," she said. "If it's okay with you I'm not going to stay too much longer here. My head's thumping."

Henry put his hand on her shoulder. "I hope your friend is okay," he said.

India smiled gratefully. "So do I. So do I."

21

Luella sat in a cab on her way back from the hospital staring out through the rain-soaked window into the bleak night. It had been a relief not to be allowed in to see Peter, she mused. At least now she had a few hours to get over the shock before she saw him tomorrow. She would hopefully deal with things more rationally after some sleep. In the hours since Peter's sister had called, she had run the gamut of emotions, from terror and panic to suspense, relief and then anger. She was drained.

Climbing into bed a little while later, Luella sank into a fitful sleep and woke again when it was still dark. She lay torturing herself with the thought that this crisis was somehow her fault, that she should have spotted the signs, and that they should have seen a counselor together months back. Maybe then she would have handled things better. Maybe Peter wouldn't have felt so isolated.

And what now? she thought. Where do we go from here? We have to move things forward. Something has to change. We really can't carry on like this.

Luella dragged out of bed and showered. She dressed, forced herself to eat a piece of toast with her coffee, and drove back to the hospital. She'd been there over an hour by the time Peter was discharged.

"We have to wait here to sign some forms," he told her.

"God Peter, what's happening to us?" she murmured,

gesturing around her at the peeling paintwork in the neon-lit hospital corridor. "It's like some kind of alternate universe. Are you sure you're okay? You look really bad."

"I'm fine. I just need a shave," he said. "They don't give you a lot of after-care when you've tried to kill yourself."

"I still think you should come back to the house with me."

Peter looked at her. "I'm not going to do it again if that's what you're worried about."

"Do you realize how lucky you are that Maisie found you in time?"

"Lucky?" He sighed heavily. "I suppose so. She came by this morning. She's furious with me."

A door swung open, and a harassed middle-aged nurse hurried toward them.

"Sign here," she said handing him a clipboard with his discharge papers. Peter signed the pages and handed them back to her.

"Okay. You can go now, Mr. Laing. It'd be nice if we don't see you back here again," she said turning on her heel.

"So much for her counseling techniques," Luella muttered, giving Peter her arm as he stood up. "I'm going to drive you back and I'm going to stay over. Maisie could do with some sleep and I've nothing else to do tomorrow. I was supposed to be in New York at the *Faux Fashion* show."

"Oh god, Lu, I'm so sorry. I'm really sorry."

"Yes, well...it was a relief if I'm honest about it," she said as they walked slowly down the endless corridor and out to the crowded car park.

They drove the mile to Peter's sister's house in silence where she greeted them at the door looking worn, her hair scraped back in an unflattering ponytail.

"Hey. Come in," she said wearily.

"I'm going to bed if that's all right," Peter said.

"Fine by me. I don't want to talk to you anyway," Maisie snapped. "Do you want a cup of tea, Luella?"

Peter dragged himself up the stairs and they heard the bedroom door click.

"Is it okay with you if I sleep over, Maisie? I'll be fine on the couch," Luella said, taking off her coat. "I thought as you were up all last night you might like to get some rest. I'll be here if he needs anything."

"I'd be glad of that," Maisie said. "I'm absolutely wiped. Must be the aftershock. Selfish bastard. What if I'd found him lying there dead? He didn't think of that, did he? He made a god-awful mess too. Threw up all over the place, all over my new rug. Sorry. You don't need to know. Did you say you want a cup of tea?"

Luella followed her into the kitchen where she filled a teapot with scalding water and pulled out a couple of mugs. "Sugar?"

"No thanks. Milk please," she said, opening the door to the garden. "Give me a minute. I need a cigarette."

"God I needed that," she said, pulling out a chair a few minutes later.

"So, Lu. What's going on with the pair of you?" Maisie asked her gently.

"How do you mean?" Luella said, taking a sip of tea.

"I know you're having a rocky time of it and I haven't wanted to get stuck in the middle. That's why I've not been in touch. I assume there must be another woman; he's always on the phone and he's been away most weekends.

"It's complicated."

"Isn't it always. When Jack left me it took a year to get the truth out of him."

"Even more complicated than that."

Her sister-in-law looked at her quizzically. "How so? Please tell me it isn't you. Are you having an affair? Tell me you're not."

"No. Not me." Luella took another mouthful of tea.

"What then? You can't come this far and not tell me. I have a right to know. He nearly killed himself in my house."

"Peter." She took a deep breath. "Peter's gay, Maisie."

"He's what? Sorry? What? You've been married for twenty years for god's sake." Maisie jumped up, a look of complete disbelief on her face.

"He's been having an affair with a man for several years," Luella continued.

"Several YEARS? You knew?"

"No, of course not. He told me a few months back."

"Lu, this is blowing my mind. I mean, he's my brother. I'm finding this impossible to take in."

"I'm sorry you had to find out this way. I really am."

"You're going to have to give me a minute." Maisie paced the kitchen a few times then sat back down again.

"You know there was only ever you for him. You were the only one. I can honestly say I never gave a moment's thought to Peter's sexuality until this minute. It's not anything that was even on my radar. You were always around weren't you? You've always been part of our family ever since I can remember."

She held Luella's hand across the table. "This must be so awful for you. I know you love him. I'm so sorry, so sorry."

"I probably should have told you before now, but I kind of left that for Peter to explain. I'm sorry to have broken this to you so clumsily."

"It's okay. I understand. It must be so hard for you. Do you know the man he's been seeing? Is it serious?"

"I know who he is, but I've never spoken to him," Luella said quietly.

"Aren't you curious? Don't you want to? I mean, if you found out about another woman, you'd be around there like a shot to give her an earful. At least that's what I did when Jack left me," she added.

"I've asked myself that a lot. I was scared. Whenever I thought about it…you know, the physical part…I didn't want to see him. I didn't want to imagine them together. Peter loves him, Maisie. He says he's been the only one. I don't understand that kind of love. I don't judge it. I just don't understand it."

"Me either. We have to get Peter to talk to us," she said. "I feel so bad. I've been so angry. I suppose because he scared me so much. I still can't take this in. I love the bones of him."

"Yes. I love him too," Luella said, her eyes misty.

"Look at the pair of us," Maisie said smiling weakly through her tears. "Here, have a Kleenex."

"Thanks."

Luella blew her nose. "I have to get Peter to talk to me. It's part of the reason I'm staying over. I was hoping we could talk properly in the morning. We've been trying, but it's been hard. This kind of issue doesn't come with a manual, and I don't think I've been handling it the right way. Well, clearly I haven't."

"I'm sure you've done the best you could. Don't blame yourself, Lu. It's nobody's fault. I mean, I never guessed he was that depressed and he's been living with me."

"Maisie, do you have anything stronger than tea? I could really use a brandy."

"Absolutely," Maisie said, jumping up and reaching into a cupboard. "There's Remy left over from last Christmas. Here," she said, pouring it into two snifter glasses. "I could use a vodka, but Peter drank it all, two bottles of it the other night. I really am amazed he isn't dead with that amount of booze and all those pills. Poor Peter. Imagine the strain of living with that secret all these years."

"Yes. It's unthinkable," Luella agreed, knocking back the shot.

~ ~ ~

"We will be landing in London shortly, Miss Butler. Would you like anything before we turn the seat belt signs on?"

Roused from an unexpectedly deep sleep, India sat up

and looked around her in a daze. "An orange juice please. Do you know what time it is?"

"Local time is six thirty." The flight attendant smiled at her. "We've arranged transport and an escort to get you through immigration as quickly as possible."

'Thank you." India smiled. "I hadn't planned on sleeping so long."

"It's good that you did. It makes the whole trip go so much faster, doesn't it?"

Still groggy, India grabbed her jeans and T-shirt from the cupboard in front of her and went to the bathroom to change out of the oversized airline pajamas and freshen up. Coming back to the seat, she sipped on her drink.

It had been an overwhelming relief to see the text from Damien the previous night on the drive back to the St. Regis. She and Annie had hugged each other at the news. Sarah had had her little girl. She was underweight but otherwise healthy. There was something about Sarah being in intensive care but apparently that was normal after an emergency procedure. A few hours from now, she would be at the hospital. It was hard to imagine her friend with a baby. She felt a flutter of excitement at the thought.

India was driven through the arrivals hall on a buggy, whisked through immigration, and at baggage claim, her case was one of the first off the plane. A driver was waiting for her and the traffic was light on the way to the hospital. Arriving at the maternity ward, she was directed to a private room.

"She may be sleeping," the nurse whispered, pushing open the door a little. "Let me look in and see."

India heard Sarah's voice. "Please. I'd like to see her."

"Just for a few minutes then," the nurse said gently.

"Hi Sarah," India whispered, creeping into the darkened room, carefully sidestepping a heart monitor and saline drip and leaning over to her. "How are you? Where's the baby?" she asked seeing the bassinette was empty.

"I'm okay," Sarah whispered. "The pain killers are awesome, but when they wear off I feel like they've used a machete on me."

"I'm so sorry you had to go through that. Where's the baby?"

"They've taken her away for the night," she said. "I need to sleep. Damien's gone home. He was up all night. He's exhausted..."

Sarah attempted to raise herself up, winced, and lay down again.

"I came straight here from the plane. I wanted to see you as soon as I could." India smiled. "You need to rest. I'll come back in the morning."

"Great," Sarah murmured, closing her eyes.

India left the room. That isn't at all how Sarah planned it, she thought. She was so in love with the idea of a natural home birth.

22

———

"Did you see the coverage, Samantha? I've worked on this for six fucking months and what happens? One short paragraph. That's it – nothing else about the show and fuck all about Luella. Okay. Get over here to The Greenwich as in *now*."

"Sure, Henry," Samantha said, throwing her phone into her raincoat pocket, racing across the street and flagging down a cab. She opened the *New York Times* and flicked the pages until she saw Jean-Luc's photograph beneath the headline:

Fashion Designer Jean-Luc Under Investigation.

She Googled TMZ. It was carrying an image of Jean-Luc in his sleeveless vest with the headline:

Has Jean-Luc Lost His Shirt to the IRS?

The Huffington Post carried a single photograph of Annabelle with a couple of lines of irrelevant copy and a short piece on Jean-Luc with a list of his celebrity fans including Kate Moss and Justin Timberlake, images of his recent collection and some speculation about the charges. There was no mention of Luella's book.

"Thanks," she shouted to the driver looking up. "You can drop me here."

Running into the hotel, she dashed through the lobby and into the sitting room. "I have an idea," she gasped. "You're going to love me for this. I know how we can get some focus on Luella." She pulled a chair directly in front of Henry.

"Go on." Henry pushed away his iPad on the coffee table and looked at her. "All ideas welcome."

"Well, we know the reason Luella didn't make it to the show don't we. I mean, there's a story there, right?"

Henry looked at her quizzically.

"Well?" she said.

"You know the reason?"

"Of course. Walls have ears don't you know."

He shook his head. "I didn't know you knew, Samantha. I'm at a loss for words."

"So you think it's a good idea? I mean, it's a human-interest story. The *Mail* would run it for sure. It's got everything – suicide attempt, fashion show, distressed wife – and we can let them have..."

"Samantha," Henry interrupted. "Samantha. You are talking about Luella. Luella. If you think I am going to leak information about her private life at any time and especially when she's vulnerable, you must be out of your mind."

"But it'll work. It'll get publicity and you've always said there's no such thing as bad publicity." She pushed back a strand of hair from her forehead. "That's what you're always saying."

Henry stood up. "Working for me is clearly a waste of your talents, Samantha. You need to get working with *Us Weekly* or find yourself a job with *The Sun*," he said.

"What?"

"Am I not making myself clear? You're fired. Get the fuck out of here. Get on the next plane. I want you out of the office before I get back."

He picked up his things and stormed out of the room.

~~ ~~ ~~

Luella and Peter were in Maisie's sitting room perched stiffly across from one another on the long couches in front of the fire. He looked haggard, still unshaven, the furrows between his eyes giving him the appearance of a much older man.

"How're you feeling today?" Luella asked gently.

"My throat's raw and my chest hurts. I have a filthy headache. I'm depressed and ashamed. Apart from that I feel fine," he said with a forced smile.

"At least you haven't lost your sense of humor," she said. "Peter. I'm washed out too. Let's talk honestly and properly. Tell me the whole story. Tell me how you met him and what it's been like. I promise not to overreact like I did. I've just realized what it might have been like to lose you completely. It was an awful thought. I've been so angry; I was obsessing about all the lies you must have told me, but if you'd...well if Maisie hadn't found you in time, if the worst had happened, I don't think I'd have ever recovered."

She leaned forward, threw another log onto the fire and watched as it caught the flame. She sat back and looked calmly at her husband. "Tell me. I'm listening," she said with a deep sigh. "I'm ready. I really am. You are my soul mate. I can't believe you've kept this secret to yourself all these years. I knew we were having intimacy problems, and I should have talked to you about that long before now. I've looked at myself hard. I've been married to my work, and I've played my part in all of this too you know."

Peter looked at her with fierce intensity as she spoke.

"Whatever you tell me, Peter, I won't judge you. I won't blame you. I love you. You're not on your own in this. I can't bear the thought that you felt so desperate."

"Thank you, Lu. I do appreciate that very much...I do. So...where do I start? Where?" He sat back and ran his hands through his hair clenching them behind his head.

"Start from the beginning."

"Okay. I was in Paris," he began slowly. "I was in Paris for work...We clinched the deal and went out to celebrate. We went to The Moulin Rouge because a few of the women wanted to go and see the cancan. I was relieved the guys didn't want to go to a strip club.

"The Moulin Rouge. I didn't know it was still open."

"Yes. It's a burlesque show still. It was packed and we had to split up and sit at different tables from each other. He began coughing. "Sorry. This isn't easy for me."

"Take your time. I'm not going anywhere," Luella murmured.

"So...I've been fighting these feelings for so long, torturing myself with guilt. I still can't look you in the face and tell you what the feeling is like. I don't even want to hear myself describe it."

"You don't have to. Tell me as much as you feel comfortable sharing."

There was a long silence. Luella crossed one leg tightly over the other and straightened her back. She clamped her hands around her knee until her knuckles were white and she held her breath.

"I was sitting opposite him and I can't really say anything more than that I looked at him and he looked at me. We didn't even speak....I stood up. I somehow knew he would follow me. We got into his car." Peter paused, his voice barely audible. "We went back to his hotel," he said.

Luella closed her eyes tightly, hugged her knee, and took her time answering him. "And that was the first time that it had ever happened to you?"

"Yes. Lu, I can't explain it any better. I couldn't push it away like I usually do. It was a bolt of electricity. It was so powerful. It was as if we didn't need words." Peter stopped speaking, lost in the memory. Luella waited.

"He sent a letter and flowers to my hotel the next day. He sent more the day after and again the day after that. He kept asking to see me and eventually well...I did. I saw him again," he said quietly. "I was in Paris for a month. We spent the weekends at galleries and museums. He introduced me to a world I didn't know existed, to art, to design, architecture. My life, our life was so different...All I'd seen up until then was my work, the bank, making money, doing deals. I fell in love with Paris through his eyes. I fell in love with him." He looked at Luella, his face creased with pain. " Lu. I'm sorry. I couldn't help myself."

They sat in silence for a few moments, his words hanging in the air. Luella uncrossed her legs and shifted on the cushion.

"I can't believe you were able to keep this secret when you were feeling like that. How could I possibly not have seen it? Where was I? Where was my head?"

"Writing, Lu. You are always writing. I think you stopped seeing me. I love you, Lu. I've always loved you, but it's a different kind of love. I never wanted to hurt you. I never meant for this to happen."

Luella could see Peter's hands were shaking. She got up and crouched down in front of him. Reaching across, she held them in hers. "I understand. I understand. I really do. Peter, it's okay, you know. I get it. The important thing is that we are going to stay in each other's lives. I want that too."

She leaned up and kissed his cheek. "I went to the hotel, to Le Meurice when I was in Paris a few months ago."

"You did? Why?"

"Ever since I found the letters I was drawn to it, curious I guess. I don't really know why. Peter, you should know that I only read one letter. I want you to know that. They were never written for me to read."

"Thank you. Thank you for that, Lu."

"You know, Peter. I have a feeling that maybe deep down I knew all along and I just didn't want to face losing you."

"Really?"

"Yes. Yes. I think I always felt something was not quite right, not this exactly, but something. Maybe it was a lack of passion, some distance between us I can't really explain. Pete, you said it yourself. We were young. I was young. What did I know? What DO I know? You're the only person I've ever slept with too. Think about that."

Peter smiled. He stroked the side of her face gently.

"Yes, and that's another reason I never in a million years wanted for this to happen."

Luella squeezed his hand and stood up. "Peter. Does Jean-Luc know who I am?"

"Yes."

"And he still agreed to host the show? That amazes me."

"He didn't know when he signed up for it. The invitation came from his old college; he did his post grad year at LIFT. All he knew was he'd agreed to host a student show about ethical fashion. Later, when he made the connection with you, he said it was too late to pull out. He couldn't let them down. It's why at first I couldn't tell you who he was. I thought it best for the whole thing to go ahead and explain later."

"But then you changed your mind?"

"I've been worried sick that the business with the CID was going to come out and the press would dig around and connect me with him and you'd find out and then and the show would...I don't know what I was thinking to be honest."

"I can see that. Peter, are you sure you haven't been dishonest? Has he been dishonest?"

"No." He looked her straight in the eye. "No. I promise."

"I don't know why I should believe you but I do."

"It's true. It'll all check out. The worst thing they'd find is that he doesn't pay attention to his investments. Someone may have acted improperly, but it isn't him and he'll be able to prove it."

"So why were you worried about your job?"

"I wasn't really. I was trying to find a reason to avoid

telling you his name. I don't know, Lu. I've not been able to think straight. Ever since you found the letters, it's been the weirdest thing. I was relieved I didn't have to pretend anymore but I've been terrified. I'm scared of what this means long term. I don't know where this leads."

"Will you tell Jean-Luc that you've been this desperate? Will he understand?"

"I don't know. I hope so. I think he'll feel like you did, that he's let me down somehow, but nobody has let me down. I've just been weak. He isn't pushing me to make any decisions right now."

"What kind of decisions?"

"He's talked about us living together. He's often talked about me moving to the Paris office. I could transfer, but..."

"I think we need a cup of tea," Luella said, steadying herself against the mantelpiece, a wave of sadness washing over her now that he was talking in practical terms. "Let's talk some more if you aren't too tired. Give me a minute for all of this to sink in properly. I'll put on the kettle."

Luella went out to the veranda, lit a cigarette, and walked across to the vegetable garden. She bent down and picked a handful of rosemary, rubbing it between her fingers to release the scent as she sat down on a bench. She looked back at the house that Maisie had inherited from Peter's mother and around at the garden she had played in so often as a kid. The rabbit hutch was still there next to the bike shed and the apple tree with the sturdy branch where they'd hung their rope swing. Everywhere she looked there was a memory, and in the flash of a moment she understood that no matter what lay in front of them, whatever different paths they would take, she and Peter would always be connected.

This is what love means, she thought. It means letting go. I have to let him go with love.

She twisted her wedding ring around on her finger, noticing how thin the band had worn over the years. She sat for a little while longer before going back up to the house to make the tea.

23

——

India was woken from a deep sleep by a garbage truck in the street below. Lying in bed, watching the stippled patterns of sunlight across the walls, she reflected on the previous few days. She would call Henry this morning and thank him properly for being so understanding about leaving New York. The show had been a huge success and she'd played an important part in that, hadn't she? Sarah was going to be fine and the baby too. She pulled the duvet up around her chin, snuggled down with a contented sigh, and was asleep again within minutes.

A few hours later, she was finishing getting dressed when Henry called.

"Hey, India. I'm back in London. Is your friend okay?"

"Thanks, Henry. She is," she said. "She's had a little girl. Five pounds five ounces. I'm going back to the hospital in a few minutes."

"You must be very relieved. You've been on my mind. My cousin had an emergency c-section and I know it can be serious stuff. I hate to be blunt about this, but can you let me know how much more time off you need?"

"I don't," India said pulling on her jacket. "Just today."

"Great because we need to talk. I've fired Samantha."

"You have? Samantha? Really? Why?"

"It's a long story. How about you come to the office in the morning. I'll fill you in and we can look at where we go from here."

"Sounds like a plan," India said. "Do you know how Luella is? How's her husband?"

"She's okay. I spoke to her last night. Peter's going to be fine too. Horrible business though."

"Yes. That's for sure."

"Okay. I'll see you in the morning."

India checked her hair in the hall mirror, put her phone and keys in her purse, threw on her raincoat, and left for the train station, stopping at a nearby florist on her way. Sarah was awake when she put her head around the door of the hospital room.

"How're you feeling?" she asked, resting the arrangement of pink peonies on a table and pulling over a chair to the side of the bed. "I'll find some water for them in a minute."

"Thank you. They're lovely," Sarah said bursting into tears. "I feel awful. I'm sorry Indie, but I can't stop crying."

"Is the baby okay? Where is she?" India asked, suddenly concerned to see the bassinette still empty.

"She's being fed. She's tiny. She needs special care, but they say she's not in danger; they just want to get her weight up so they're bottle-feeding her. I can't even do that part right," Sarah added, beginning to cry again.

"Sarah, you must be worn out."

"I can't stop crying. What's wrong with me?" Sarah blubbered, turning her head to the wall. "I should be all excited. I'm supposed to be overwhelmed with these feelings of love. Where's my maternal instinct? When I look at the baby, I don't feel anything. All I want to do is sleep."

"I'm sure it's only because of the operation. Your hormones must be going crazy. Tell me what happened."

"Can you pass me some of those?" Sarah asked, hoisting herself up on her elbows slowly and pointing to a box of tissues.

"Thanks," she said, blowing her nose loudly. "I had these contractions. The baby's head hadn't engaged so I wasn't dilating and I was in so much pain that Damien called the hospital and they said to bring me in. When they put me on the monitor they suddenly went into emergency mode. The cord was around her neck and they raced me down the corridor on a gurney and wouldn't let Damien come with me. Then all I remember is being in surgery and somehow it was all so wrong. I'm a nurse. I'm not the one who's supposed to be on the table. I was terrified lying there not sure what was happening. I thought I was going to die."

"I'm sure. I'm sure it must have been horrific, but you're safe and the baby's healthy. You must be having a delayed reaction to the shock of it all."

"Maybe. It's a nightmare in here. They wake me up every few hours in the night and pump me full of antibiotics. I feel like I just want to die."

"You'll feel better in a few days, I'm sure. Your body's taken a beating, that's all."

"Nothing's ready at home," Sarah sighed. "I was too superstitious to buy so much as a box of diapers until I was thirty-eight weeks. Damien can't or won't take time off work. What am I going to do? Was I insane to think I could have a baby all on my own?"

India looked at her friend and smiled sympathetically. "You're not on your own, Sarah. You have Damien and you have me. Give me a list; it'll only take me an hour to get anything you need. Right now, all you have to think about is bonding with the baby. With Alana, right?"

At the mention of her name, Sarah brightened a little. "Alana. That's right. Press that button next to you and see if the nurse will bring her in."

India made the call and Sarah lay back down and drifted in and out of sleep while they waited. Eventually a midwife arrived cradling the newborn. She woke Sarah gently and put the baby into her arms. India leaned over and gasped at the tiny bundle, at her shock of black hair, scrunched up face and her perfect tiny hands, marveling at how delicate she was.

Holding back tears, she murmured softly, "Hello, Alana. Welcome to the world." She turned to her friend "Sarah, she is so beautiful." she murmured.

"Yes," Sarah answered, looking at India. "I'm sorry. I can't."

Turning to the nurse, she said, "Could you take her away again please? I need to go back to sleep. I'm sorry."

~~ ~~ ~~

India came into Henry's office the next morning and tried to push from her mind all images of the last time they had been in there alone together. She was failing miserably. He swung around in his leather chair, took his legs off his desk ,and stood up.

"So, Henry?" India said, sitting down and attempting to ignore the strength in his thigh muscles and the breadth of his shoulders as he walked toward the window.

"I don't think you've met Joel Lichtenstein, my partner, yet. Have you?" he said.

"I did briefly a while ago. He was on his way to Cannes."

"Ah! Right. Well, Joel hired Samantha a couple of years back after she'd interned for him. She was an international student here. We've been gradually giving her more responsibility. She was much more than a receptionist, as you know."

"And?"

"She came up with a suggestion that took the wind out of me." Henry recounted the story and India shook her head.

"That's callous," she said. "Sounds like she'd sell her granny."

"I agree." He nodded.

"Anyway, this now leaves me with a problem. Samantha was from Switzerland. She spoke fluent French and she's been setting up the meetings with the Paris Fashion Institute. She was probably hoping to score a job there now that I stop to think about it. Anyway, you don't speak much French do you?"

"Sadly not." India sighed. "Un petit peu."

"Yeah! I thought I remembered that. But I need you in Paris for a couple of days. We have to hold those meetings while *Faux Fashion* is fresh on the shelves and the publishers are still excited. Luella doesn't want to be away in the next couple of weeks for obvious reasons."

He crossed the room and leaned against her side of the desk.

"Sorry. I'm not following," India said, looking up at him. "You want me to go to Paris? I just told you I don't speak much French."

"I want you to come with me to the meetings."

"But again, you just pointed out that I don't speak French."

"It's a PR thing. It's not important. They all speak English, but opening the meetings in French is the polite way to do business there. You can describe the educational benefits of the projects. You've lived and breathed it these last few months, and two of us presenting together will be a stronger pitch."

"Okay." She hesitated. "When do you have to go?"

"End of next week, in ten days' time."

"I think that'll be okay," she said, hoping she was conveying a studied response and that he hadn't noticed her breathing had become shallow the closer he was to her. "How many days will we need to be there?"

"Three I reckon. Possibly four. Are you up for it?"

"Yes," she said. "Happy to help." Oui oui! Oui! OUI! she thought. I'm going back to Paris. Le vais revenir a Paris. Wahoo!

"Perfect. Patricia will book us tickets," he said hopping up and going around to the back of his desk. "I'm keeping her on. She's working out well. Are you happy to stay in Hotel de l'Abbaye again?"

"Absolutely. I loved it there," she said. "Henry, what do you think about Jean-Luc? I saw the newspapers. Do you know what that's all about?"

"I don't know a lot of the details. I know it has something to do with his financial advisers and he's being used to get bigger headlines. I bet he's like a lot of successful people. They leave the money stuff to managers, who sometimes get greedy. Jean-Luc is the talent. He doesn't strike me as a crook, but I've been wrong about people before."

"Okay. I hope you're right. I like him," India said, getting up. "Henry, I'm going to go to my desk and catch up on things. I've a ton of e-mails to send to the colleges. Did you send a letter of congratulation to the winners?"

"Yes, and I spoke to them too. We shot the videos the day you left. Everyone was on a high. Sorry you had to miss that. I've sent flowers to Annabelle and to the college deans. All taken care of. Didn't I copy you in?"

"You probably did. As I said, I'm way behind on my e-mails."

"Okay. Catch you later," Henry said as she stood up to leave. "Oh! And India."

"Yes?" she said, turning back as she reached the door.

"We want to extend your contract. You've proved to be a real asset. We're happy to renegotiate the terms. Are you good 'til the end of the year?"

India grinned at him. "Thank you, Henry. Yes. I am. I'm loving this job."

"It shows," he said.

India resisted the urge to throw herself into his arms and hug him. She smiled and left the room.

On her way to visit Sarah that evening, she mused on the fact that Henry had been so quick to protect Luella. I like that, she thought. I like that in a man. In fact, there's a lot I like about that man, now that I think of it. A lot.

Roger was sitting with Sarah when she arrived at the hospital. She looked fragile in her hospital gown and slippers, her face free from makeup, her eyes hollow from lack of sleep.

"Hey. Great to see you India," he said, standing up to give her a hug. "It's been ages. How's it going?"

"Good. Lovely to see you, Roger. So how's the patient?" she said to Sarah. "And how are you today?" she crooned to the baby.

"I'm okay. We're okay," Sarah said. "They reckon we can go home in a few more days as long as she keeps gaining weight. It's funny saying 'we.'"

"That's great," India beamed. "Is Damien coming this evening?"

Roger shot India a look as if to say, "Don't go there."

"Not today," she said. "He's working."

"Oh! Look at the time," Roger interrupted. "Here, take my chair. I'm going to leave you two to have a chat."

"Thanks, Rog." Sarah smiled, looking over to the table and gesturing to the oversized stuffed animal. "And thank you for the teddy bear."

India sat down on the chair when the door closed behind him. "Did you get much sleep last night?"

"Not really. But I feel a bit more human. They had me walking around today. I'm like a granny. I feel as if I've been sawed in two, which is pretty much what's happened."

"You look a lot better though. It's good to see you out of bed, Sarah."

"Yes. Well, I'm sorry for my meltdown."

"I think you had every right to have a meltdown. Don't beat yourself up. Is Damien going to stay with you when you get out? You're going to need help."

Sarah hesitated. "I don't think so," she sighed.

"Okay if I camp out with you then? I'm going to be away a few days with work the following week, but I can help you over the hump."

Sarah's look spoke volumes. "That'd be wonderful, Indie. Thank you."

"No need to thank me." India smiled. "I'm being selfish. I want Alana to get to know her Aunt India."

"Indie. Can I ask you something?

"Sure."

"Will you be her godmother?"

"Of course. Of course, I will. Absolutely. In fact, I will be her fairy godmother. She will be the best dressed little girl in town."

"Thank you." Sarah smiled. "I'd give you a hug but my stitches hurt too much."

∼∼∼

India checked her inbox and saw there was an e-mail from Luella changing where she wanted them to meet and asking her to come to her house. She was fine with that. It was close to Sarah's and she could go straight on afterward.

Luella greeted her at the door, casual in a pair of blue jeans and an oversized cashmere sweater. "Great to see you, India. Come in. Cup of tea?"

"Yes, please," India said, taking off her coat and putting it on the hall-stand. "It's really cold out there today."

"Margaret," Luella shouted through to the kitchen. "Be a love and make a pot of tea before you go, will you? India and I are going to sit by the fire."

India followed Luella through into the sitting room and warmed her hands at the grate. "This is such a lovely room, Luella," she said looking around. "You have some beautiful paintings."

"The paintings are Peter's," Luella said. "He collects watercolors. The books are mostly mine. I should show you my Alice in Wonderland collection before you leave. I've been collecting them since I was a kid."

Margaret set out a tray with tea and biscuits. "I'm off now, Luella," her assistant said. "Do you need anything else? I've scanned all the photographs from the book signings. I'll archive them tomorrow."

"No. I'm fine. Thanks, Margaret. Good morning's work."

"Okay. Bye then. Nice to see you, India."

Luella sat forward to lift her cup. "India, thank you so

much for stepping in for me at the show. I heard you did a marvelous job. I can't wait to see the footage. I also heard Henry's extended your contract. I'm very happy about that."

"Me too," India answered. "I'm amazed how much fun this has been. It doesn't really feel like work at all. I can't wait to get to planning the Paris show with you."

"Biscuit?" Luella said, offering her the plate of shortbread. "India, thank you for stepping in next week as well. I'm exhausted after the book tour. We did ten book signings in as many days on top of the media blitz and then...well, you know what happened. I don't need to bore you with the details, but it's been a very stressful time, to put it mildly."

"I'm sure." India nodded.

"I know you and Henry will manage perfectly well without me. By the time you get back here, things will hopefully be more sorted out," she said. "I'm way behind on my next book. I really appreciate not having to travel right now."

"Luella, I'm delighted to be going back to Paris, I promise you. It's not a hardship, just so you know," she added. "I know we've not known each other all that long, but I understand you're having a rough time of it, and if you ever want to talk about anything, I'm here."

"That's good to know," Luella said, looking into the middle distance dreamily. "Funny isn't it? I worked so hard to build up to the fashion show and to making *Faux Fashion* a commercial success, but suddenly it doesn't seem important. I don't feel driven in the same way. If all this stopped tomorrow I think I'd be okay with it."

Snapping out of her thoughts, she forced herself back to the moment. "Okay. Sorry. Fill me in on what I've been missing. Henry said he has things in hand to maximize the online promotions. Where are we up to?"

As India was leaving a few hours later, a tall man in a gray overcoat walked up the path. He nodded to her as they passed each other.

That must be Peter, she thought, turning around and seeing him use a key to open Luella's front door. What a good-looking man.

Peter went into the sitting room. "Who was that I just saw?" he asked, taking off his coat and throwing it over the back of an armchair.

"India Butler, the education consultant. She was collecting some papers. She's going to Paris with Henry."

"How are you, Lu?" he said.

"I'm okay." She looked up from tidying the tea tray in front of her. "You?"

Peter sat down on the armchair across from her. "I'm beginning to get it together. Thank you for being there for me, Lu. I will always regret putting you through all this. I'm so grateful to you and Maisie for all the support."

"We love you very much. I think you know that. Let's try to forget about it. It's behind us now."

"I told Jean-Luc what I'd done," Peter said quietly.

"And?"

"Turns out he understood better than I thought he would. He's been there himself."

"Really? You mean?"

"Yes. He tried to kill himself when he was about twenty, when his first love affair ended. Artistic temperament I suppose. He's very dramatic. Cut himself, then panicked and called for help."

Luella sat down across from him. "That's awful...Peter, dreadful. You know, I've been thinking. You should take some time off. Spend some time with him. It is what you want isn't it? I mean, you want to be with him, to live with him, to see if it'll work out don't you?"

"Yes, I do. It's why I wanted to see you." He paused. "I'm going to France, to Provence for a while. I wanted to tell you rather than phone, and I was thinking about Christmas. I don't like the thought of you being on your own."

"I'll be fine," she said. "Susie and Phil have invited me

for the whole of that weekend. They always have a crowd of people around for Christmas dinner, her 'waifs and strays' as she calls them. Have you squared the time off with the bank then?"

"Yes. They owed me a bunch of time. I'm taking a month's leave."

"And Jean-Luc? Is he in the clear with the bank?"

"Pretty much. These things take time, but it turns out he's lost a shitload of money through mismanagement. They know who they need to go after. It's not him. Don't worry, Lu. Our money, your money's safe."

"It's a relief to hear you say it, but actually I haven't been too worried. I trusted you on that one. You're too sensible with money to mess that up. I overreacted, but let's move on, put all that behind us."

She stood up and lifted the tray. "I have soup ready. Let's get something to eat."

Peter followed her into the kitchen and leaned against the wall. "What do we do next, Lu?" he asked.

"You mean about us?"

"Yes."

"I don't know," she said, putting down the tray and wiping her hands on a towel. "But you know what I think?" She walked over and looked up at him.

"Go on," he said.

"I think we'll be just fine. That's what I think. No matter who I might meet or what happens with you and Jean-Luc, you will always be my best friend. Always."

"And you will always be my soul-mate," he said, looking deep into her eyes. "Always."

~ ~ ~

A tiny whimper made India sit up from where she'd been napping on Sarah's couch. She leaned across to the cradle at her side.

"Shhh. Shhh. Shush," she whispered. "It's not time for your feeding yet."

Gently rocking the wicker bassinette, she watched as the baby closed her eyes, then opened them and cried again the second the motion stopped. The past week had been a serious learning curve for India. Volunteering to help Sarah, she had imagined a few evenings singing the child lullabies at bedtime and warming chicken soup for her friend. The reality had been a lot more prosaic. Seven straight days of sterilizing bottles, changing diapers, changing clothes, averaging three hours of sleep a night and making endless dashes into Mothercare for yet more supplies had left her achingly tired.

It amazed India that one miniscule human being could cause such exhaustion, require so much attention, and create such chaos. She'd found it impossible to get any routine established for Sarah, who'd taken full advantage of having her there and had spent most of the time in bed. Her doctors had given her medication to help with the postnatal depression and India could see Sarah's mood was lifting.

By the end of her stay, India joked that she was beginning to feel postnatally depressed herself. She was counting the minutes until she could go into the office for a full day. She was done. So done that she felt pretty certain it'd be a good ten years until she ever felt broody again, and by then she'd be looking at adoption in a system that required nothing more than a monthly donation to a child in a developing country.

The baby continued to whimper. India picked her up and took her upstairs to Sarah, who sat up slowly, stretched out her arms, and took the baby and the bottle from her.

"Sorry to wake you. Are you two going to be okay on your own for the rest of the morning? The nurse will be here in a couple of hours. I've left a fresh set of clothes out for the baby, and there's a quiche in the fridge for you for lunch. Why don't you get dressed before then?"

"Okay." Sarah smiled. "I think I will today. Thanks for everything, Indie. We'll be fine 'til she gets here. Thanks again. You've been wonderful. Have a great trip."

India hesitated a minute to make sure Sarah didn't fall back asleep, then confident she was okay, went downstairs, packed her bag, and called a cab for home.

Climbing under the welcoming sheets of her own bed that night, India reflected on Sarah's situation. Things would improve for her, she felt certain. Sarah was too independent to be under par for too long. A professional baby nurse would have the child in a regular sleep pattern in no time at all. Drifting off to sleep, India reflected on how much their lives had changed in the last few months.

24

—

Sitting on the train on the way to the airport a few days later, India was buzzing with excitement at the prospect of going back to Paris and to Hotel de l'Abbaye. This is strictly a business trip, she told herself. What happened months ago is ancient history, an insane moment best forgotten...not easily forgotten though, she thought, crossing the terminal and checking in at the Air France desk quickly, where for once her bag was the correct size and weight for carry-on.

Walking into the business-class lounge, she had a flashback to the last time she'd flown with Henry. At the memory, she resisted the glass of chardonnay she craved to steady her nerves before the flight and poured herself a cup of tea instead. She caught sight of him stretched out in a seat by the window as she struggled to open a creamer.

He looks decidedly European today, India thought, taking in his navy overcoat, Berluti loafers and his worn Lotuff satchel. He looked up over the top of his reading glasses and put down a copy of *Le Monde* as she approached him.

"Hey. Have a seat," he said, lifting his overnight bag off a chair. "We're boarding in fifteen minutes."

"Thanks," she said, taking off her woolen coat and folding it carefully at her side.

"We've been invited for dinner tonight," he said.

"That's nice. Who with?" she asked as casually as she

could manage. I'm going to Paris, I'm going to dinner in Paris, wahoo!

"An old friend of mine," he said. "He's a professor at the Sorbonne. He and his wife have an apartment around the corner from our hotel. She's a photographer. I think you'll like them."

"Great," India said. "Do they speak English?"

"Of course. Don't worry, and anyway you get by don't you?"

"Yes," India said. "But I'm better when I'm with people I don't know. I get all self-conscious otherwise."

"Well, don't worry. They're lovely and the food will be wonderful. Did you get a chance to prep for the meetings? I know you were staying with your friend and her baby. How is she by the way?"

"She's okay. She'll be fine. And yes, I got into the office for a few hours yesterday, so I'm pretty much up to speed. I am so looking forward to this part of the project. I expect the show will be very different from the one in New York."

"Yes. It'll be a hell of a lot more avant-garde, that's for sure and even if it isn't, the French publicists will hype it up so we all think it is."

"How's Luella?" India asked. " haven't seen her all week."

"She's okay. Better than she's been for a while actually. How much did she tell you?"

"Nothing really. She just said she was tired and glad not to be making this trip."

"I've known her and Peter for quite a while," he said, sliding his newspaper into the side of his satchel. "In a million years, I never would have guessed he was gay."

He sat back again and smiled at her. "She's pleased you're taking the pressure off her coming on this trip."

"I'm happy to be able to. I can't imagine how tough things have been for her. Of course, I never knew her before all this happened," India said, wincing at the steaming tea and setting down the cup.

"She's a lot more serious these days that's for sure, but stick around and you'll get to know us all a lot better. Oh! Look, we're boarding early. That's our flight up on the screen," he said, getting up and stretching.

India followed Henry through the lounge, down the stairs, and outside to the tarmac and the waiting plane. They climbed the narrow steps and were directed to the first row. India was relieved to see there were three seats across and the middle one had been deliberately left empty for the comfort of business class travelers. Getting on board, she'd been anticipating the agony of sitting squashed up next to Henry. The fallout from their last flight together was burned into her psyche.

Once airborne, the flight attendants did their rounds with the drinks and snacks trolley and before she knew it, the short flight was over and they were striding along the glass-walled arrivals lounge of Charles de Gaulle Airport. Getting through passport control took a while. The arrangement reminded India of a dressage performance, where the horses prance around cones and take the longest route over the shortest distance.

They made a dash for the waiting car through a deluge and climbed into the rear seats of a Peugot. Why does it always rain the first day I'm in Paris? she thought. Damn it, I don't have an umbrella.

"We should be there in plenty of time to relax before dinner," Henry said as they approached the Champs-Élysées lined with Christmas market stalls.

"How pretty" India exclaimed, admiring the holiday lights wrapped around the chestnut trees. "Look, they make the shape of champagne glasses. How very French. Oh! Yes I recognize where we are now."

Walking into the hotel foyer, it felt to India as if no time at all had elapsed since she had last been there. She almost expected Luella to appear down the narrow carpeted corridor

as she made her way to her room. And what a room this was
– the room Samantha had reserved for Luella. India marveled at the elaborate wallpaper with its colorful humming-
birds, the sepia prints, the curtained closets, and the marble
bathroom, but it was the tiny conservatory with its view of
the garden courtyard and its mahogany writing desk, velvet
armchair, and coffee table that made India suddenly ache
for something she couldn't quite place for a moment. She
allowed the thought that maybe it would be perfect if she
were not alone. If she were not by herself, she would have
leapt on the bed with delight while Adam popped the cork
on that bottle of champagne and filled the two tall-stemmed
glasses.

She went into the conservatory. The last time I was in
Paris I was alone as well and that was way back at Easter.
She sighed. Can it really be all those months since I saw
him? Why am I torturing myself like this? It's madness.

She pushed open the window and heard a wood pigeon
cooing against the background hum of traffic. Bien sûr.
Je suis en Paris, she thought, closing the window quickly
against the blast of icy air. Je sius ici.

Unpacking some toiletries in the bathroom, she arranged
her shampoo and conditioner on a narrow shelf and caught
sight of her reflection in the mirror.

"Right," she said out loud, before undressing and stepping into the shower. "I'm going to wash that man right out
of my hair maintenant, tout de suite or whatever is French
for 'right now.'"

Henry was waiting for India in the sitting room when
she went in a couple of hours later. He looked fresh in a
navy cashmere sweater, striped shirt and a pair of blue jeans.

"Hi," he greeted her. "Shall we have a quick drink before
we go out?"

"That'd be lovely," she said. "Vin blanc, s'il vous plait."

Henry went over to the corner bar as India sank into the
plush velvet armchair in front of the fire. She was pleased

she had chosen her black Agnes B wraparound dress but was wondering if following Ines's rules was taking some of the fun out of dressing up. The other women in the room were wearing black too, she observed.

Henry sat down across from her a few minutes later as the barman put placeholders on the low table in front of them.

"Merci Monsieur." India smiled. "Denis Oui?"

"Oui, Denis. Welcome back, Miss Butler," he said pouring her wine. "Will there be anything else? Would you like some olives?"

"Non. Merci, Denis. Mais. Saus peut etre, on parle en Francais? Je suis ici apprendre le Francais."

He laughed.

"Of course, madame. Whatever you would like."

"That's hysterical," India whispered when he had left. "I ask him to speak in French because I'm trying to learn it and he answers me in English!"

"Too funny," Henry said, "but I thought you said you were self-conscious speaking French in front of people you know."

"I am. But that was one of my stock phrases from my language course. I thought I'd give it a whirl. I shall be tight as a clam for the rest of the evening."

Henry laughed.

"Salute," he said, raising his glass.

"Salute," she said, lifting hers.

"So let me fill you in a little on my friend Joseph and Melanie, his wife," he said. "I know them from way back. Joseph was a friend of my mother's. Melanie is much younger, but they're really good together."

"I think I remember you telling me your mother was French."

"Yes."

"So did you grow up here then?"

"No." Henry sipped his wine and leaned back in the

chair. "My dad's English. My parents separated a few years ago, and she came back to Brittany. I went to school in London, but we used to take our vacations here. She was keen that I didn't lose the connection to the culture. I have a sister, Jacqueline, who moved back here. She lives in Marseille."

India realized this was the first time Henry had spoken of his personal life to her. He's such a different person when you get him out of work mode, she thought. She wondered if he had ever been married, but now was not the time to ask.

"What does she do?" she asked. "Is she married?"

"Yes. She's a research scientist at Aix Marseilles University. She's very smart. It was talking to her about her work that gave me the idea for the *Faux Fashion* show. So how about you? I'm sorry I didn't get more of a chance to get to know your sister. She's charming."

"Yes. Annie's the best," India said. "I'm very proud of her."

They sat chatting companionably for a little while longer before walking the short distance to the house, which was across the square and hidden behind old city walls. Going through the tall wooden gate into an old stone courtyard, India had a feeling of nostalgia, a connection, a forgotten memory she couldn't place. They approached the front doorstep and as Henry jangled the bell, she took in the pungent scent of Fois de Bois.

A woman of about her own age, extremely slender in blue jeans and a white T-shirt opened the door. Her hair had been pulled into a tousled chignon. She wore little makeup and no jewelry except for a simple gold wedding band. She was, India thought, the epitome of quintessential French chic.

"Lovely to meet you, India. Come in," she said with an almost imperceptible accent. "Henry's told me all about the project you're working on together. I can't wait to hear more."

She kissed Henry on either cheek and swapped into French. "Henry, go through to the sitting room; Joseph's attempting to light the fire in there. He could do with some help."

India gasped as she entered the kitchen. Everywhere she looked, there was something more quirky or beautiful than the next. She took in the stand-alone range and the deep ceramic sink in a glance, the painted shelving piled with jugs and bowls, the antique dresser, the stripped mahogany table with mismatched chairs, the rusted candelabras and the delicate tableware glistening in the candlelight.

It was everything India ached for, that air of 'benign neglect,' where nothing is too considered, nothing formulaic, everything sitting together in comfortable harmony. This kitchen spoke of family history, of nights spent in animated conversation and intense arguments over the relative merits of Proust and Camus.

"Please sit down," Melanie said, lifting some magazines from a ladderback chair. "Wine?"

"Thanks," India said, sitting down.

Melanie gestured to the bottle of white and India nodded.

"We'll be eating soon. I've made a cassolet and Joseph has prepared some asparagus. Have you been to Paris often?"

"Not as often as I would like," India said, "though I love it. I feel in another lifetime I must have been French."

Melanie smiled. "Ah! Yes. We have done a good job of branding ourselves, but you do know we are not the most innovative and that our confidence is superficial."

"How so?" India was intrigued.

"If you look closely you will see that we stick by the rules. Of course we all understand what the rules are."

This was a little enigmatic for India, but she nodded in what she hoped was a sage manner. The two women made light conversation as Melanie pulled out dishes from the range. After a while, they were joined by the men, who were deep in conversation. Henry smiled over at her as he sat down at the table.

"Come and join us," he said, popping an olive into his mouth.

220 Letter from Paris

India went over and sat down next to him.

As Henry had promised, his friends were charming and relaxed. They put her at ease, chatting in English and including her in the conversation, which ranged from plans for the holidays to Melanie's latest project and India's love of Rodin. Over a delicious chocolate mousse served in miniscule dishes, Joseph regaled India with tales of Henry's mother and his awkwardness as a boy. Henry took it all in stride and after a course of delicious cheeses, they took their glasses and sat by the fire in the sitting room.

"If you aren't too busy, I'd like to take you to Musée Jaquemart Andre," Melanie said turning to India. "It's a wonderful collection. You would love it. You can't do it in a day of course, unless you're an American tourist," she added with a smile. "But I could show you the Winter Gardens."

"That would be lovely," India said.

"Sorry India, we have the days booked out," Henry interjected. "Next time."

Next time? Next time? There's going to be a next time. Je reviens, she thought with a little whoop.

"He's the boss," she said to Melanie, "but next time for sure. I would like to see it. I'd love to get to know Paris from a Parisian. That would be wonderful."

By the time Henry and India left their house, it was raining again. They ran much of the way under a shared umbrella. This reminded India so much of a scene in *Midnight in Paris* that it required serious effort for her not to throw herself into Henry's arms when they arrived back breathless and panting on the steps of the hotel.

"Great dinner," he said, stepping into the foyer and shaking off the umbrella before folding it in a stand by the Christmas tree.

"Wonderful. It really was. Thank you so much for taking me," India said loosening her scarf. "I really enjoyed myself."

"Me too. I'm pleased you and Melanie hit it off. I had a feeling you would. That fire looks very inviting," he said, hesitating for a moment as they walked toward the sitting room, which was bathed in a golden glow.

"It does look very cozy," India said. I would SO be up for a nightcap with you. She thought.

"Oh! Well." He said, turning toward the elevator. "Good night.. Early start tomorrow. Sleep well."

25

The next few days were busy. Henry had set up meetings with the Paris Institute and with Parsons Paris. There was much talk of summer programs and links with the Fashion Institute in New York and LIFT. India was regretting not having had time to research the schools more fully. She discovered with relief that several of the people she met were even less prepared than herself. The conversation drifted off topic frequently and the short meetings inevitably ended up in a restaurant.

Their hosts were all keen to show off the city and its cuisine to the best advantage. At Le Café de l'Homme, she and Henry sampled Pate Lorrain while enjoying spectacularly stunning views of the Eiffel Tower. They tasted beef tartar at Cru and traditional sausage and rack of lamb at Chez George. Clearly, the French were not leaning toward a vegetarian diet anytime soon, India mused.

These extremely long lunches, involving wine on most occasions, left India somewhat spaced out for the afternoon meetings. She made a mental note to stick to Evian each time but wasn't having much success.

"The meetings don't ever seem to reach any conclusions," she told Henry after tea at Chez Paul as they were walking back to the hotel.

"We're here to meet people in person," he said. "In my experience the French are not as hooked on Le Skype as us.

Virtual reality is not their thing."

"I've also noticed fewer people on cell phones in restaurants." She nodded. "How do you think it's all going?"

"Couldn't be better. We make a good team, Miss Butler," he said with a smile as they went into the lobby and collected their keys. "Catch you later. I've a call to make to New York, and I must remember to tell Luella that Jean-Luc wants to speak to her."

"They never met did they?" India said. "Luella had been looking forward to that. I wonder if her nephew got to meet him. With everything else that happened that night I forgot all about him."

"That's an easy fix. We can arrange it. Good thought. Catch you for dinner," Henry said, walking toward the elevator.

India went to her room. After tossing her coat and scarf on the bed, she walked across to the mahogany writing desk and sat down. Looking into the courtyard, she remembered the last time she had been in Paris. How she had seen Luella sitting out there in the rain and how they had talked about her book and about endings. Maybe she even wrote one of them at this desk, she mused.

Picking up a couple of sheets of handmade Melodies Graphiques notepaper, she took the lid off her fountain pen and wrote the date. Rolling the pen between her fingers and thumb, she rested her hand on her chin and gazed out of the window at the trees sparkling with tiny white lights, the branches swaying in the breeze.

Endings are new beginnings, she reassured herself, remembering the quote from Joseph Campbell that Luella had used to end her novel. *We must be willing to let go of the life we have planned so as to accept the life that is waiting for us.*

She began writing. After a while, she carefully folded the letter into an envelope and addressed it. She went down the hallway quickly and handed it to Jean-Paul to post before she had time to change her mind.

~~ ~~ ~~

"Hi Henry," she said, sitting down in front of the fire a few hours later and lifting the glass of wine he had waiting for her on the coffee table. She leaned back savoring the heavy scent of smoldering pine logs admiring the fresh display of star anise on the console next to her. "It all looks so festive doesn't it? Here's to our last night in Paris. Santé."

"We'll be back soon enough," he said. "I've set up meetings at Eva Zingoni's workshops for January. I'd like to involve her in the show in some way."

"You mentioned her yesterday, so I checked her out. She recycles French textiles from all the major fashion houses. I can't wait to see the fabrics. She worked at Balenciaga didn't she?"

"Yes, and she has quite the celebrity following now. Nicole Kidman's a huge fan."

"So, were you happy with how the meeting with Karmi Organic went today?"

"Very," he said. "Well done you. I had no idea you were so up to speed on their products."

"I'm a fast study." India smiled. "It seems Karmi is ahead of the curve in France with their vegetable dyes. I love the effects they create. My enthusiasm was genuine."

"It showed." Henry nodded.

"I love the Kora Organics line too."

"Good thought."

"Great. I'm pleased I'm being useful. So where are we eating tonight?" she asked, confident that her all-black ensemble would be appropriate anywhere.

"There's a little bistro around the corner, Au bon Saint-Pourcain. I think you'll like it," he said. "It's tiny, as in really tiny, the size of Melanie's living room, and the lace curtains haven't been washed since Napoleon's wedding. Francois the owner is an old friend of my family, runs it with his daughter. He cooks. She waits tables. He doesn't speak a word of

English, never been out of the country. It's time you tried out your French properly."

"Is this your idea of entertainment, Mr. Cowan? Watching me make a complete idiot of myself?"

"Not at all. I think you may fare better than you think. Either way, I want you to get a flavor of a neighborhood place. It'll be fun and, of course, the food is great."

"Okay. I'm up for it," India said, secretly delighted at the opportunity. "But you'll have to help me out if I get stuck."

"Bien sûr." He grinned.

They finished their drinks and walked the short distance to the restaurant where Francois, a middle-age burly man in an oversized apron, leapt from behind a counter and held the door for them. He pumped Henry's hand, greeting him like a long lost relative, barely pausing between breaths. India doubted she would understand him, even if he were speaking English. He turned his attention to her.

"Enchante, madame," he said. Then turning back to Henry he continued, "Votre ami est tres belle. Ma fille sera bientot la qu'elle doit rencontrer. Asseyez vous. Seme Asseoir, votre place habituelle."

India understood the gist and gave him her widest smile. He took their coats, ushered them over to a rickety wooden table facing the door, and pulled out an old battered chair for India. She sat down, delighted at the welcome but somewhat taken aback by the décor. As Henry said, the drapes had seen better days, the paintwork was peeling, and the tiles were chipped. Behind Henry was a rack crammed with books and newspapers. A few couples at adjoining tables glanced up, smiled, and looked away again.

Francois brought over two glasses of Saint Pourcain house wine in small glass mugs.

"This is the wine selection." Henry laughed, thanking Francois and looking across at the chalkboard. "The menu never changes either. What do you fancy? I usually have the soup and the chicken cassolet."

India took Henry's lead and ordered the same meal.

"So now we speak only in French," Henry said. "Rules of the game."

"Okay. Well... Je m'appelle, India." She laughed. "J'aime la France."

"Moi aussi. Pourquoi?"

"Pasque il est tres agreeable."

"Comment?"

They continued in this vein, India tripping over her words, Henry helping. Henry encouraging, India relaxing into it, Henry cracking up at her attempts, India floundering out of her depth. Their food arrived and more wine was drunk. The evening went by fast.

"Qui etait delicieux," India said, pushing away her cheese plate. "C'est souffi. Merci."

"Moi aussi...Damn. I've left my wallet at the hotel," Henry said, forgetting to speak in French and fumbling around his inside pocket.

"I have mine," India said, reaching for her purse.

"It's cash only," he said. "Francois would be fine with me paying next time, but I want to give him something extra for the holidays and we're leaving first thing tomorrow. Wait here. I'll be back in ten minutes. Sorry about this. Have another glass of wine."

Francois looked over. India caught his eye. "Ou est la toilette s'il vous plait?" she asked him.

"A bas, madame," he said and began escorting her toward the kitchen, through a passageway, and outside of the building. He opened the lavatory door for her with the smile of a mischievous schoolboy.

India looked aghast at the pit in the ground, a gaping hole surrounded by flat tiles. Henry promised an authentic experience, but this is taking things to a whole new level, she thought, considering the logistical implications in front of her.

Francois continued speaking in a torrent of French. "Je pense que Madame que votre jupe peut etre un peu serre." He chuckled.

India had no clue what he was saying. He was miming now, a mime that was leaving little to the imagination, pointing at her four-inch pumps and pencil skirt. What am I doing? she thought. I'm on the street in Paris, discussing, well kind of discussing how to take a pee. Is he offering to help me? What am I supposed to hold onto? I am SO not going to hold onto him. Okay, this is not happening.

She shook her head and began speaking pidgin French. "Non. Non Monsieur. Je voudrais...il est le old-fashioned toilette. Je need," – she mimed the action for sitting – "mais je suis desparu. Ou et la toilette Americano?" Wrong, she thought. That sounds like I'm in Starbucks. Damn I really do need to use the loo. Some loo. Any loo. Just not THIS loo.

Seeing the desperation in her eyes, Francois took pity on her and pointed up the street. "L'hotel dans le coin," he said.

"Merci. Merci," she answered, teetering off up the cobbled street, praying for all she was worth that this was not his idea of a joke. She raced through the foyer of the modern hotel and tore down a long hallway.

It's like a game show; surreal, she thought as each corridor led onto another and there was no sign of an exit or restroom. Just as returning to the latrine was looking like a serious option, she saw the sign.

India walked back up the street slowly, attempting to avoid the potholes. She pushed back her hair and took a deep breath before opening the door to the bistro. It was empty now except for Francois and Henry, who were sitting together at the table drinking cognac. Neither of them made the least attempt to hide their amusement as she walked in.

"Sorry, India," Henry said. "I completely forgot to tell you."

India laughed. "Okay, Henry. Game on," she said, sitting down opposite him. "You have been warned. I will find a way."

"I have no doubt." He grinned. "I shall be watching my back at all times."

"Day and night I suggest. Merci, Francois," she said, lifting her glass.

"Santé Monsieur. J'aime le restaurant. J'aime Paris, mais je n'aime pas la toilette."

For once India was grateful not to understand his reply. She was pretty certain it was politically incorrect at the very least. Francois left the table and began settling up the till. Henry and India looked across at each other. Neither of them spoke. Henry held her gaze.

"On y va? Shall we?" he said, pushing back the chair. "Bonsoir, Francois. Bonnes Fêtes."

"Monsieur, Madame. Revenir bientot." Francois grinned, holding out India's coat for her.

Out on the street, Henry turned to her. "Are you tired?"

"No," India said. "Wide awake."

"Shall we walk to the river? It's a beautiful night."

India looked up at the Van Gogh sky. "It's absolutely perfect," she agreed. "Starry Starry Night. It is really starting to feel like Christmas. Yes, let's walk a little. I can't go too far in these shoes."

~ ~ ~

A homeless guy was washing his shirt in the park lake as Luella dropped speed from her run and broke into a walk. She carried on quickly past the spilling garbage cans and the young man asleep on a bench. A woman dragged by, pushing a shopping cart laden with empty plastic bottles and miscellaneous bags. Parks have to be the most depressing places on earth in the early morning, she thought.

If she looked in one direction the world was a beautiful place: the stark outline of trees bare of leaves, the lake partly iced over, the wide expanses of lawn dewy from melted frost, the sun breaking though thin clouds. Closer up, all you could see was a city's hidden shame, human misery, displaced people who had fallen through society's slats.

She stopped at Starbucks for a latte and croissant and bought her usual Sunday papers at the newsstand. Walking past the gaggle of teenage girls at the bus stop, she stopped in her tracks, recognizing the red-headed girl in the white anorak. The girl looked up and caught her eye for a second. Luella gave her a wide smile and walked on. How strange, she thought. How strange that you will never know how I've carried you in my heart all these months and even written a fictional life for you.

Back home after her shower, Luella watched the clock as the hours dragged by. She sorted through files, cleared the clutter from drawers, shredded papers, and rearranged the shelving in her home office. At last, as the sun went down, the phone rang dead on cue. She rested an armful of books on the coffee table and hesitated before picking up. She lowered herself into a chair.

"Jean-Luc?" she said quietly.

"Luella?"

"Yes."

There was a long pause. "I am so grateful you agreed to talk to me," he said.

"Of course."

"I want you to know that Peter has told me how you encouraged him to come stay with me. So few people would be as understanding. I want you to know and to tell you I appreciate that very much. I am sorry you have been hurt."

"I have been hurt," she said calmly. "Very. But what am I to do? My husband loves you. I want him to be happy. He won't be happy if there's animosity between us."

"That is true, Luella," Jean-Luc answered. "He has been in agony. He loves you too."

Luella's throat tightened. There was a deafening silence. How strange that she could think of little more to say to the man who had torn her life apart.

"Look after him, Jean-Luc," she said quietly. "He's fragile."

"I know. Je comprends. I understand."

"Goodbye, Jean-Luc."

Luella put down the phone. Fighting back tears, she lit a cigarette, took a drag, and stubbed it out. "That's the last cigarette I'm ever having," she vowed, grinding it into the ashtray. She put her head in her hands, leaned on her desk and cried until she had no more tears left. Sitting up and grabbing a tissue, she fell back in the chair thoroughly spent, her face a streaming mess, her eyes swollen. Standing up took every ounce of her strength. She went into the kitchen and poured a glass of water, then walked over to the French windows. She stood watching a squirrel race up and down the side of a tree before closing the drapes.

Turning and crossing the hallway, she went back to her office, sat down at her desk, and opened her laptop. The plotline in front of her was still sketchy. She wasn't following her usual template. She was writing differently lately, digging deeper within herself.

She began to type, her fingers flying deftly over the keys. It was several hours later before she looked up. For the first time in many months, she felt a lightness of spirit and a sense of relief. Powering down her computer, she turned off the light and went up the stairs. Tonight she knew she would be able to sleep. Tonight she might even dream.

26

A dam sat at his kitchen counter sifting through the mail that had built up in the months he had been in Europe. His Hollywood apartment felt cold and neglected after lying empty so long. He closed the window to shut out the wail of sirens in the street below. Flicking over a couple of holiday cards, he spotted a hand-addressed envelope with a line of French postage stamps. Slicing it open carefully, he pulled out the letter and began to read.

Hotel de l'Abbaye Paris December 15th

Dear Adam,

I'm leaving Paris in the morning to go home to London. I've been thinking about you a lot, about 'us' while I've been here. We've shared so much over the last couple of years that I couldn't bear the idea that things had ended on a bad note. I understand why you were mad at me and I'm sorry.

I want to thank you for all the lovely times we've had. I think back to that summer in LA, how we met, all the beach walks, the craziness with the paparazzi and then St. Petersburg; do you remember my boots?

Making love in the snow? And London, you remember Browns Hotel? I could go on. I have so many great memories of our time together.

Adam, I respect that your work is important to you. You're immensely talented and deserve all the acclaim for what you do. I really do understand the strains the lifestyle puts you under. I've seen Annie and Joss go through so much too and I read the press (as you know to your cost). I just don't think I was built for it. I'm sorry I didn't trust you. You have been wonderful to me and I owed you more than reflex reactions and bad temper. I have simply found the long distance thing too much.

I've been on something of a journey myself recently. I love my new job and I can see a future in it even when the current projects have finished. I know I'm in the right place with my own career. I'll even get to spend more time in France over the next few months. My French is coming on really well.

Adam, what I'm really saying is thank you. I think if we'd both been able to be in the same place for any length of time we could have made a real go of it, but it wasn't to be.

I wish you so much happiness and I send my love.

Happy Holidays
Bonnes Fêtes
India

Adam picked up the phone and dialed India. It went straight to voice mail.

~ ~ ~

"I think a few more and we're done," India said, admiring her handiwork.

She was sitting on the cozy couch in Sarah's sitting room tying red satin ribbon into festive bows. The baby was asleep by a silver tree decorated with tiny white lights. Damien was noticeably absent these days, but Sarah seemed happy and content.

"Alana has me, her granddad, and her fairy godmother. Who else could she possibly need right now?" she'd said.

"Have you seen much of Luella since you got back from Paris?"

"I've seen her a few times," India answered. "I think her husband's moved out. She said he's gone to Provence for the holidays, but she told me deep down they both know he's not coming back."

"Maybe we should invite her around for drinks or something over the holidays. I'd like to meet her."

"Good idea," India said. "I'll do that. Okay. Where do you want the snow globe and this monstrosity to go?" She laughed, pulling a box toward her and holding up a pottery Santa Claus. "These photographs will be for posterity, remember."

"Mantelpiece, please," Sarah said firmly. "'Tis the season for bad taste."

"I've ordered the turkey, and I'll make the stuffing and get the veg ready at home next week. This is going to be a wonderful Christmas," India said, standing back to assess the arrangement. "I plan on arriving in my glad rags and I expect the same from you. I'm thinking red of course for our photo shoot."

"Of course." Sarah smiled. "So how're you feeling, Indie? You seem great."

"How do you mean?" India said, looking away from her and fiddling with a fir cone.

"You know what I mean. About Adam of course."

"A little fragile I suppose, but I feel good about it too. I've done the right thing; *we've* done the right thing."

India stretched out a string of tinsel along the mantel and placed another white cone on top. "He might have been telling the truth about that girl in Vegas, but ever since he had that fling after that summer I left Los Angeles, I've been waiting for the other shoe to drop."

"I've wondered for a while how long you could take the strain of it," Sarah said. "It was really starting to show."

"I know. You read about Hollywood couples breaking up every five minutes, don't you? I'm simply not cut out for it, Sarah. I hated the goodbyes, the waiting, being on my own so much."

"But the good news is you ended it properly, without anyone getting hurt."

"True. It's still a bit raw. I'm feeling okay though. I know it's the right thing. I think writing the letter really helped. Sometimes it's the only way to say exactly what you mean."

"I can see that," Sarah said through a mouthful of chocolate. "Want one?"

"Thanks," India said, taking the box. "Sometimes I think I was more in love with the idea of Adam Brooks than the reality. I'm not sure we had that much in common when it comes down to it."

"Well, you've plenty in common with Henry, that's for sure." Sarah smiled, lifting the baby into her arms. "She has, hasn't she, Alana?" she said, jigging the baby over her shoulder in front of the log fire.

"Enough on that Sarah, thank you very much," India said in tones of mock outrage. "Stop fishing; we work together. We're just friends, honestly. I'm enjoying this job far too much to jeopardize it."

"I can see that. I've never heard you talk about anything

the way you do about the shows and all the trips. You're obviously in your element."

"I am. I really am. I never imagined there was a job in the world that I could love this much, and it turns out I'm really good at it too."

She paused. "I shall be taking it very slowly with Henry," she said. "There's too much at stake for me."

"Such wisdom from one so young." Sarah laughed.

"Okay," India said, lifting her purse. "I was going to wait until next week to give you this, but I just couldn't. Let me show you the cutest dress I bought for Alana. You're going to flip over it."

She handed her friend a delicately wrapped package. "It's from Bon Point," she said. "From Paris of course."

"Here. Hold the baby," Sarah said. "I still can't get the hang of doing everything with one hand." She gasped as she pulled out a powder-pink dress with a delicate hand-embroidered collar.

"She'll grow out of it in five minutes it's so tiny," India said, "but then I thought she could use it to dress up her dolls."

"Thank you. It's exquisite," Sarah said folding it carefully and giving India a hug. "Thank you."

"So I'd better get off. I think we've done a wonderful job here, don't you?" she said, glancing around the room twinkling in the firelight.

"Night-night Alana." She kissed the baby on the forehead and handed her back to Sarah.

"See you two soon," she shouted, closing the door behind her. "Merry Christmas."

It seemed to India as she walked the short distance from the subway to her street, that change happened when you stopped drifting and took control. That's what Sarah had done wasn't it? She had wanted a baby badly enough to rewrite the script. No matter what the future might hold for her, she had listened to her heart and taken a leap of faith in herself. India put the light on in the hallway, took off her coat, and went through to the bathroom to shower.

Of course, I took control too, she thought later that evening as she set the kitchen table for one and arranged tall candles with fresh holly and ivy as a centerpiece.

She pulled the quiche from the oven and tossed the salad. Opening a bottle of merlot, she left the cork to the side of it the way they always did in French restaurants.

The End

Acknowledgements

My thanks first and foremost go to Lou Aronica, who cajoled and nagged me (in the nicest possible way of course) to write this book. Thank you for giving me the opportunity to be published again and for encouraging me every step of the way.

Jodi Rose, where do I begin? Thank you for your insights and humor and for picking up on all my English dialogue and translating it into American. You helped bring the characters to life, mercilessly editing my tendency toward flowery language, banning all "amber liquids" and limiting the number of chicken casseroles eaten as well as the number of times people were allowed to "drain" their glasses. Working with you never feels like work.

Rand Rusher, for your insights, warmth and humor.

Claudia Barwell, for getting me into a writing cycle and suggestions on character development

Mark Shelmerdine, for encouragement and the generous offer of hosting the book party. Yes, please.

Matt Goldman and Renee Rolleri for awarding me the 2012 New York Literary Torch Award. It was a great honor.

Love and thanks to all the "Derry Girls." Especially to Jenni Doherty and Ursula McHugh for the warmth of your welcome for me and my work. You have no idea how grateful I am to you all.

Merci Beaucoup to all the wonderful staff at the Hotel de l'Abbaye in Saint Germain and especially for letting me have the room with the conservatory each visit.

Thank you to the vegans in my family who inspire me with their commitment to an issue they believe in passionately – Neil Robinson, John Robinson, Allison Robinson, Cat Robinson.

This time around I simply didn't have time to share the drafts with friends who offered to read them, but I am so grateful to you for all the cheerleading and support you gave me by keeping India alive and well – Jane Arnell, Patti Diane Baker, Tony Barton, Ann Dickson, Roma Downey, Bryn Freedman, Bronya Galef, Lena Gannon, Lani Hall, Sheran James, Carol King, Diane McCarter, Avril More, Bernie McMahon, Mel McMahon, Mimi Peak, Sharon Harroun-Peirce, Bob Peirce, Lynn Pompeii, Ron Pompeii, Chris Ranck, Amy Rappaport, Diana Revson, Beryl Roberts, Dorothy Storer, Paul Wright.

Thank you Barbara Aronica-Buck for another exquisite cover.

Endless thanks to Brenda Cullerton for your sharp insights and encouragement.

Finally a huge thank-you to Ken, James, and Kate Robinson. This book is for you with all my love.